Ms. FORTUNE

Drive Me Wild, #1

AMY BOOKER

eBook ISBN: 979-8-9859875-6-0

Print ISBN: 979-8-9865651-1-8

Published by Renaissan Publishing, Cuyahoga Falls, Ohio

www.amybookerauthor.com

Renaissan
Publishing

To my Constant Readers:
Thank you for continuing with me
on my writing journey.

Author's Note

If you've read my previous books, you'll know that the chapter names are all song titles. Music has been an integral part of my life, and it always sets the mood. Whether it's the overall energy of the song, the lyrics, or even just the title, that tone carries through into my written words on the page. The playlist and a link can be found at the back of each book, or you can find them on my website: www.amybookerauthor.com.

Chapter 1

Is Everybody Going Crazy?

Brandon

"We've got a problem, Mr. Carmichael." My assistant Diane's voice over the intercom in my office sounds more peeved than usual, which is a feat. While I don't know what's got her all riled up, I could sure do without more problems today.

I lean back in my chair with a long sigh, rubbing the bridge of my nose, irrationally thinking it might fend off an oncoming headache. I am not happy. Our stock is taking a nosedive ahead of our annual meeting, and outside of the rumors of possible insider trading, which I hope to God are false, nobody can tell me why the markets are so jumpy. What else could go wrong today?

"What is it, Diane?" I try to keep my own irritation at bay, but damn, it's hard.

"Apparently, Victor Blake of Mischief Motors passed away." She sounds like this is highly inconvenient for her, but I'm stunned. Victor wasn't just a business colleague; he was a friend. "So, with his business now up in the air, we're scrambling for car service for all the board members for the upcoming meeting. Since our meeting always coincides with the Consumer Electronics Show in Vegas, finding a substitute is proving...difficult."

I'm shocked. Victor and I were unlikely friends, but besides my using his car service exclusively, we would have lunch together a couple times a year when I was in town, mostly to discuss cars. Especially classic cars. His knowledge of almost any vehicle from any era was astounding, and his stories of various cars he'd owned over the years were always colorful.

"Why are we substituting Mischief Motors? Are they completely out of business now? Did they cancel our reservations?" Victor never talked about his family, other than saying he had daughters, but they were never around the business that I saw. I don't know what he planned, if anything, for his company once he left this mortal coil. I can't imagine he didn't have *any* plan. Victor was too forward-thinking for that.

Diane hesitates, "No, they didn't cancel. I just thought...."

"Well, don't. As far as I'm concerned, it's business as usual until we hear otherwise." *Shit.* That was harsh. I'm taking my emotions out on the wrong people. "Sorry, Diane. That was rude of me. Can you come to my office, please?" This intercom conversation bullshit always gets on my nerves. I prefer face-to-face conversations where I can read people's body language. She's only five fucking feet from the door anyway. *Geez. News of Victor's death is hitting me harder than I thought.*

Diane knocks once and then comes in, her pencil skirt making walking a trial of how fast a person can move six inches at a time. It's almost comical to watch, but I'm not in the mood now. She is such a forced persona, trying extremely hard to pull off the sexy librarian look, with her red hair up in a bun and oversized glasses on her nose. Sure, she's got the costume down, but it's so obviously forced, it's a complete turn-off. Not that I would ever consider an employee *that* way, but as a man... it's just not there for me. Authenticity wins for me every time.

She sits across the desk from me, notebook and pen poised at the ready. This is why she's my assistant. She's excellent at what she does. Not because she's pretty.

"What do you know about Victor Blake's death? Anything? Cause?" As many Vegas folks do, he lived hard, but he was still relatively young and seemed fit.

"Massive heart attack."

Well, alrighty then. That would definitely do it.

"And his daughters? Have you heard anything about them?"

She shakes her head, "No, but I can find out for you." She glances at me over the glasses I don't think she even needs. "Did you want to send flowers or a card? Perhaps a donation in his name somewhere?"

She makes it sound so fucking impersonal. As if it's another transaction that needs to be completed. A box to mark on a checklist. It rubs me the wrong way. Victor was a person, and a good one at that. And a friend. She should know this. He deserves more than some flowers and words.

"Sure, all of the above. But find out the funeral arrangements and get me there. And yes, if you can obtain any information on Victor's daughters, that would be appreciated as well. I'd like to extend my condolences to them personally."

"Anything...else?" She asks, biting on the end of her pen suggestively. It's so overt and, at this point, silly, how hard she tries to get into my pants. She's been trying for the entire three years she's worked for me. That's commitment, at least. I admire the tenacity.

"No. Thanks, Diane. That's all for now." I turn to the wall of TVs behind my desk with all the financial news channels on. Despite the upsetting news about Victor, I have a corporation to run. And today, that's a particularly tough job, just made even harder.

The crawler on each screen predicts doom and gloom for my company, LC Consolidated, the largest microchip manufacturer in the world. And not a single one is correct. The business has never been stronger. Someone important must have sold off a chunk of stock, throwing everyone into pandemonium, and I need to find out who and why, because the government is about to be up my ass with a microscope. Which, in turn, will have my shareholders raging with moral panic even more than they are.

A few minutes later, Diane is back on the intercom,

"Mr. Carmichael, I sent the information you requested regarding the Blake daughters to your email."

Damn. That was quick.

"Thanks, Diane."

"Also, the business is still running, so our reservations are still being honored for the upcoming meeting."

"Who's in charge now?" I'm curious who would take the helm of the Mischief Motors empire. "Do you know?"

"It's all in the email I sent. His daughters, Normandy and Chelsie Blake, have inherited equal controlling interests in the company."

Interesting. I wonder if these women or girls, hell if I know how old they are, know the first thing about running a business. I guess I'll soon find out.

"Thanks again, Diane."

I open the first attachment to the email with the Blake daughters' information and am instantly blown away. When I open the file, I find a picture of Normandy Blake, who is the most beautiful woman I have ever laid eyes on. Victor wasn't much to look at, so I did not expect his offspring to be so breathtaking. While beautiful, the long blonde hair, sharp jawline, and cheekbones are nothing compared to her intelligent dark eyes. I could see myself getting lost in those eyes for an unreasonable amount of time.

She also looks like she doesn't take any bullshit. I don't know where this picture was taken, but she seems to be in an intense conversation with someone. I like women who can hold their end. I think I might like this Normandy Blake.

She's thirty-one, so a few years younger than me, I can handle that. Went to live with her mother when her parents divorced when she was pretty young. Then moved permanently to Sacramento after college. A Stanford business grad, which isn't too shabby. Maybe she won't wreck her father's business after all. Not that I assumed she would in the first place. Bonus points because she runs her own business consulting firm, turning around lost causes, and focuses on women-owned businesses. Very nice.

I'm starting to regret not talking about our families to each other when Victor and I would have lunch. I would have liked to learn more about Normandy directly from him, instead of an impersonal private investigation firm with just facts and figures. I'm almost offended that he kept her existence from me. But I haven't been the relationship kind of guy for a few years now.

The sister, Chelsie, is another story. Similar features to Normandy, though a little darker. Definitely a different mother. Twenty-five. A string of dead-end casino jobs. To each their own. I'm not one to judge. I'm curious how that dynamic will play out at Mischief Motors between the two sisters. They seem like they couldn't be more opposite in lifestyles.

"Mr. Carmichael, I have the funeral arrangements for you. I've sent you an email."

You don't need to tell me you sent me a fucking email. I can see it.

"Thanks, Diane." My clenched jaw barely lets the words out. I could be a ventriloquist with how hard my teeth are shut together. I know it doesn't stop my frustration from coming through my voice.

I'm a billionaire. At 34, I'm still considered one of the youngest billionaires ever, and I run one of the most successful companies in the world. Until Alexandr Wang came along, I was the youngest to reach that milestone at 25. And moments like this, where I'm annoyed by my fucking assistant being good at her job, make me question how the fuck I got here in the first place. Never mind all the hard work I've put in to be where I am. When the pressure gets to me, and I'm a dick for no reason like this, I don't deserve a penny.

Chapter 2
Fell On Black Days

Normandy

T his can't be right. These books cannot be right. There is no way my father left his business in such shambles.

"On the bright side, the ex-wives won't be paid another dime now." The accountant for the company, Sora, is trying to cheer me up, but it will take a hell of a lot more than that. "It looks like most of the money from the business went to them."

One of those ex-wives is my mother. She never mentioned that Dad was still paying alimony. She didn't live like it either.

"But at least the business is yours free and clear. Well, yours and Chelsie's." He pushes his glasses up higher in classic nerd fashion. "So, there's not a mafia loan shark after you or anything. It's just the typical line of vendors with their hands out for what's due." His laugh is nervous and is not comforting at all.

"Great. That makes this all so much better." I can't keep the sarcasm from my tone no matter how much I try. Ever since my dad died, I've been on the edge of a migraine trying to put the pieces of his life back together and figure out what to do with it all.

I've had to put my life in Sacramento, including my business consulting job, on hold to come here to deal with all of this. My half-sister Chelsie does not have a mind for business and basically volunteered me to straighten everything out. The control freak in me is perfectly happy with this, but the grieving side just wants to curl up and cry my eyes out and let someone else, *anyone* else, handle all of this. Keeping busy has kept the tears at bay so far but discovering the mess the business is in is threatening to change that fast.

"The good news is your father's biggest account, LC Consolidated's, annual reservation is coming up. That will relieve a lot of this pressure. Temporarily, at least." He frowns with guilt, like any of this is his fault. I know it's all my father's doing.

My father was a hopeless romantic in a city full of sin. He always fell for the wrong woman for the wrong reasons and paid for it dearly in more ways than one. And it appears he continued to pay for it long after the marriages were left in ashes. Luckily, Chelsie and I are the only products of the failed marriages, all four of them. Otherwise, this nightmare could be worse. I can deal with Chelsie. We've always gotten along, though we've never been what I would consider close. We both understood what a cluster our families were and had no delusions on that front.

"What's so important about LC Consolidated's reservation?" I know the company. *Everybody* knows the company. It's one of the biggest tech conglomerates in the world. But I don't understand the connection to our business.

"Their annual charity ball and meeting is coming up in a couple of weeks. Mischief handles all the transportation for the company's Board of Directors."

I raise an eyebrow. That could be a decent injection of funds into this cadaverous company. If these numbers are to be believed, we need all the business we can drum up.

"We handle their business often?" It sounds like this is a standing order or something. I know there are accounts with frequent or regular users, but I never thought my father dealt with the likes of LC Consolidated.

"As far as I know, yes. They use Mischief exclusively." He clears his throat nervously. Sora doesn't seem like the kind of guy who gets nervous easily. "Well, at least they used to." That sounds ominous.

"What do you mean, '*used to?*'" We can't lose any business right now. Especially someone as important as

LC Consolidated. "Why wouldn't we still have their business?"

He adjusts his tie, looking at the exits as though he wishes he were running out of one of them right now. *If I'm stuck here, so are you, buddy.*

"Since we're fielding the business calls temporarily, we had a call earlier from the CEO's office inquiring about the status of the business. They seemed a little concerned."

"The CEO?" I know the company but I can't think of who the CEO is off the top of my head.

"Brandon Carmichael?" He quirks an eyebrow. "Surely, you've heard of him before?"

I shift in my seat a little. Of course. What woman doesn't know Brandon Carmichael? Besides being one of the wealthiest men in the universe, he's also one of the most attractive. Sometimes life just isn't fair. I doubt any of this is coming directly from him, though. He's probably got people to deal with this stuff for him. Shit, he most likely has people to deal with his people.

And now they're concerned about us? Of course, they'd be concerned. Hell, *I'm* concerned.

"But they didn't cancel, right?"

"No. They haven't canceled." Sora nods, appeasing my worry.

I can hear the *'yet'* not spoken. He doesn't need to say it. I have to get things back to normal for this company as soon as humanly possible.

"Do you think it's in jeopardy? Should I try to speak to their CEO or something?" I cringe at the thought of having to grovel to keep business, but I don't see much choice here.

Sora eyes me curiously, not sure what to make of me. I'm definitely not what he was expecting.

"It wouldn't hurt to have a conversation, I'm sure. But..." He drifts off, his features clouding slightly. I can't read what it means.

"But, what? Is there something else I should know?"

"Well, just know LC Consolidated has its own troubles right now. The stock tanked today, and there are rumors of insider trading."

This is shocking, even to me, who keeps tabs on all of the Fortune 500s. For one of the biggest companies in the world to have that kind of scandal is almost beyond consideration. It makes me wonder if *we* should be doing business with *them* if they're now wrapped up in a scandal. We can't afford a misstep at this point.

"Should I be worried about our association with them? I don't want to tarnish the business's name by working with criminals."

Sora laughs lightly, the corners of his eyes crinkling. It's the first sign he's a real human being I've seen from him since coming to his office to go over my father's accounts. Until now, he's been all business.

"I don't think you need to worry. LC Consolidated is strong enough to weather a pretty big storm."

The way he says that makes me envious. As though we're weak and couldn't handle any kind of storm in comparison. Not even a brief rain shower or a strong gust of wind. I get that we're in a precarious situation. There's no need to twist the knife.

"So, I just need to make sure that LC Consolidated stays our customer." I stand and prepare to leave with a nod to Sora. "I think I can do that." *I hope I can do that.*

He shakes my hand with a kind smile.

"I'm sure Mischief Motors is in good hands with you, Ms. Blake. I look forward to working with you. I wish it were under better circumstances. And again, my condolences to you and your sister on your sudden loss. Your father was a fine man and will be missed."

"Thank you for saying so." The familiar pang of grief crashes into me again. I made it through this whole meeting without crying or even getting misty-eyed. I've been too wrapped up in all the issues the business has to think about the loss. But now, I can feel my eyes stinging with unshed tears, and my throat tightens as I strain to keep the sob in my chest at bay.

I leave the accountant's office no happier than when I went in. I am more determined than ever to pull Mischief Motors together. My father may not have been the savviest businessman in the world, but he knew how to build a company from the ground up. He was a people person, something I am absolutely not but will need to work on fast if we have any shot at staying afloat. I have other ideas that might help us as well, but first and foremost, I need to talk with Chelsie. We need to lay down some ground rules and define our roles in all this.

We weren't close growing up with as little as we saw each other, but we've always been friendly. When we found out we both inherited the company, we were both shocked. We are vastly different people. Being co-owners could get tricky between us.

I think I can handle Chelsie; I'm not too worried about her. Brandon Carmichael? That's an entirely different story. Hopefully, I won't need to deal with him personally. I can handle admin people, the richest man in the world? No, thank you very much.

Chapter 3

Black Honey

Brandon

The LC Consolidated saga continues as the insider trading rumors come to fruition in the worst possible way. My ex-girlfriend, Eve Cromwell, is now being investigated by the SEC for insider trading, and I'm not surprised. Apparently, she caught wind of an acquisition we are making and decided to buy up their stock on the cheap. I have no idea where she heard about the takeover, but it wasn't from me. When we were together, I figured out pretty fast her interest in me wasn't personal. It was strictly a financial transaction on her part. It's too bad, she appeared to have all the ingredients to make a great person. Well, all except one – a soul.

Now I need to find out who she got the information from, and it should be easy. For a large corporation, we have a relatively small Board of directors. Our Executive Management team is tight as well. However, I don't see any of them giving up information. So that means someone from the acquisition team is most likely the culprit. With the SEC's approval, I've already got two of our private investigation firms on the case. It's incredible how much more a private citizen can do to expose crime than the government.

I'm not complaining, though. Ever since the rumors surfaced, I've been in damage control mode, which isn't easy when you know who's at fault but can't say it out loud yet to the public. All I can do is spout the old *"we're cooperating with investigators..."* blah blah blah. It's frustrating, to say the least. I want to shout from the rooftops, *'My ex is a bitch from hell who only cares about where to get her next Birkin bag and who will be dumb enough to buy it for her. And, by the way, she's about to be arrested for insider trading.'*

What I'm not looking forward to is all of the relationship questions that will come along for the ride on this. We broke up over eight months ago, and I don't think I've talked to her since, except at a charity event or two. Come to think of it, I don't think we even spoke at those. I have nothing to say to her. Well, no, I'd like to tell her off for making my life a living hell right now, but she's not worth the air required for me to speak.

Am I being tough on Eve? You're damned right I

am. Anyone who puts my company in jeopardy will feel the full force of my wrath. I've worked too damned hard and given up way too much for shit like this to screw everything up. Besides, I have more employees than I can count, relying on me to keep us afloat, productive, and profitable, so they can have food on the table, a roof over their heads, and a stable home life. That is a lot of people I am responsible for in their happiness and well-being. I don't take that lightly. No, I take it personally.

So, when someone tries to game the system or exploit a loophole, or as in this case, take unfair advantage of my company's transactions, I will not sit idly by. I will do whatever it takes to find the perpetrator and ensure they are punished while ensuring the status quo finds itself painlessly for those affected.

I'm not a saint. I didn't become a billionaire by being Mr. Nice Guy. But I didn't do it by cheating, either. I didn't hurt anyone along the way, and I like to think I still have my soul intact. Whether or not that's true is yet to be seen, but I'm going with that until proven otherwise.

"Mr. Carmichael? I have Normandy Blake of Mischief Motors on the line for you," Diane's annoyed voice interrupts my thoughts. "With our discussion the other day, I thought you'd want to take this call."

Normandy Blake? The newly discovered most beautiful woman on the planet is calling me? For a second, I'm speechless. I've had dinner with Presidents and Prime Ministers, but the name Normandy Blake somehow has the power to throw my nerves into a bee's nest.

"Mr. Carmichael?" Diane repeats, now sounding annoyed with me.

"Yes. Put her through," I finally say, shaking my head and gathering myself. I swear my palms are starting to sweat, and I haven't even spoken to the woman yet. I let the phone ring twice, taking a deep breath before answering. "Ms. Blake, how good of you to call. This is Brandon Carmichael."

It's too formal. I can hear how stilted my voice sounds. I don't know why this woman is getting to me like this. We haven't even met yet.

"Mr. Carmichael, thank you for taking my call." She's all business. I guess she's picking up on my tone, but I sense a bit of nervousness in her voice. "I wanted to thank you for your charitable donation to the Heart Association in my father's name. It meant a lot."

"Of course. My condolences to you on your family's loss. Your father was a good man and a friend. I was deeply saddened to learn of his sudden passing."

"You were friends with my father?" She sounds surprised. I suppose it's not the likeliest of scenarios.

"We were friends, yes."

"That's so strange. My dad never mentioned that he knew you."

"Well, to be fair, he never talked about you either." I cringe inwardly as the words come out. That sounded way too harsh. "I mean... I knew he had daughters, but he didn't like talking about his personal life." I hope I recover quickly enough. The last thing I want to do is offend her during our first conversation.

She laughs softly, and I can almost picture it in my

mind. Her dark eyes crinkling with her smile. I pull up her photo on my computer, admiring her beauty again.

"Touché. He didn't like talking about himself. He was always more interested in whoever he was with." I can tell the smile leaves her voice, and a touch of sadness creeps in. I have the feeling emotions aren't something she shares willingly.

"I'll actually be there tomorrow for the funeral service, so I'll be able to offer my condolences to you in person." I don't know why I'm hoping this cheers her up. Though the circumstances are horrible, I know I'm excited to meet her. I have no idea why anyone would be excited to meet me, but it's something to say.

"Oh? I wasn't aware you arranged a car...." She's back to her business voice and now sounds irked.

"Yeah, my assistant told me it would be better to use another service this trip since you're dealing with the funeral and everything." I get the sense this might have been a wrong move. At least as far as Normandy is concerned.

"Oh." She's quiet for a moment. "That was...thoughtful."

Now I'm sure it was a wrong move. She definitely isn't happy with my decision, but changing now wouldn't help at this point, either. I can't think of how to salvage this conversation.

"Would you care to have dinner with me while I'm in town?" And as soon as I say the words, again, I want to take them back. I don't know what the fuck is wrong with me. It's like I have foot-in-mouth disease or something, and I can't stop saying stupid shit. "Tomorrow after the service or the next day? If you're free?" *Jesus Christ, I sound pathetic.*

She doesn't answer for a long moment, and I can't tell what's happening. Did I cross a line, maybe? I probably did. You don't ask someone to go to dinner after their father's damned funeral. What the hell was I thinking?

"Um...I think I'll pass this time. But thank you."

Yup. I've fucked this up every which way. You'd think I would know the proper etiquette for asking a woman out and *not* doing it right after their father dies.

"I apologize." I don't know how to dig myself out of this one. "That was callous of me to ask now. I just thought...never mind. Forgive me."

"Yeah... okay." The trepidation in her voice makes me think she now considers me a creep or something. "Well, thanks again for the donation. I should get going...."

"Right. Of course. I'm sure you're busy with arrangements and everything. I look forward to meeting you in person tomorrow." And after this entire discussion, saying that last bit *really* makes me sound like a perv. I can't win.

"Sure. You too. Goodbye, Mr. Carmichael."

"Bran-" the call disconnects. "-don." I look down at the phone in my hand, shocked. "Call me Brandon." *Wow. She just hung up on me.* I don't think I've been hung up on in over ten years.

One thing is for sure, tomorrow is going to be interesting.

Chapter 4

Hearts Hard to Find

Normandy

What the heck was that all about? Asking me to dinner? And who knew my dad was friends with one of the wealthiest men in the world? He never said a word about it. But then again, he never talked about his business. And now I have said rich man showing up tomorrow, and I don't know what to expect with him asking me to dinner. I hope he got the hint that I am not interested. I've got enough to handle with the business, funeral, and estate and no time to worry about the hot-shot billionaire Brandon Carmichael, who may or may not be a white-collar criminal chasing my tail.

The outpouring of sympathy we're receiving from the community since my dad's death is mind-blowing. The overwhelming number of cards, flowers, calls, donations, and even people stopping by the business to express their condolences has been a lot to take in. And that is just the locals. Tomorrow, a slew of people will be here to pay their respects. While Mischief is a reasonably small company, my father built up an elite client base, including some big named people from around the world. It's surprising but also genuinely touching to see how many lives my father impacted.

My face is starting to hurt from the smile I constantly force when I meet these people. I want to go back to my dad's house, where I'm staying, drink a large glass of wine, and think about something else for a minute. *Anything* else. Hell, maybe I should have taken Brandon up on his offer for dinner. The thought makes me laugh out loud to myself. *Me and Brandon Carmichael. It's preposterous.*

"I'll have whatever you're having," my half-sister Chelsie grumbles as she walks into the office I've temporarily taken over here at Mischief Motors and falls back into one of the chairs across from me. She looks like she's having a rough day, though I can't imagine why. It's not like she's doing anything productive to help with any of the problems around here. But then, I took everything over when I arrived like the idiotic control freak I am, so being angry about any of it is equally dumb.

"Oh, I'm having a mental breakdown. You want some?" I give her the smile I've plastered on my face for a few days. I'm sure it completely lacks any real emotion at this point.

"You are definitely wearing some Eau de Psycho with that crazy grin on your face." Chelsie always looks put together in that Vegas kind of way. Her hair is tousled perfectly, and her makeup is just on this side of heavy-handed but is still gorgeous. Her outfit, while totally age-appropriate, is a tad more revealing than anything I would wear. "How many people came by today?" She leans back and crosses her stilettoed feet on the desk. Someone could put an eye out with those things. I don't know how the hell she walks in them.

"Not that many today. Tomorrow will be the big one." I'm trying to sound more confident about everything than I am. As if I have everything under control when that couldn't be farther from the truth. Between the two of us, I need to take command of this sinking ship and right it. "Did you know Brandon Carmichael and Dad were friends? He's coming for the service tomorrow."

She blinks at me like I've grown a second head, her brows raising in surprise.

"I did not know any of that. Wow." Her feet slide off the desk, and she leans forward, suddenly excited. "How do you know he's coming? Have you talked to him?"

I'm almost pushed back by the force of her excitement rushing at me.

"Yeah, I just got off the phone with him." I scrunch my nose to show my distaste. "He asked me out to dinner. Can you believe that? We're burying my dad, I mean, *our* dad tomorrow, and he wants to go on a date? That's just plain weird. I don't care how rich the guy is, that's just wrong on so many levels."

Chelsie's expression tells me she might disagree with my assessment of the billionaire.

"He asked you to dinner? And wait, you said no? To Brandon Carmichael?" Her shock and disbelief at my rejection of him baffle me. How can she think what he did was okay?

"Yes. Brandon Carmichael. The creeper who thinks it's appropriate to go on dates after funerals. What aren't you getting about that part?" I shake my head at her, still not sure if I'm communicating the wrongness of it all properly.

"Norm, it's freaking *Brandon Carmichael*. What aren't *you* getting about *that*?" She throws her hands up in exasperation. She's the only one who gets away with calling me 'Norm.' Since we were kids, she's called me that, and it's too late to ask her to stop now. Everyone else either calls me 'Mandy' or uses my full name.

"I'm sorry, my father just died, and the company he left is on the brink of bankruptcy. Maybe that's why I'm not thinking about dating right now." I can't help the angry tone of my voice.

This pulls her up, and her eyes go wide. I have to turn away from her. I've not told her how bad things are because I've been hoping to find a solution sooner rather than later.

"Are you serious, Norm?" She swallows hard, and guilt takes over her features. Her shoulders drop under the weight. "Is it as bad as that? Bankruptcy?"

I stare down at my hands on the desk, fidgeting with a

pen. I really didn't want to get into this with Chelsie if I didn't have to. I guess I have to now.

"It's pretty bad, Chels." I sigh heavily, looking around our dad's office at the pictures on the wall of some of his favorite cars over the years. Some real classics, and some rare ones as well. He sure did love his cars. Enough to build a business out of driving them. "Maybe not bankruptcy bad, *yet*. But it's close. We might have to sell off some of the classic inventory if things don't get better soon."

She gasps, and a hand flies over her mouth.

"No. Don't say that. Dad loved those cars. Hell, I love those cars." She turns to study the pictures on the wall along with me, her eyes tearing up. If she starts crying, I really will have that mental breakdown I mentioned a little while ago. "What can I do to help?"

I stare at her blankly for a minute, not sure I heard her correctly. Did she just offer to help with the business? I can't even imagine how she could. She's only worked casino jobs, and mainly as a waitress. I don't see how those skills could translate to a car service.

"I don't know...." I stammer, still shocked she's even offering. "How do you think you can help?"

She straightens in her seat, pushing her shoulders back, and clears her throat, ready to make her case. I'm all ears. She nods at the pictures on the walls.

"I know cars." She pauses. "Well, I know *those* cars. I would go with Dad to buy them, and he would tell me all about them, what to look for in the different makes and models, what was a reasonable price, etc., and how not to get screwed over by the sellers. It was kind of our thing." The tears are back in her eyes and now in her voice too.

I didn't know they would go together to buy the cars. Shit, I didn't know much of anything about their relationship at all. A pang of jealousy sparks in my chest, knowing they had a special connection I didn't have. The only thing remotely special my dad did with me was play cards. Though, in Vegas, that's not all that special. He taught me how to play poker and how to play it well. He'd have me sit for a few hands during his bi-weekly card games with his friends, and I would usually win.

"Okay, well, that could be extremely helpful. Do you know much about the newer models? Or just the classics? How would you like to be in charge of the fleet inventory?"

"Both." There's a confidence back in her demeanor and a new sparkle in her eye I love seeing. This could be good for both of us. "I think I'd be pretty good at that, actually."

"Perfect. Once we're back open for business next week, you'll need to review everything and see what we can liquidate. If we can sell even a few, it'll help a lot."

She smiles, but it's bittersweet. I can tell she has mixed feelings about selling any of the inventory. Chelsie isn't usually so sentimental. Ever since she graduated from high school, she's become a sort of badass with little to no emotion. When it comes to our dad or these cars, that's different.

"Every one of those cars has a story," she sighs.

"Well, you can tell them to me as you hand over their sales checks." I grin at her, a genuine smile this time, and she rolls her eyes at me. She'll soon learn there isn't any room for sentimentality when it comes to this business. That was our father's downfall, and it won't be mine. If I can, I learn from mistakes, mine and everyone else's. And I'll do everything in my power not to repeat them.

The morning of the funeral is nothing but chaos as I've become the go-to person for absolutely everything now relating to my dad and his business, not to mention the funeral. None of his ex-wives are willing to help with the service, and my own mother, who was my dad's first wife, won't even be coming for the funeral. None of them are. They all wanted to avoid running into each other. My mother never remarried, and I think she held a torch for him. News of his death hit her harder than I thought it would. A lot harder. She moved to Utah when I turned eighteen and went off to college, saying that Vegas had too many sad memories for her. I understand all of it, but it's still frustrating that everything surrounding my dad has now seemingly dropped into my lap.

When Chelsie and I arrive at the funeral home, we're shocked at the number of cars waiting to join the procession to the cemetery. We have difficulty getting through them all to reach the main funeral home building.

Chelsie started crying before we left the house and hasn't stopped, but I can't shed a single tear for some reason. I can sense the tears bottled up inside, but releasing them isn't an option. I need to be strong for

Chelsie and everyone else attending. That will be my job today, being a rock for everybody. I'll break down in private later.

Once we park and make our way into the funeral home, I can't help but notice what seems to be a large contingent of security guards hanging around. *Is that part of the funeral?* I don't remember that being on the list of services offered, but I guess I understand it. There are a few famous people attending today. Maybe they brought their own security.

"I don't care who your boss is, there's a set order for the car procession, and I'm not about to change it for anyone," a loud female voice says from just inside the doors. I'd know that voice anywhere. It's Bianca Torino, the Lead Driver at Mischief Motors, who doesn't take shit from anybody. From her tone, I can tell she's about to break into Italian, and I'd hate to be the guy she's arguing with when that happens. The tall brick wall of a man she's arguing with has gone pale and looks like he wants to hide under a rock somewhere. I need to intervene. We can't have fights breaking out at my dad's funeral.

"What's the problem here, Bianca?" The guy she was talking to gives me a withering but grateful look for interceding.

She tears her glare away from him to face me. "This guy's asshat boss thinks he's special and wants to move up behind your car. I told him the order is set, and I am not changing it."

I hadn't even thought about the order of the cars because who gives a shit? We're all going to the same place.

"Who is your asshat boss?" I ask the gentleman, who now shrinks under my focused attention. He wasn't expecting a tag team, but this seems very important to Bianca, and I'll back her up no matter what. "And does he not know we're all going to the same cemetery? It's not a race."

"I'm the asshat," a recently familiar voice says from behind me. I can't help it, but goosebumps rise on my skin as I hear him. The billionaire himself. Of course, he'd want special treatment.

"Oh, Mr. Carmichael. I didn't realize it was you," Bianca starts, but I hold up a hand to silence her as I turn to face him. I don't care how rich he is, he can't change everything for his own convenience.

I am not at all prepared for the sight of him in person. I've seen pictures of him, everyone in the world has, but they don't do him justice. Tall, dark hair, impeccably styled, intelligent dark eyes, but they seem to spark with humor, squared jaw, and hints of dimples if he were to smile. And, he fills out a suit like nobody's business. Up close, he's almost too perfect for words.

You're mad at him right now, don't forget.

"Mr. Carmichael, unfortunately, there is a pre-set order for the procession I'm not comfortable with changing last minute. I'm sorry if this inconveniences you." It's evident in my voice I'm not sorry at all. I hate guys like him who throw their clout around like confetti. I grew up hating bullies, and sickening amounts of money are just another form of it.

"No, you're quite right. I understand. It was a request from my security detail, but I'm fine wherever I am in line. Don't worry." He's contrite, but there's still that spark in his eyes I can't read.

I examine him closer, making sure he's not patronizing me. It doesn't appear he is, which is one measly point for him, but I'm still not won over.

"Is there a security issue we should be concerned about with you here?" His mention of the request being from his security now brings everyone's safety into question for me. The last thing I need is some crazy person crashing the funeral.

He puts his hands up. "No, not at all. It's... an insurance thing. Nothing for anyone to worry about."

"You're insured? Like, your body is insured?" Bianca is incredulous, and I'm right there with her. I've never heard of such a thing, but what do I know about billionaires? Nada.

His embarrassed smile in response nearly breaks through my dislike of him.

"Well, I know it sounds nuts and extremely egotistical, but if something happened to me, world markets would kind of go crazy." He shrugs his shoulders with a hint of a blush on his cheeks.

"Well, there goes that idea...." I mutter under my breath, turning away briefly, but Bianca hears me and chokes out a laugh, covering it with a forced coughing fit. I give her a sideways glance, encouraging her to keep her shit together. It doesn't look as though Brandon heard me, however, thank God.

"I'm Brandon Carmichael, by the way. You must be Normandy." He steps closer and holds out a hand for me to shake, his eyes now full of compassion. "My sincere condolences on your family's loss. Your father was one-of-a-kind." He nods at Chelsie to include her as well.

As he nears, I catch the scent of his cologne that smells so exquisite it probably costs more than my car. My knees start to wobble as I take his hand into my own, and the feel of his skin against mine brings back the goosebumps from earlier. I pull away quickly, not wanting my reaction to him to cloud my thoughts of the day. Plus, I'm confusing myself with the differences in my intellectual and physical responses to him. Part of me wants to jump his bones, but most of me wants nothing to do with him.

"It was nice of you to come today. Thank you." I turn to Chelsie and Bianca. "Right, shall we, ladies?" I hold out an arm, indicating we should get moving and away from this awkwardness as soon as possible. Chelsie, who has been sniffling throughout the ordeal, flashes a weak smile at Brandon as we pass, and I inwardly cringe. I'm most likely being too harsh on him. He can't help he's disturbingly rich, but he should know at least *some* funeral etiquette.

It's pretty simple: You don't ask people on dates, and you don't ask for special treatment.

Chapter 5

Babylon

Brandon

So, Normandy Blake's first impression of me is I'm an insensitive asshole who, not only is some kind of weird creeper, but also so full of himself he thinks he should get preferential treatment at her father's funeral. Not how I wanted any of this to go. I had wanted to apologize for asking her out on the phone but couldn't think of a way to do that without offending her further. Plus, she never gave me a chance; she was in a hurry to get away from me.

Looking at everything from her point of view, I get it. It looks bad. I admit that much. However, she isn't giving me much chance to fix any of it. She makes up her mind about people a little too hastily. I like to give people the benefit of the doubt, at least at first. If they prove me wrong later, then I deal with it. Not everyone puts their best foot forward in the first meeting. Surely, she understands that much. At least, I thought she would. I was obviously wrong. Normandy Blake is turning out to be a bit of an ice queen.

After the funeral, a small gathering develops at the Mischief Motors depot. My security team has done a great job keeping the small legion of press at bay, and I hope that keeps up throughout the day. I don't want anyone here swept up in my current media storm surrounding Eve's insider trading fiasco. I'm told she will be arrested in the next few days, and I still don't know what that fallout will look like.

I know several people from business or charity functions here, so I'm at least not standing in the corner like a wallflower. At a lull in one conversation, I excuse myself and wander the garage, checking out some of the cars Victor has amassed over the years. It's quite an impressive fleet with a nice mix of classic and newer luxury cars. He always did have fine taste in automobiles.

"See anything you like? I might be able to get you a deal." I turn and find Chelsie Blake eyeing me with curiosity. Her expression is almost hopeful, and I'm unsure what to make of it. Are they looking to sell off Victor's cars?

"Are these for sale? I was under the impression you and Normandy were keeping the business going. Is that not the case?" It would be sad if the business Victor built for so long was dismantled so quickly after his death.

"They might be, depending on the car and the offer." She's looking a little nervous now, like she doesn't want to part with any of them, making me confused.

"Well, tell me which ones are, and I'll take a look. How's that?"

She glances around, assessing the cars, her eyes wide with clear panic, and she's now anxiously wringing her hands.

"Let me think...." She bites her bottom lip, turning one way, then another, her eyes shining with unshed tears. I can't take it anymore. I place a calming hand on her shoulder.

"Chelsie. It's okay. You don't need to show me any cars."

"No, no. I need to sell some of these; I just don't know which ones to pick."

My hand instinctively drops from her shoulder in shock. She *needs* to sell?

"What do you mean, exactly?"

She glances around again, and I think she's checking if anyone is nearby before speaking.

"I probably shouldn't be telling you this. Norm would have my head if she knew, so you can't say anything. Okay?" I nod as I lean in to hear her better. "Apparently, our dad wasn't the best businessman, and the company isn't doing so well. Norm suggested maybe liquidating some of the inventory to get us back on track, and I'm in charge of that since I know all the cars."

"I see...." I rub my chin as I consider this. I had no idea Victor was a shoddy businessman. He always seemed to have it together whenever I saw him. Of course, people only show you what they want you to see. This puts Normandy's cold shoulder in a different light. She's been dealing with all of this on top of the funeral and whatever was going on in her previous life in Sacramento. It's a lot all at once, I'm sure. I examine the surrounding cars and note this can't be all of them. "Where's the rest of the inventory?" There are a few particular classics that aren't here I might be interested in *if* they still have them.

"There are three other garages housing the more unique cars." She hesitates, eyeing me cautiously. "Are you sure you want to see them?"

"Absolutely." I nod. "There were a few cars I've used before I'm particularly fond of. If they're available, of course."

Chelsie starts walking toward a back exit, and I follow her. "Oh? Which ones were they? I'll be able to tell which garage they're in."

As we step outside, we're hit with the cool desert air. When you think about Vegas in the desert, you think of hot weather, but it can be chilly in the winter. And even the summer nights can be cold compared to the triple-digit temperatures of the daytime. I'm originally from Chicago, where it's only cold when it's below freezing. These mid-fifties are downright balmy.

"There was an Impala? Not sure of the year, but it was gold."

"Oh, Betty! I know which one you're talking about. Follow me." She takes off toward another garage nearby, and I jog to catch up with her. How she's walking so fast in those heels is impressive.

I can spy my security detail surreptitiously repositioning themselves out of the corner of my eye. I've gotten used to it, though, and it doesn't usually bother me anymore. For some reason, today is different. Their presence is almost as stifling as my damned tie.

"Betty?" I wasn't aware the car had a name.

"What? Oh yeah, my dad named every car he bought. They're all female, now that I think about it. I wonder why that is."

"Actually, I think that practice has something to do with boats and ships and sea goddesses or something, but I'm not sure." Useless trivia like that hides in the corners of my brain, just waiting to come out and fill awkward silences whenever needed. Unfortunately, it's also typically incomplete.

"Weird," she mutters, punching a code into the keypad by the entrance of the next garage over and opening the door.

When I take a look around, I spot Betty right away, and she's still gorgeous.

"There she is." I smile and start making my way toward her location in the corner. Her sharp front angles and shiny chrome bumper stick out prominently in the row of cars. Chelsie follows behind me, her heels clicking on the checkerboard tile floor.

"So, Betty is a 1967 Chevy Impala SS hardtop fastback. If I remember correctly, she's got a turbo-jet V8 engine and a 4-speed manual transmission. Power steering, but manual brakes. My dad bought her at a local auction. A pretty decent bidding war was waged to win her, but he was determined. He had to have her."

"I completely understand why. Betty and I are well acquainted." I walk around to the other side, studying the impeccable paint job and the classic lines of the fastback. I rented this car a few years ago from Victor during a stay for my company's annual meeting, and it was the most fun I've had driving in a very long time. I went into the desert toward the Hoover Dam and opened her up on the highway. It was the last time I think I felt remotely free.

"Brandon?" Chelsie sounds like she's been trying to get my attention. I must have zoned out remembering that drive.

"Yeah. Sorry."

"Did you want to take her for a ride? I can grab the keys...."

"No need. How much do you want for her?" It almost sounds like I'm buying a person. Creepy. I don't need a test drive. I know this car. I want this car. And like Victor, I'll do what it takes to get it.

Chelsie seems surprised by my jumping right into the sale, but I'm not one to fuck around. If I want something, I get it. Plain and simple.

She studies me briefly, considering what to quote for a price. I have a feeling I'm about to be fleeced, but if it means good old Betty is mine, I'm okay with it.

"One Hundred and Fifty thousand." She thrusts her chin out, expecting me to haggle her down in price and ready to argue her case. I almost feel bad that I'm making this too easy for her.

"Sold." I know the car isn't worth quite that much, but if it helps Victor's daughters keep the business going, I'm all in. "I'll have my assistant, Diane, contact you for the wire transfer information if it's different from our normal business setup, and arrange delivery tomorrow if that's okay?"

Chelsie is speechless for a minute as my words sink in. She had no clue I'd be such a pushover. She stares at me with her mouth open. My grandmother would have said something about her catching flies, but I can't remember the exact phrasing, so I don't repeat it. She finally nods slightly.

"Oh, and wasn't there an Aston Martin Vanquish? or Superleggera? I can't remember which one, but it was a beauty. Is that still around? If so, I'd like to take a look at that one if you have the time. I know this is strange with the funeral and everything."

She snaps out of her stupor and catches up with what I've said. Shaking her head, she says, "Yeah, there's a Vanquish in the next garage. Her name is Tina...." Her voice trails off as she walks back to the exit, and I again follow her.

When I came to this funeral, I didn't know I'd be in the market to buy cars, but it feels good to give back a little bit in Victor's honor. I think he'd be happy I'm helping his daughters the only way I know. Now, if only I could get Normandy to see me as I am, I'd feel better about everything.

Chapter 6

Unspun

Normandy

As I view my half-sister leave the main garage with Brandon Carmichael hot on her heels, a rush of heat etches its way through my spine. What in the world are they doing? And where are they going together? In the middle of a post-funeral reception?

Chelsie seemed excited about Brandon coming today, but I didn't expect her to go after him so blatantly. I'm not sure why, but a spike of jealousy hits my heart. Chelsie and I have very different tastes in men, so I'm surprised at her interest in Brandon. Of course, there are at least one billion reasons she'd be interested. Not that I think Chelsie is necessarily shallow, but wealth of that magnitude is attractive to some people. People like Chelsie.

"I am sorry for your loss, Ms. Blake." A rough voice breaks me out of my thoughts. I turn and find an older gentleman, about my late father's age, his face sun-weathered and in an extremely outdated suit, with an unlit cigar in one hand. Definitely a Vegas local, and the back of my brain tickles that he's familiar to me somehow, but I can't pinpoint it. "Old Vic was always a tough competitor, but he was fair. I'll give him that."

"Oh?" I'm curious what kind of rival this man was to my dad. "How did you two know each other?" The way he rakes his eyes over me makes me super uncomfortable. I take a small step away from him, trying to keep it discreet and not offend him. As a woman, I hate that I have to do this, but here we are.

"We were sort of adversaries, if you will. Always fighting against each other for the good cars at auction and such, among other business dealings." He puts the cigar in his mouth and extends a nicotine-stained hand for me to shake. "I'm Louie Calnetta. I run Calnetta Cars over in Henderson."

That name does ring a small bell in my head, I think I have heard it before, but I couldn't say when or why. I begrudgingly take his hand to shake and quickly withdraw mine from his vice-like grip.

"Thank you for coming today, Mr. Calnetta." I give him a small smile and curt nod and move to walk past him, but he steps in my way, blocking me.

"What's your hurry, honey?" He puts the hand I just shook onto my arm and squeezes. Tightly. Too tightly. "I wanted to talk to you about what happens next at Mischief Motors now that Victor is gone, and perhaps offer you a proposition. A business proposition, that is." He smirks as if he's made some sort of funny joke. I am not amused in the slightest.

I glare down at his hand on me, then up at him. The audacity of this man to lay a finger on me is more shocking than anything else. I pry his hand off my arm, still holding his gaze.

"Mr. Calnetta, as I'm sure you can appreciate, I don't think today is the day to discuss our mutual business interests."

The next thing I know, there's a gentleman next to me in a suit, placing a hand under an elbow and turning me slightly.

"Ms. Blake, you're needed in the other room." He nods at Mr. Calnetta, pushes me away from him, and leads me into my office. Shutting the door, he says, "I'm sorry, Ms. Blake, but Mr. Carmichael asked me to keep an eye on you, and it appeared that the man you were speaking with was being aggressive. I didn't want to make a scene, so I figured getting you away from him would be the best course of action. I hope you don't mind my interference."

I don't even have a second to register what just happened. Aggressive? Yeah, I guess that was one way to put it. Too forward is more like it, but I've handled jerks like him before. While I'm glad I'm now away from Mr. Calnetta, I could have taken care of myself perfectly well.

"Who are you?" He's a middle-aged man with dark skin, a bald head, a graying beard, and an all-business air about him. He hasn't given me a name or told me anything about who he is or why he's here, pushing me into my office. "And what are you doing here? Why are you watching me? Brandon said what...?"

"I'm sorry, ma'am, I'm Randall Keyes. I'm on the security team for Mr. Carmichael. He asked me to watch over you today." He gives me what he must think is a smile but comes off more like a toothy scowl. I don't know what to make of him or this whole situation.

I examine him more closely. He has a definite military demeanor. Now that I look, he's obviously carrying a gun in a shoulder holster under his suit jacket.

"Did Mr. Carmichael happen to tell you *why* you are supposed to babysit me today?" I am bristling at the idea of being 'watched' by anyone, especially by someone ordered to do it by Brandon. This man is just doing his job, so complaining to him would be rude and useless.

He pushes his shoulders back, and I note that he's still blocking the doorway. If I wanted to leave this office right now, I'd need to go through him. I'm not sure what kind of resistance he would put up, if any.

"No, ma'am, he did not."

"I see." There is a window from the office into the inner garage, but the blinds covering it are shut, so I couldn't look out if I wanted to. "If I were to walk past you right now and out the door, would you let me?" I'm starting to feel claustrophobic at the idea of being held here against my will. My heart is beginning to speed up with anxiety. I'm not sure if this is worse than having to deal with lecherous Mr. Calnetta or not.

"You're free to go as you please, Ms. Blake. I was

merely removing you from the other situation." He steps aside, clearing my route to the door.

I let out my breath slowly, glad that I at least have the choice. I didn't even ask for an ID or something to prove he is who he says he is. The gun he's carrying is ID enough for me at the moment. I'm letting my instinct guide me on this one, and I get the feeling he's telling me the truth.

Now that I'm away from the crowd in the garage, the quiet of the office hits me. This is the first quiet moment I've had all day, revealing how tired I am. I can almost hear the headache coming on. Before that happens, I need to deal with Brandon.

"Is it possible for you to get your boss in here for a little chat?" I'm keeping my expression neutral, but I think Randall senses my irritation, and he looks a little nervous. I'm not sure who he's worried about, Brandon or me. Maybe both.

"I'll see what I can do. Excuse me." He steps out of the office, but his voice carries through the door. I can't tell what he's saying, but he's brief and is back in a few moments. "He'll be here shortly."

"Thank you, Randall. I appreciate that." I wave to the door behind him. "I'm sorry, would you mind...?"

He almost bows to me. "Of course. I'll be right outside if you need me." And poof, he's gone. Apparently, guarding the door to my office. It's the oddest sensation I've ever felt. Like I'm in a cage and have the key, but if I use it, I'll be in some kind of danger.

There's a slight knock on my office door, and then Brandon walks in, swiftly closing the door behind him. I had put my head down on my arms on my desk for a moment while I waited and almost fell asleep. His rushing in startles me, and it must show on my face.

"I'm sorry; I should have waited for you to call me in." He always seems to be apologizing. But then, he always seems to have something to apologize for.

"It's fine," I mutter, resting my elbows on my desk with my face in my hands, trying to gather myself. My internal batteries are drained, and I barely have the energy to have this conversation, but it needs to happen. "Please have a seat, Brandon." I wave at the chairs across from me for him to sit.

He's a little nonplussed I'm directing him around my office, but he'd better get used to it. He's on my turf now, not in some fancy boardroom where he calls all the shots. We play by my rules here. He takes a seat, and when I finally look at him, my stomach does a flip, and a flutter quickens in my chest that wants to disobey everything I'm telling myself to do in response to him – like, ignore the fact that he's hotter than Hades.

"Randall mentioned an incident out in the garage. Are you okay?" His voice is soft and low. If I let myself, I might believe he sounds genuinely concerned. I study him closer, my tired eyes examining his, trying to figure out what his game is. As handsome as he is, I can't bring myself to trust him for some reason.

"Why did you have Randall babysitting me?" I rest

my chin on my fist, narrowing my eyes at him. "Did I somehow give you a reason to believe I can't take care of myself?"

I am not a woman to be 'taken care of,' nor would I ever want to be. I have the feeling Brandon is used to getting his way when it comes to women, and that includes keeping tabs on them through his security team. Just the thought of it bristles my sensibilities.

Surprised at my displeased tone, he sits a little straighter in his seat. He's probably not used to people questioning his actions.

"I beg your pardon?" He has the good grace to at least feign confusion. "I didn't have Randall babysit you. I asked him to monitor the surroundings for irregularities. That's all."

I purse my lips and frown. I don't like liars, no matter how little the lie may be.

"Randall said you asked him to, quote, "watch over me."" I lean back and cross my arms over my chest. "Are you saying your employee would lie to me?"

Color drains from his face, and he swallows hard. He's on the verge of glaring at me now, but at the same time, I catch a fire behind his eyes, expressing something completely different. Something entirely carnal is going on there, and a shiver rushes through me.

"What would you like me to say, Normandy?" He crosses his own arms, matching my annoyed stance. "Yes, I asked him to ensure you weren't harassed today. It was mostly to keep the press away, but apparently, there were assholes allowed in here today too."

"I can deal with assholes." I raise an eyebrow at him,

indicating I might be doing that right now with him, considering I just caught him in a lie.

He nods and smirks as if he just told himself a joke. I'm not amused. I'm not seeing how any of this is funny. Not today of all days. He composes himself, and his jaw sets in a hard line. A muscle twitches as though he's steeling himself for what he's about to say.

"Of course. I'm sure you can." He pulls on his tie, dragging my eyes to his chest, and I have to snap my eyes up to his quickly to stop myself from envisioning the buttons of his shirt coming undone.

What the hell? One minute I want to strangle him with his own tie, the next, I want to rip it off him. I need to keep myself in check.

"And can I ask what you were doing with my sister?" I'm honestly more curious than anything. I try to sound more protective than jealous.

He eyes me before answering, measuring me. I can't help but squirm internally under the weight of his gaze. It's as though he can see through me, right into me, and I can't hide. I don't like the sensation.

"She was showing me some cars that were being liquidated, so I purchased a couple that have been favorites of mine over the years." He hesitates, then asks, "Is that alright? She made it sound as though it was your directive to sell some of the inventory. If that isn't the case, I'm fine with--"

"No. That's great. She is in charge of the inventory and can do what she wants with it." I try to sound indifferent, but inside I'm doing cartwheels that Chelsie pulled off a sale so fast. "I hope you're satisfied with the vehicles you've picked." I try to manage a smile, but it's an effort. I'm so damned exhausted, and this entire conversation has been a roller coaster. I can't do much more verbal sparring with him.

"I'd like to repay the favor." He leans forward, elbows on his knees, his stare intense. "Are you sure I can't take you to dinner while I'm in town for the next few days? I know things are pretty crazy for you right now, and I realize asking you the other day was inappropriate. But I really would like to get to know you, if you'd let me."

I can't believe this man. How can he look at me in my current state and think I even have the slightest interest in dating anyone? And how does he know I don't already have a boyfriend? Is it that obvious I don't? I must have 'spinster' etched on my forehead or something.

"What makes you think I want to get to know you?" I try to sound bored, but inside, my blood is pumping hard, and I can't tell if it's from anger, anxiety, or plain old attraction. Brandon seems to force me to feel every single emotion all at once, confusing the shit out of me.

He looks surprised but then smiles to himself again. I want in on these inside jokes of his. They seem so entertaining.

"Wishful thinking, I guess." He stands, shoving his hands into his pants pockets. He gazes down at me with his dark but amused eyes, and I'm exposed again. "I can take a hint, though. I wouldn't be where I am today if I couldn't read the room." He smiles, and sure enough, there are dimples. God damn it, there are dimples.

I stand and hold a hand out to him, forcing a smile of my own I don't feel. I don't feel anything right now, to be fair. That's not his fault, though. This day is just catching up with me.

"Thanks for coming today, Brandon."

He shakes my hand with a nod and a small smile before leaving. If I didn't know better, I'd say he even blushed a little bit.

I don't know what to make of him. If I'm being honest with myself, most of my hesitation is because I have no clue what a handsome billionaire like Brandon Carmichael would ever see in someone like me. I'm not a celebrity or anything; I'm sure he's got a laundry list of more qualified candidates. That fact alone is what makes me utterly suspicious. It must be some sort of game for him, like a cat playing with a mouse. And I don't want to play.

Chapter 7

Boilermaker

Brandon

When we arrive at my home on the furthest western edge of Las Vegas, where my property is next to the Red Rock Canyon National Reserve, I find a note from my local house manager, Sophie, letting me know the refrigerator has been stocked and other various house-related nonsense I have zero interest in. I love Sophie, she's worked for me for years and has run this house impeccably, but she can be a bit much. I'm surprised she didn't remind me to brush my teeth and turn out the lights before I go to bed.

I am being such a dick. I don't know why I'm so annoyed tonight. Being angry at Sophie for doing her job? That's so unlike me. I think Normandy Blake has a lot to do with it. She's gotten under my skin but obviously wants nothing to do with me. I don't know what to do with that. It sounds shitty and self-centered, but I'm not used to women rejecting me. It's just a fact of my life. Women see me, and they see dollar signs, and any potential 'no' becomes a 'yes.' It's not my fault, but it's also why I haven't even been close to marriage. If anyone is interested in me, there is no way for me to know they're not just after my money, and so far, they have been.

Normandy is very different from any other woman I've met. It's more than clear she doesn't want me, let alone any of my money. And that is God-damned attractive. She did seem to have a tinge of jealousy in her voice, though, when she asked what I was doing with her sister. That was interesting. Or did I imagine that? Again, more wishful thinking. She was annoyed with me for some reason, but I wish I understood what the reason was. Could she hate people with money that much? I suppose it's possible.

I take off my suit jacket and tie, pour myself a couple fingers of bourbon, and open up the back terrace doors. I start up the crystal firepit in the middle of the patio, warming my hands near the flames briefly. Sitting on one of the lounge chairs, I lean back and take in the fantastic sunset. I haven't done this in a long time. I don't usually have a completely clear schedule like I did today. My days are typically booked solid end to end, but I haven't even looked at my phone. I've been so preoccupied all day with thoughts of Normandy that I didn't miss it. I still don't, but then I'm also still preoccupied.

I'm betting my clear day is about to come to a screeching halt. While sipping my whiskey, I spy Taylor, whose security company I recently hired to replace my old one, approaching me with his cell phone to his ear, apparently in an intense conversation with someone. I take a deep breath before he gets to me, steeling myself against the oncoming tidal wave of whatever-the-fuck has gone wrong now.

"Mr. Carmichael, I have LCC's VP of PR, Maggie, for you. She says it's urgent." He holds the phone out to me.

"That's a lot of initials, Taylor. It *must* be important. Thanks." I smirk as I take the phone from him, and he returns the smile and nods in agreement at the ridiculousness of it all. He's been with me for a few months and seems like a down-to-earth guy. I lean back again, close my eyes for a second, then get to it. "What's up, Maggie? Isn't it past your bedtime in NYC?" I just had to throw in a few more initials.

"Eve's been arrested." Her voice is flat and lacking any emotion whatsoever. A chill runs down my spine at her words. So, it's started, then. I knew this was coming, but I thought the SEC would give me a head's up. Perhaps they did try to contact me, but my phone's been off all damned day. *Shit.*

"Okay..." I'm not sure what else to say. I thought I was prepared for this , but I misjudged myself. "What's the fallout? I've been off the grid all day."

"It's not good, Brandon. The press *and* the public are starting to turn on you. Generally, we have one or the other, but never both like this. The socials are going berserk."

"Wait, what? Turning on *me*? Why? I didn't have anything to do with this. I fucking helped the SEC figure out it was Eve in the first fucking place." I jump up, startling Taylor, and start pacing the patio, making a circuit around the pool, not caring how fucking cold it is away from the fire pit. My blood is boiling at this point, and I need to cool off.

Maggie goes silent, letting me process the news for a minute.

Once I have my temper under control, I ask, "So what's next then? Should I care about this? The truth of everything will come out soon, no?"

"Should you care? Brandon, you do realize the shareholders' meeting is in two weeks, right? The Board could propose a vote of no confidence against you. This is something we need to get ahead of. First and foremost, call an emergency Board meeting to fill everyone in on the investigation. After consulting with Legal, I'll prepare press releases and a speech for the press conference we should have right after the Board meeting."

"Right. Okay. That sounds good." I'm still shocked this has all turned on me somehow. I never in my wildest dreams saw this coming. My brain has again switched to damage control, which I've been doing way too much lately. "Have Legal get back with me too. If we've somehow misstepped here, I might have a bone to pick with them."

"Will do." Maggie hesitates for a moment. The skin

on the back of my neck prickles. I have the feeling I'm also not going to like what she says next.

"What is it, Maggie? I can tell you've got something else. Spill."

"Do you have a date for the charity gala the night before the annual meeting this year? I really don't think you should go stag again. You need to separate yourself from Eve as soon as possible, and a new love interest or companion would help tons."

My mind goes to Normandy Blake, but I cringe, remembering her blatant dismissal of me earlier in the day. I've asked her out twice and been shot down each time. I don't know if I can survive a third time. Or, maybe the third time could be the charm?

"I'll need to think on that one, Maggie. Thanks for the insight, though." I'm not comfortable recruiting a date just to improve my optics with the public. That's not me. I've never done it, and I don't see myself starting now. I can appreciate Maggie's point, however. Distancing myself from Eve needs to happen. *Fast.*

The following day I'm up before the crack of dawn, preparing for a video conference with the rest of the Board of Directors. Since we're all scattered around the country, scheduling last minute is a nightmare, but Diane manages to nail down a time in the early morning. I have our attorneys join the call to help put everyone's mind at ease that things are under control and there's nothing legally we need to worry about. The only issue we're genuinely facing is the court of public opinion, which has been spun out of control. But, I assure everyone, it's fixable. I hope to God I'm right.

I spend the next few hours doing press interviews with various business news outlets, reassuring the public of the same thing, and those responsible for any crimes will be punished with my blessing and cooperation. I sidestep the relationship questions as smoothly as I can.

The next thing I know, it's the end of the day, and Sophie, who has been hovering outside my office door on and off all day, finally bursts in with a plate of food for me.

"You skipped lunch. You shouldn't do that." Sophie is an older woman, a former nightclub owner during the halcyon days of Vegas, who never stops caring for other people. I've heard stories of all the girls she picked up off the street and gave jobs and temporary shelter until they got back on their feet. She earned the nickname "Saint Sophie" during that time and still deserves it. Her nightclub closed years ago, but when she's not working for me, she's volunteering at the youth homeless shelter downtown. She's a ball of kinetic energy. I don't know where she gets it from.

"Well, I didn't have much choice today, unfortunately." I lean back in my chair, rubbing my temples to fend off another oncoming headache. "The world needs saving." I glance up at her and grin.

"I'm telling you. You are Bruce Wayne, and I'm your Alfred. I swear I will find your bat suit one of these days."

I knew that was coming, but it still makes me chuckle. "And I keep telling you, I am no superhero. Quite the opposite. I'm somebody's arch-nemesis, I'm sure. I just haven't met them yet." I instantly think of Normandy and her clear dislike of me. *Or maybe I already have.*

Taylor knocks on the open door. "Mr. Carmichael, we're making the arrangements to pick up the cars you purchased from Mischief Motors...did you want to come along? Or just have us retrieve them? We're leaving shortly."

I don't need to be asked twice. After today, I could use some hot rod therapy and maybe even a glimpse of Normandy to top it all off. I jump to my feet. "I'm in."

"But your dinner...." Sophie calls after me, disappointed at another skipped meal.

"Keep it in the fridge. I'll heat it up when I come back. I promise."

Food is currently the last thing on my mind.

Chapter 8

Smile

Normandy

I shut my office door and am heading toward the exit when Chelsie calls me from behind.

"Where are you going?"

"Home. Well, Dad's house." I'm still not used to staying there, and it doesn't feel like home, but I don't know what to call it half the time. I also don't know what I'm doing long-term yet, and my life in Sacramento is on pause indefinitely while I clean things up here. When I came back here after Dad died, I had no idea my life would change so dramatically. Sometimes I want to send for all my things, and other times I want to run back there and never look back. "Why? What's up? Want to grab some dinner or something?"

She's a little amped up, her cheeks flush with color. *What on earth has her in such a state?*

"You can't leave. Brandon's on his way to pick up his cars." She almost jumps up and down with excitement. Chelsie has been so proud all day with the sales she made, and she should be. The prices she got for the cars were astronomical. I can't believe Brandon didn't know he was overpaying. That's one more stupid point for him, but he's still in the negative as far as I'm concerned.

"I don't need to be here for that. I'm sure you can handle it." I start heading for the exit again, determined not to get caught up in her whirlwind. "The funds came through this morning, and you know how to transfer a title. I'll see you tomorrow."

"But..." She almost sounds timid, as though she doesn't want to handle it alone. Before I can say anything else encouraging, the door opens, and Brandon walks into the garage, pulling off his sunglasses with another gentleman behind him.

He's not in a suit this time, but a light gray button-down shirt with rolled sleeves and jeans that hug lean but powerful-looking thighs. His hair isn't as styled as it was yesterday, but it's still perfectly disheveled. The day-old stubble on his face makes my fingers instantly itch to touch it and run a finger along his jawline to see if it's as rough as it looks. My mouth goes dry, and I need to stop before walking right into him. He grins at me with a megawatt smile as though he's happy to see me, and those god-damned dimples send a tremor through me. *Holy shit, this man.*

"Normandy, it's so good to see you. I was hoping you'd still be here." He holds a hand out to me, and I reluctantly take it briefly, but I pull away before I can melt into a puddle at his feet from his touch. I can't let myself give in to this physical attraction to him.

"Oh? Why is that?" I can't imagine what he wants with me. I've made myself pretty clear with him. At least, I think I have.

"I have a business proposition for you, actually." He slides his sunglasses onto the collar of his shirt and shoves his hands deep into his jeans pockets. If I didn't know better, I'd say he was nervous. What the hell could he be anxious about relating to business? He's Brandon Fucking Carmichael, for Christ's sake. And what business could he possibly have with me?

I cross my arms and raise an eyebrow at him, intrigued. "I'm listening...."

"Nope. Not here." His eyes sparkle with mischief. "Dinner. I'll only discuss it with you over dinner."

Of course, there's a catch. I would have been shocked if there wasn't one. I really don't want anything to do with him right now. I saw the news last night about his ex-girlfriend getting arrested and had to investigate it more today. My curiosity overtook me, and I couldn't help it. I wanted to see what kind of woman Brandon would date, and Eve Cromwell is about 20,000 leagues above me on the status ladder, at least compared to me and my little solo consulting firm. Sure, she's a criminal, but she's gorgeous and filthy rich. She'll probably buy herself a simple slap on the wrist.

When I don't respond right away, he takes my silence for consideration.

"Business only. I swear." I notice then that one of his dimples is higher and deeper than the other, and the imperfection only exaggerates his perfection, as if that makes any sense. My brain is running on a hamster wheel of thoughts; go, don't go, go, don't go.

"Fine." I finally say, trying to shut up my brain more than anything else. Plus, if I go this one time, I can get him to stop asking, and we can both go on with our lives. Also, with what he overpaid for the cars he bought, I do feel like I kind of owe him, though he could easily afford it. The thought pisses off my inner feminist, but I give in. "Business only," I repeat, making sure he's clear on the objective.

Chelsie has made her way to us and has a sly smile of her own playing on her lips. If I didn't know better, I'd think she was in on this ambush, but I don't think she was. She's probably just happy to see me so annoyed. She always did get a kick out of watching other people's drama. She holds out a set of keys to Brandon and drops them into his outstretched hand.

"Have a nice dinner." Her bright eyes twinkle with mirth. I thoroughly dislike my half-sister right now. "Betty is right out in the lot for you. Gassed up and ready to go."

"Thank you, Chelsie." Brandon turns to the guy behind him, who I think is part of his security team. "You can handle the paperwork? I'll see you back at the house later."

"But, sir..." the gentleman is startled at this announcement, and I think Brandon is going off-script. This isn't what was planned.

"I'll be fine, Taylor. It's okay." Brandon turns to me next, ignoring the growing concern of his security guard. "Shall we?"

I switch my gaze between the two men, unsure what to do now. I guess Brandon has the right to ditch his security detail if he wants to. And, if he feels safe without them with whatever he has planned, I guess I should too. I nod and move to follow him, and he opens the door for me, his grin broader than before. *Those god-damned dimples.*

Out in the lot, I start heading to my car to follow him. He gently grabs my arm and stops, forcing me to stop with him.

"Where are you going?" He's confused, though I don't know why.

"To get my car to follow you...?"

"Come with Betty and me." That crooked smile on his face is infectious, but I force myself not to reciprocate. "It'll be fun."

"Fun? I thought this was a business dinner." I had a feeling he was going to derail that idea.

"It is." Those dimples are lethal weapons, and he knows what he's doing with them. There's something I think is hope in his eyes, but I don't understand it. I don't get anything about this man. "But the way *to* the business dinner can be fun, can't it?"

I cross my arms again. I can't help it. I need to know what his game is.

"Why are you doing this?"

"Doing what? Taking you to dinner?" He's playing coy, and it's so damned cute I have to bite the inside of my cheek so I don't smile back at him.

"Ugh. Fine. Let's go." I brush past him toward the gold car named "Betty." He hurries to beat me to the car and opens the passenger door for me. He even bows slightly as I approach. I just shake my head.

Before he gets in the car, he makes a quick phone call. Once inside, his nearness becomes magnified as we're cocooned together, his light cologne mixing with the leather of the interior. My senses seem heightened whenever he's near me, and I mean *all* of my senses. I've never experienced anything like it before, and I don't know if I like it. I feel like I'm a bit out of control when I'm around him, which bothers the crap out of me.

"The restaurant we're going to is literally just up the road, so you won't be far from your car." He turns the key, and the engine roars to life, rumbling beneath us like a newly-tamed predator. The grin on his face at the sound is like a little kid on Christmas morning, and I can't help but smile now. I catch myself before he notices, though, and turn to look out the passenger side window as he pulls onto the road.

Brandon drives carefully, not pushing the car's limits like I thought he would. His restraint is surprising but admirable. Mischief Motors is very close to the airport, and after maybe five minutes of driving north, with the bright lights of the strip beckoning in the distance, he pulls into the lot of a familiar upscale Italian restaurant. While I haven't been here in years, my dad would bring me here for special occasions like birthdays or graduations. I can't help but tear up a little bit at the memories we made here.

"Are you okay?" Brandon's turned off the car and is studying me with concern.

"Yeah. I'm fine."

"You don't look fine. You look upset."

Under his intense gaze, I feel seen but also exposed. My volatile history of making bad choices in men has taught me not to allow this closeness. But something about Brandon makes me want to open up to him. I know in my heart and my head that would be a mistake. Doing that will only open me up to hurt. And not just me, him too.

I push open the door and step out. I don't want to discuss my grief with Brandon. We are not friends. We're barely acquaintances. I don't even know why I agreed to this. This is supposed to be a business dinner, so let's get down to business.

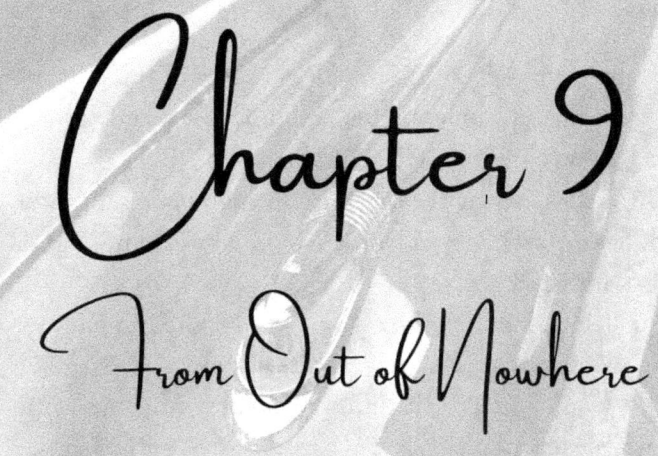

Chapter 9

From Out of Nowhere

Brandon

So, the Ice Queen still hasn't thawed to me yet. This is turning out to be more difficult than I initially thought. I guess I need to try harder but fuck if I know how to do that. I am not used to working so hard for a woman's attention. I haven't had to chase someone like this since my first year at Harvard. And Normandy Blake is not like anyone I've ever been interested in. I sense that there are sensitive and vulnerable layers to her that she hasn't shown anyone, and uncovering what those are is intriguing.

I catch up with her in time to open the door to the restaurant for her. Chivalry is not dead for me and treating a woman well shouldn't be a thing of the past. In my book, making someone feel cared for or taken care of isn't a bad thing. It's how it should be.

Regardless of my intentions, Normandy frowns, and she nods begrudgingly at me as she walks past and enters the restaurant. Baby steps.

I called ahead, and the owner, Maria, is waiting for us when we walk in. I'm not appropriately dressed as I usually would be, and it didn't even dawn on me until now when she shakes her head as she scowls at my jeans.

"Brandon, *tesoro*. What am I going to do with you?" Her scowl turns quickly into a grin as she holds her arms out to invite me into a warm hug. I have to lean down to reach her; she's so short. When I pull away, she eyes Normandy carefully, giving her the full once-over but ending with a nod of approval. "*Moglie*, no?"

"No," Normandy laughs nervously, a pink flush running up her neck into her cheeks. "Definitely *not* his wife."

Maria and I share a look, both of us surprised Normandy understands Italian. Maria winks at me as though she knows better, but as I glance over to Normandy, the flush looks to be more from anger than embarrassment or nerves. That's not a good sign.

We're led through the restaurant to a private booth in the back, away from other tables or prying eyes. As soon as we sit down, a traditional tomato and bread soup is delivered, and wine is poured.

"I'll be back shortly with your entrees," Maria says, smiling widely, and she turns away toward the kitchen.

Normandy looks after her, confused. "We didn't tell her what we wanted...."

I can't help but chuckle. "Maria knows what you want, even if you don't. It's a gift of hers."

"Oh...okay." She twists her wine glass on the table by the stem, staring at it intently. "So, what is this business proposition you have for me?" Her dark eyes snap up to mine, and they're just as intense as the photo I have of her. Her self-confidence is beautiful, and everything she does is passionate. I like that about her.

"Getting right to it, huh?" I laugh, but even I can hear the nerves in it. I don't know what it is about Normandy Blake that undoes me whenever I speak to her. It's as though her entire aura short circuits my brain.

She doesn't reply and keeps her gaze steady. Waiting for me to go on. How can I warm her to me if she won't give me a chance?

"As you may or may not know, LC Consolidated hosts a charity gala every year before our annual meeting."

"I am aware. From what I've seen in our books, it's one of Mischief Motor's busier nights." She shrugs silently, but then her eyes tighten, and she's a little panicked. "Is the ball being called off with your girlfriend's arrest?"

"Ex-girlfriend. And no."

Her shoulders sag in relief, and I take a minute to examine her closer. I wasn't sure what would happen when she took over the business, but I'm happy to see her concern. She really does have her company's best interest in mind and takes her position seriously. I admire that. Victor would be proud of her.

"Ok, good."

"Though that particular item is related...."

An eyebrow ticks up. And damn. Skeptical Normandy is hot. "Oh? How so?"

"According to my Vice President of Public Relations, I need to separate myself from my ex as much as possible. I'm proposing for you to act as my girlfriend until after the gala. Four dates maximum, including the gala, and then we can go our separate ways. I'm willing to pay you if you want, you can name your price, but I think the publicity from it might also benefit your company. It would put Mischief Motors on the map, for sure."

She had been about to take a sip of wine but now holds her glass two inches from her mouth, which has now dropped open in shock. She still hasn't moved. I had expected a reaction like this and am not surprised by it. But maybe I didn't word it right? Or I wasn't clear?

"I know it sounds crazy, but if you think about it, we can benefit each other from some positive publicity. Don't you think?" I realize I hadn't actually asked her a question until now. Maybe this will get a response from her.

She slowly lowers her wine glass to the table, never breaking eye contact with me. The skin on the back of my neck prickles. I think if looks could kill, I'd be laid out in this booth like a victim of an old-school mafia hit.

"Did you just offer me money... for a date?"

I'm not so sure about the laws in Vegas surrounding prostitution, but holy shit. The way she said it makes what I offered sound downright awful and possibly even illegal. I rake my hands down my face, trying to think of how to salvage this. I've really stuck my foot in it this time.

"When you say it like that, it sounds pretty bad...."

"Pretty bad?" Her tone is so cold; I feel frostbite starting on my skin. She throws her napkin on the table and slides out of the booth. "You may be able to buy whatever you want, but you can't buy me. Let's get that clear right now." She points a finger at me, stopping me from saying anything. "You, Mr. God-damned Billionaire, couldn't afford me. And even if you could? I still wouldn't go out with you."

Her words sting, but more than that, I need to correct her thinking I was trying to buy her somehow.

"Normandy, wait." I jump up and maneuver around her, stopping her from leaving the private back area. If we're going to get into it, it needs to be here, where no one else can see. And that's for both of us, not just me. "Please. Hear me out. That came out completely wrong. I would never, ever, pay to date you."

She crosses her arms, a stance I see too often from her. This is all going straight to shit.

I take a breath and try again. "I am very sorry, Normandy. More than you can possibly know at this moment. But before I dig this hole any deeper, can we please sit back down and talk this through?" I hold an arm out, indicating the booth.

I don't blame her for her reaction. I fucked this whole thing up, and I'm usually so good with words. Being around Normandy takes all of that away. I'm reduced to a blubbering idiot whenever I'm around her, and I don't get it. I shouldn't feel anything for her. She's been crystal clear; she wants nothing to do with me. I can't stop myself, though. And I can't seem to keep my cool around her.

She gives me the wariest look I've ever gotten from a woman and turns to sit down again.

"This is against my better judgment, by the way."

"Duly noted." I do appreciate that she's giving me this time to fix everything. Now, I just need to figure out how to do that without pissing her off. "And, thank you."

Chapter 10

Vertigo

Normandy

I can't believe I'm still here. I should have walked out as soon as he said, "name your price." I don't have a price. I cannot be bought. So why I'm sitting across from this jerk, expecting him to somehow convince me to stay, I have no idea. I pull my phone out of my purse, anticipating the need to call for a car should this get any worse.

"Mr. Carmichael, while I'm grateful for your purchases today, I don't think that entitles you to...."

"Wait, what?" He seems shocked at my inference, as if he didn't just offer me money for dates as some sort of quid pro quo. "I am not entitled to anything here. Trust me, I completely fucked up what I am trying to ask of you. This could not have gone any more wrong if I tried." He chuckles to himself and rakes a hand through his hair, and the dimples make another appearance. *Damn it, those dimples can't save him every time.*

I don't like that I'm reacting to him this way or giving in like this when I know I should walk away. Shit, I should most likely run as far from him as I can. But he mentioned this might help our business too, and if that's possible, I need to consider it. Even if it is with this asshole. However, I have to figure out a way to be in his presence and not get weak-kneed at the same time. That's proving more difficult than I imagined.

"First and foremost, you should know that I have a strict policy of not dating clients or employees, and well, you're a client." I just made up the policy, but it's my business; I can do that sort of thing.

"Well, these aren't going to be real dates, right? So, it shouldn't count against your policy. It's strictly marketing."

Damn him and his loopholes.

"So, what's your plan?" I keep my tone professional. This is a business transaction, only not in the way he thinks. "But understand there will be no money exchanged. I don't want your money." That much needs to be clear. I can't believe I have to be saying these things.

He physically slumps in relief and reaches across the table to take my hand. My first instinct is to pull away, but he grips tighter, trapping my hand in his. When I meet his eyes, something passes between us. I don't know what it is, but it makes me squirm a little inside. When

Brandon Carmichael really looks at you, you feel seen. I'm unsure what to do with that, so I do nothing.

"I understand." He still hasn't let go of me, and now his thumb runs across my knuckles. I'm surprised his hands are slightly rough, not soft as I assumed they would be. "I'm thinking three or four very public dates before the gala. My PR team can leak location details to the press, no problem. You can pick what and where those dates are if you want. And we can use your company's cars with whatever branding you want to use to get the name out there for Mischief Motors, though once your name gets out, it will be attached to your company, obviously."

Good God. The press. I can't believe I'm actually considering this. This is insanity. But how complicated could it be to go on pretend dates with him and attend a gala? And then I can have absolutely nothing to do with him. And our business can finally be on track after Dad left it in such shambles. I glance down at our hands still joined on the table and consider the offer. It would probably be great for business to have Brandon's name attached to it. It would lend us some credibility. And, my dad was friends with him, so perhaps he isn't all bad.

He takes my silence for the hesitation it is and goes on. "Look, I know I have given you the absolute worst first impression a person can give the last few days. I don't know what the hell is going on with me. Something about you makes me trip over myself and say stupid shit, and I don't know why. Can we start over?" He lets go of my hand but holds his out again in greeting. "Hi, I'm

Brandon Carmichael, CEO of LC Consolidated. Nice to meet you."

The dimples are out again in full force, and now there's a twinkle in his eyes sparkling with humor and something else. Something sexy that is so beguiling, I can't help but smile back, but it feels like a con in my head. I shake his hand enthusiastically.

"Hello, Mr. Carmichael. I'm Normandy Blake, Co-owner of Mischief Motors. Don't fuck with me or my business, or you'll regret it." I smile wide, almost baring my teeth like a cornered wolf. I drop his hand and pick up my wine glass. "If I agree to this, there need to be parameters. *Two* dates and the gala, no more. And no kissing or anything of the sort. Nothing more than hand-holding and maybe a hug here or there. And I do not speak to the press. That's it. Those are my terms."

The disappointment that washes over him is almost comical. He wasn't expecting rules or boundaries to be put down. What did he expect? But then, he did offer me money; so his ideas were pretty screwed up to start with.

He swallows hard but nods, taking a swig of his own wine. "That's a decent opening salvo." The grin spreading on his face is so playful and devious that my stomach flips, wondering what the deviant part of it could be. He's enjoying this game way too much. But I might be too.

"Opening salvo?" I arch a brow at him.

"Yes. We're negotiating, aren't we? That was a good start. Now it's my turn."

The way he says those words makes my skin vibrate with an electric current. I should not be reacting this way.

"Let's hear it."

"*Three* dates and the gala, hand holding is fine, but kisses allowed from the second date on. And lots of hugs. I'm a hugger." The dimples flash again, damn it. He has to know what those are doing to me. "And, one informal press Q&A."

I narrow my gaze at him. "Two dates plus the gala, hand holding is okay, a single kiss on the cheek in front of the press at the gala, zero Q&A, and *maybe* a few public hugs. Final offer." I meet his eyes, both of us highly amused now by this so-called 'negotiation.'

"And I reserve the right to amend these terms, with your agreement, of course, should the need arise."

"Need?" I can't help but laugh.

"Yes. I may need to kiss you before the gala. I reserve the right to make that happen."

"For the record, if this is all fake for the press, why would we need to kiss?" *Damn. The thought is becoming more and more intriguing, though.*

"Don't people kiss in public anymore? Is romance truly that dead? Whatever happened to good old PDA?"

I roll my eyes at him. "Fine. But only with my permission."

"Oh, you'll agree. You might even instigate it yourself."

"We'll see about that, Mr. Carmichael." He's so damned confident.

"We will indeed, Ms. Blake." His eyes brighten with excitement from our interplay. "So, are we in agreement?"

I consider him before answering. What the hell am I

getting myself into? Agreeing to date Brandon Carmichael? Sure, they will be fake dates, but it can still be dangerous. And with the press maelstrom around him right now, it could get crazy. Am I prepared for that? I think of my dad's business and how hard he worked to make it a success. Maybe there's a reason why we met at my dad's funeral. Maybe he brought us together somehow from the other side. That is something he totally would do; he was such a hopeless romantic. And though this situation is definitely hopeless, the thought settles everything in my mind. I need to do whatever I can to keep his legacy going.

"We have an agreement." My stomach tightens as I say the words, feeling like I've just signed my own death warrant. I hope I'm doing the right thing.

The smolder in his return gaze could melt me right here if I let it. Luckily, the owner comes out with our food just then, saving me from having to respond. Saving me from myself.

Chapter 11

Lemon to a Knife Fight

Brandon

I can't believe I dug myself out of that hole. Actually, it was more than a hole, it was a fucking crater the size of Montana, and I somehow clawed my way out of it. I still don't know how I did it, but I am not about to question it either.

Maria brings our dinners; sure enough, she knows precisely what each of us will love. Normandy is impressed with Maria's selection for her, and after her first bite, she closes her eyes and moans.

"Oh my God. This is heaven."

Watching her at that moment, eyes closed and groaning in ecstasy, is almost more than I can handle. I am not prepared. I can only stare at her, imagining her under me with the same expression on her face, those sounds in her throat as I make love to her.

"Sorry, this food is amazing." Her words snap me out of my x-rated daydream, and I refocus on her. She's blushing as though she knows what I was thinking, but she has no idea.... "I haven't been here in so long. I forgot how good the food is."

"So, you've been here before?" I don't even know what I'm asking; words are just coming out. I'm still stuck in the perverse thoughts of a second ago.

"Oh yeah, this was our special occasion place when I was younger." She looks around at the carpet and artwork, presumably searching for similarities or changes. "Lots of birthdays were spent here." She gets a far-off look in her eyes as though she's remembering particular moments fondly. At this moment, with that expression, she's even more stunning now than she was moaning about the food a second ago. My breath almost catches as I take her in.

I need to be careful here. I admit that so far, Normandy Blake has been a challenge, but one I've been game to meet. And, one I think I've overcome, or am about to, if our dating agreement is any indication. But I'm not sure what my end goal is with her. Am I just doing this to make it through the Eve scandal relatively unscathed? I could be that cold, couldn't I? That indifferent? The idea of using Normandy tightens my chest in a way I'm not used to. I barely know her, yet I'm already afraid of hurting her? I might need to get my head checked.

It takes me a second, but I notice Normandy has gotten quiet. When I glance over, her head is down, and she's pushing the food on her plate around with her fork. A lump forms in my throat as I realize she's most likely missing her father right now.

"You know, the last time I saw Victor, he was on the phone arguing with someone, I have no clue what about, but man, he was the king of one-liners." I can't help but chuckle, remembering the incident. "He said, "*Louie,*" or "*Lou,*" something like that, I can't remember exactly, *"I started this business with nothing, and I still have most of it. I'd like to keep it that way."* He sure had a way of turning negatives into positives, even in the middle of arguments."

She snaps her eyes up to mine, she's not laughing, and her brow furrows. "Did you say, Louie? Did you get the last name?"

"No." I shrug. "I don't think he ever said it. Why?"

"There was a man at the funeral, Louie Calnetta, apparently a business rival. He was creepy, and your security guard had to move me away from him when he got too aggressive with me."

"Is that when you called me into your office to yell at me?" The smirk on my face is involuntary. The whole thing reminded me of elementary school, but the smile doesn't last long as I realize what she's said. "He was aggressive with you? How so?" I'm instantly on alert now. "Randall said there was an incident but didn't go into details. Did this guy hurt you? Nobody said anything." I'm reaching for my phone, preparing to put a hit out on this Louie guy if I need to. This is Vegas, somebody still does that, right? "If I'd known at the time, I would have done something...."

"No, he didn't hurt me. Just squeezed my arm too tight and said he wanted to talk business." She seems to shiver as she thinks about it.

Before she finishes her sentence, I text Taylor to find out everything I can about this Louie Calnetta person.

"Brandon."

"Yeah, one second." Next, I type out a text to the head of my legal department to draft an application for a restraining order to keep him away from Normandy. This asshole is going to find out what it's like to have someone get aggressive with him. We'll see how he fucking likes it.

"Brandon. What are you doing?"

"I, am taking care of it." I press send on the last text. "There. Done." I put my phone back on the table face down. I don't need to see replies yet. I know they'll get what I asked done. It's what I pay them for.

She stares at me blankly. "Taking care of what?"

"Louie Calnetta. You won't need to worry about him. I took care of it."

Her eyes widen in disbelief. "You did what? How? And more importantly, why?"

I'm a little thrown by her reaction. I figured getting this guy off her back would be a good thing, a welcome thing. But of course, Normandy has other ideas.

"I'm having my security find out what they can about this asshole, and my lawyers are getting a protective order prepared to keep him away from you."

"Are you being serious? A restraining order? That's a bit extreme."

I grab her hand, and again she doesn't pull away. I like it. Way more than I probably should. "As my girlfriend, fake or otherwise, you should know I won't put up with anyone fucking with you. If someone crosses that line, they're going to regret it. That's all." I shrug. It's the truth. I will not put up with anyone messing with her or her business. Not while I'm around, anyway.

She doesn't say anything but gives me an unreadable look. She's got a great poker face. I'd hate to get into a high-stakes hand with her. I have a feeling she'd take me for everything I've got, and I'd let her.

Chapter 12

Vultures

Normandy

What the hell have I gotten myself into? Did he seriously order his legal team to get a restraining order for Louie Calnetta? This is surreal. He snaps his fingers, and the world moves for him. I can't imagine wielding or even having that kind of power. While I am beyond annoyed that he thinks he can steamroll over anyone that pisses him off, I have to admit to myself I also kind of like the idea he's doing it for me. There's something about a man taking control of a situation when you just don't want to and fixing the problem without having to ask.

The fierceness in his eyes when he says he won't let anyone fuck with me flips a switch in me. He's still holding my hand, and as his intensity rises as he speaks, he grips my fingers that much tighter. It's almost too intense. I wriggle my fingers a little to loosen his grip, and he must notice he's holding on too tight because he reluctantly releases my hand. I don't know what to make of any of this. It's too much.

"I think I need to go home." I'm still unsure how I feel about what I've agreed to tonight, and I need to be somewhere without Brandon distracting me to let it all sink in. His close proximity, intense eyes, and hand-holding are clouding my thoughts. "Can you take me back to my car, please?"

Disappointment clouds his face, but he nods, signaling for the check. "Of course." His phone buzzes on the table, and a crease forms between his brows when he sees the screen. "Taylor, what's up?"

The intensity is back, and his jaw sets in a hard line. Whatever Taylor is saying isn't making him happy. When he hangs up, he scrubs his hands down his face and suddenly appears tired. Definitely not happy.

"What's wrong?" He's avoiding my eyes, and that is a red flag.

He lets out a deep sigh. "It's started already. I thought we'd be able to dictate the pace of things, but the press has other ideas."

"The press?" I don't understand what the press has to do with anything yet. We haven't done anything press-worthy.

"The vultures are congregating in the parking lot.

Apparently, somebody dining here saw us and spread the story on social media." He shakes his head in disgust. "This place is usually safe from prying eyes. I'm sorry this is starting so soon."

Maria comes by with a sad smile and lays a gentle hand on my arm. "*Cara mia*, let's get you both through the kitchen to the back door, *bene*?"

I nod and follow her to the kitchen, Brandon behind me with a hand protectively on the small of my back. He's keeping close as if he'll shield me from an attack. It's both appreciated but unsettling. I don't like the idea I need protection from anything.

I find a familiar face as we approach the back door, but he's not flashing a toothy scowl tonight. Randall stands alert, head on a swivel surveying the surrounding area. Beyond the exit is a limo only a few feet away with a door open. Randall positions himself on the other side of the car's open door, creating a privacy corridor.

"Duck lower than the top of the car door," Brandon whispers in my ear, his breath jostling my hair and tickling my neck.

I do as he instructs and bend low as I step into the limousine, Brandon right behind me.

"Girl, what have you gone and gotten yourself into?"

I glance at the front of the car and see Bianca in the driver's seat, smirking at me in the rearview mirror. Of course, this is a Mischief Motors limo. She gives me a coy wink when our eyes meet.

"That's a great question, Bianca," I smirk back at her. "Can we get out of here, please?"

"Yes, boss." She salutes me in the mirror as Randall

gets in next to her, and the divider slides up once we start moving.

As we make our way through the parking lot to the main road, I'm amazed at how many photographers there actually are, waiting for a glimpse of Brandon. I count at least ten.

"Wow. Do you ever get used to that?"

He's been staring at his phone and not paying attention to the paparazzi. He glances up and gives the crowd a brief once over, indifferent to their existence. "What? Oh, yeah, you do get used to it. Eventually." His voice is flat, no longer the intense and passionate man of a few minutes ago.

I get the feeling something more than the press is bothering him, but I don't want to get into a deep conversation with Brandon about anything right now. I'm still sorting through the fact I just had to sneak out the back of a restaurant I've been to many times in my life without incident.

After a few minutes of riding in silence, I notice we're not heading back to the depot. I do not need another surprise tonight.

"Where are we going?" I don't know why I think Brandon will know this information, he's been with me the entire time, and neither of us has been told anything.

"Taking you home." A sadness drips from his voice, and he hasn't torn his eyes away from the passing scenery since we started moving.

"But what about my car?" I need my car to get back to work tomorrow.

"Expect to be driven around from now on."

"What? Why? I have a perfectly good car." It's happening slowly, but the magnitude of tonight's events is dawning on me. I think I'm in denial, though.

"I'm sorry, Normandy." His sad eyes meet mine, and I can plainly see he means what he's saying. "Like I said, I thought we'd be able to manage the pace of this, but it's gotten ahead of me. I don't know how, but it did." He looks away again, his brows furrowing in anger now. He's mad at himself.

My heart, which has been racing since getting up from our table, finally begins to slow down. Knowing he's as upset about this as I am is a comfort, albeit a small one. Of course, I wouldn't be in this situation if not for him, so there's that too.

"It's okay." I don't know why I'm trying to make him feel better, but the sadness in his eyes and voice is too much for me to handle. Just as he shielded me on the way out of the restaurant, I have the urge to protect him from whatever is upsetting him. It's inexplicable, but it's there. Recognizing it, though, I stop myself.

During our so-called 'negotiations,' he had mentioned the press. He knew they would be a factor and upend my life like this. He even stated he thought they could handle the pacing. He's known the paparazzi would be after me but didn't warn me. Maybe I should have figured that much out myself, but he planned for them to be involved in the first place. It's only fair he let me in on the consequences of all this. I knew they'd be involved somehow, that's kind of the point of this arrangement, but it's already starting out a little insane. This is only a reputation bump for both of us anyway, right? That's all this is?

Before I can think any more of it, we're at my dad's house, and a small group of photographers is camped out on the sidewalk. Luckily, my father's house is older and set back from the road, with a gate. It's not the most modern of homes, in fact, it's very much stuck in the '70s, but it is reasonably private.

"Fuck," Brandon mutters.

The remote for my gate is in my car, so Bianca pulls up to the keypad, and I give her the code to enter. Once we arrive at the back of the house, Randall jumps out and blocks any sliver of a view the photographers might have from the street. Brandon exits and does the same. I take a deep breath and dash for my back door, pretty sure no one can see me from the street.

Brandon tries to grab my hand as I pass him, but I slide out of his grasp and enter the house without a glance back. Once inside, I lean back against the door, breathing heavily. I feel like I just ran through a shooting range and somehow dodged every single bullet. Before I can get too comfortable, my phone rings. It's Brandon.

"Close the blinds on your front windows."

"Shit." I hang up and make my way to the front of the house, trying to stay out of view while I move, which is near impossible. I eventually get all the blinds in the house closed, not just the ones facing the street. Even though I can't see the photographers outside, I know they're there. The sensation of being watched or under surveillance is so unnerving I jump at every little sound in the house. I get ready for bed quickly and lie there, staring at the ceiling, knowing I'll never find sleep tonight with people right outside.

I did not sign up for this. Did I?

Chapter 13

Stop the World I Wanna Get Off With You

Brandon

As Bianca drives up to my gate and speaks to the guard on the intercom, I ignore the flock of press gathering around the car. Randall jumps out and joins the other security guards, who quickly swarm in and move everyone away from us so we can drive through. Bianca's driven for me before, so she's used to the circus that can sometimes wait for me when I get home. However, tonight seems particularly crazy.

Pulling into the side portico of the estate, Bianca lowers the divider between us and stares at me in the mirror; her expression is apprehensive but also conveys a warning. I know what that look is. It's a *'don't fuck with*

Normandy, or else' look. I get it. She's been with Mischief Motors for several years and was fiercely loyal to Victor. She must know the last thing I want is to hurt Normandy. I meet her gaze and nod my understanding before stepping out of the car and into the house.

Once inside, I head straight for my office. Taylor meets me in the hallway and walks with me. I check my watch briefly; it's just after nine here, meaning it's after midnight in New York. While my employees are used to working odd hours should the need arise, and they're paid handsomely for it, I don't like bothering anyone this late or when they should be off the clock. However, I know Maggie will want to discuss the press issue as soon as possible.

"I sent you a preliminary report on Louie Calnetta, but I'm diving deeper to be thorough."

That makes me chuckle. Taylor is nothing if not thorough. He's at least learned to give me preliminary information when he used to take forever while he double and triple-checked everything. You can take a soldier out of the Marines, but you can't wholly take the Marines out of the soldier.

"Sounds good. Anything I need to know now?" I sense there's more he wants to say, but he's hesitating. "Even if it's preliminary?"

"He might be...connected."

I'm not following. I'm getting very tired, and the neurons in my brain aren't firing on all cylinders. "Connected to what? To the paparazzi showing up tonight? How could that be possible?"

"No, sir. Connected, as in...connected." He waits for

a beat for me to catch on but continues when I don't. "To organized crime, sir."

"The mob?" I laugh and turn to him outside my office door. "You're telling me the mob is still a thing? In Vegas? How cliché can you be? Are you being serious?"

"Very serious, sir." And the ferocious gleam in his eyes tells me he's not kidding around.

I enter my office, rounding my desk, trying to digest the fact that the mafia is apparently really still a thing and not just in the movies. My first concern is automatically Normandy. I fall heavily into my desk chair, buckling under the weight of the evening's events.

"What does he want with Normandy Blake? Any ideas?"

"From what I've gathered so far, Calnetta's been after Mischief Motors for years, though I don't have details or specifics yet. I assume he's playing the same game with Ms. Blake."

I study him carefully, wondering if he's thinking the same thing I am. "In light of this, are we absolutely sure about Victor's cause of death?" I can't believe I'm asking that, but tonight is full of insanity.

Taylor shifts a little and clears his throat. "I've made some inquiries with the medical examiner, but I don't have a relationship there yet. I'll keep pushing."

"Ok, good. Let me know what you can find out."

He leaves, and I jump out of my chair and start pacing at once. Something about the whole Louie Calnetta situation isn't sitting right with me, and I can't pinpoint what it is. My mind is itching as though I could think hard enough to figure it out; the answer's right in front of me, but that's not possible. It's frustrating as fuck. I do not like feeling like this. I know things are in motion, but I still feel helpless. I do not do helpless.

My phone rings, and I see it's Maggie. The press is now the furthest thing from my mind, but I guess I have to deal with it.

"Hey Maggie, what's the latest?" May as well dive right in.

"Well, Brandon, you and Ms. Blake sure have been shot out of a cannon." She doesn't sound upset like I thought she would be.

"Oh? How's that?" I can't say I like this attitude any more than if she were upset.

"The public loves Normandy. She's pulling you up by the collar of your shirt."

What an odd saying. "Can I assume that's a good thing? It sounds painful."

"Whoever it was that caught you two in the restaurant got some great pictures." She pauses as though pulling them up to view. "There's you hugging the restaurant owner. Boy, she's short, huh? Then you and Normandy holding hands at a table, deep in conversation."

I hold my breath, waiting to hear if there are any of us arguing, and Normandy almost walking out of the restaurant. Those would be hard to explain. *Oh yeah, that was when I offered her money to fucking date me.*

"Is that it?"

"Oh, that's plenty. I'd say *good job*, but I don't think you had anything to do with these, unfortunately."

"That is correct. I was unaware of anyone taking

pictures. If I had been, I would have been able to prepare Ms. Blake for the onslaught that awaited us outside the restaurant and her house. She just got trial by firing squad, and I don't think it went over too well."

Maggie sighs, "Well, it was bound to happen sooner or later once you found someone. It just happened to be sooner."

That doesn't make me feel any better. We hang up, and I consider calling Normandy to see how she's doing, but I don't want to disturb her either. I send a text instead.

> ME: *Are you doing okay? Sorry about the crazy end of the evening. Next time will be much smoother. I promise.*

I don't get a response by the time I go to bed, making me wonder if there will even be a next time.

Chapter 14

Run Rabbit Run

Normandy

T he following morning when I turn on my phone, I'm bombarded with hundreds of alerts for voicemails, text messages, and emails. I don't know most of the people sending them either. I shut the bedroom window that I leave open a crack at night, no matter how cold it gets, and as I make my way downstairs for a much-needed cup of coffee, I hear a phone ringing. I look down at the phone in my hand, but that's not the culprit. Dad still has a landline. I glance around the kitchen, trying to locate the phone, and find it on a desk built into the counter. The phone doesn't even have a Caller ID, so I can't tell who's calling. How did people function before smartphones? I would typically let an unknown number go to voicemail, but I don't think Dad has that or an answering machine. I take a chance and answer, hoping it's the most daring thing I have to do today.

"Hello?"

"Finally. Let me in." It takes me a second to register that it's Bianca's voice. I am really not awake yet.

"What? What do you mean? Let you in where?"

"Into the house, dummy." Her words coincide with knocking on the back door to the kitchen. I turn around and spy Bianca waving at me through the window on the door, a big grin on her face.

I roll my eyes, and hang up the phone, then shuffle to the door to unlock it for her. Once she storms in, I make my way to the life support machine, a.k.a., the coffee maker, for some caffeine.

"So, how's it feel?" Her Cheshire cat grin takes over half of her face as she makes herself at home on a barstool. "Normandy Blake, the new Vegas celebrity at large."

"Ugh. Don't remind me. I take it you're here to drive me to work?"

"You really want to go to work today?" She wrinkles her nose at me. "Don't you have 'billionaire girlfriend' stuff to do?"

I can't help but both scoff and cringe at the title. That is not going to fly with me.

"Yeah, no. Not a billionaire's girlfriend. Just pretending to be one on TV." I give her the fakest smile I can to prove my point.

She looks me over curiously. "Seriously? Does he know you're pretending?" She scrolls through her phone briefly, then holds it out to me. On the screen is a photo of Brandon and me at the restaurant last night, holding hands while we talked. If I didn't know any better, I would think the amorous look in his eyes was genuine. But I do know better. It's all a ploy to improve his image and boost my business. Though my heart does flutter a little at the sight of him. *Stupid heart.*

"He knows," I say, handing back her phone and taking a sip of liquid life force. I close my eyes as the warm elixir hits my soul, ensuring that I will, in fact, make it through this morning. "He's pretending too. It was his idea in the first place to help with his image during the whole insider trading thing. And I thought it would be good to push Mischief's name out there."

"Well, you certainly accomplished that. Our phones have been ringing off the hook since last night. But not for reservations, for interview requests for you. It's crazy."

I blanch at the thought of giving an interview of any kind. "That will definitely not be happening." It was explicitly not a part of our deal last night. No interviews for me. I wouldn't know what to say anyway; I don't know Brandon, not as a person. Not like a girlfriend should know their boyfriend.

I'm reminded of our negotiation last night for the parameters of our dating and future kisses, and my neck grows warm at the thought. How he looked at me and said I would eventually be the one instigating a kiss made me almost want to believe him. But then I remember he also initially offered me money to date him, and he's right back on the garbage pile of my brain, next to decaffeinated coffee, kale, underwire bras, and every other idiotic thing on the planet.

"Oh, there was a guy at the depot this morning when I picked up the car who wanted to talk to you. He said he wasn't with the press and that it had something to do with Victor." She digs through her purse and pulls out a wrinkled business card to hand me.

I glance down at the card and notice the Calnetta Cars logo on the front next to the name Frank Santangelo. His title is listed as 'Consultant.' That's dubious. When I flip the card, it reads "CALL ME" in all caps, scrawled across the back.

"He didn't give you any clue as to what it was about?" Memories of Louie Calnetta grabbing my arm flash through my mind. I don't like this.

"No, but he gave me the creeps." She shivers with an exaggerated shudder.

"Oh? Why's that? Did he say or do something?" I like this less and less.

"No, it was just a vibe I got from him. Definite creeper."

"Awesome. After the stellar ending to last night, today is starting out just as fanfuckingtastic." I turn and throw the card on the island. I am not in the mood to deal with guys like him today. "I'll be ready in 10 minutes. Let me go shower."

"Sure thing, boss." Bianca has a knack for making snarky comments sound sincere. I don't know how she does it, but it doesn't do anything to fix my mood.

I spend most of my time in the shower considering

just dropping everything here and going back to my life in Sacramento. It would be so much easier to do that. But I can't do that to Chelsie, and I can't do that to my dad's business. I'm determined to turn things around for his legacy if nothing else. He deserves that much from me since he trusted me with everything.

We make it out of my neighborhood and to the Mischief Motors depot without incident. Getting inside the lot itself is another issue. The number of photographers has multiplied exponentially overnight, and Bianca seems to have too much fun pushing them gently out of the way with the car, swearing in Italian at them all the while.

"Vaffanculo! Oh my God, these idiots. I swear they *want* to be run over." She inches forward, making super slow progress to the gate. "You see what they're doing, right?"

A mass of people with cameras leans against the car and peer through the windows. It would be difficult for me not to see what they're doing. Even though the windows are heavily tinted, it's not impossible to see in, especially with the bright Las Vegas sun shining through. It's starting to make me claustrophobic.

"Yup. I see." I sigh. I may have bitten off a *tad* more than I can chew. I wanted Mischief Motors' name out there. *Be careful what you wish for.* This is quickly becoming a nightmare. I'm going to need to do something about this. But what can I do? I can't get out of the car; I'll be mobbed.

Just then, the gates open, and our mechanic, Wayne, comes out waving his arms wildly and yelling at the photographers to move out of our way. Wayne is about a hundred and seventy-three years old and has no business working anymore. He should have retired a century ago, but he still shows up every day and takes care of the cars as if they were his own. Luckily, the photographers listen to the old man and let us through.

"Thank you, Wayne." Bianca waves at him as we pass and enter the lot without running anybody over. It's a minor miracle.

I don't know what I'm going to do about all of this. I've barely had time to read what all is being published about Brandon and me in the short drive here, and what I did see is crazy. The press has resorted to making up whatever they think will earn more clicks. One story even had me being his lover for years with a secret family, including twins. It's unreal.

"If it isn't Mrs. Carmichael, gracing us with her presence. Just a head's up, don't believe everything you read on the internet." Chelsie greets me with a healthy helping of snark as I enter my office. She's in her usual spot with her feet on my desk, scrolling on her phone. I debate telling her to clear off, but I need to pick my battles carefully. Feet on a desk, I can deal with. Secret twins? Not so much.

"Did you know I used to be a stripper?" It's almost addictive to see what insanity people can say about you. I certainly got an eye full reading some of the lies online.

"I didn't! Was that before or after you were a backup dancer for Celine Dion?"

I pretend to stop to think, considering her question. "It was between Celine and Britney."

We both burst into laughter, and it feels good to make light of the situation for a change. Let the tabloids make up whatever lies they're going to. If I let it, things like this, regardless of how ridiculous it is, could give me major anxiety. The last thing I need is to have a full-blown panic attack in front of the press. Outlets like laughter help a lot.

"Oh man," Chelsie sighs, still chuckling, "Dad would have gotten a kick out of this."

Now we both fall silent, thinking about our dad and his crazy sense of humor. He would have absolutely had a blast with this publicity fiasco. Thoughts instantly morph into emotions of missing him, and it falls quiet between us. At first, it's somber, but then it turns awkward the longer it goes.

"So, which one had me as a dancer? That's kind of original, at least." I sit in the chair beside her and cross my feet on the desk next to hers. We didn't get a chance to be very sisterly to each other when we were younger, so it's nice to experience moments like this on occasion where it feels like we do share a family.

"*Blindsided,* of course. They said you were "*Following in her mother's footsteps.*""

"Ugh. They're the worst. And now they're bringing my mom into it? Good Lord. She is not going to be happy." As I say this, I'm reminded that Bianca told me the phone was ringing like mad with press inquiries. I haven't heard a single phone ring since I've been in the building. "Why haven't the phones been ringing?"

She shrinks slightly at my question as though she doesn't think I'll like her answer. I'm starting to think I won't like it either.

"I had all the calls forwarded to an answering service." She cringes, expecting a harsh response from me. "I hope that's okay. It was too crazy to handle here."

"Actually, that was brilliant." I nod, considering. "We're getting the real business calls or messages, right?"

"Well, theoretically, yes. But there haven't been any legitimate business calls yet."

I close my eyes and count to ten in my head. Did I do the wrong thing? Is this entire Brandon Carmichael scheme blowing up in my face? I hadn't considered that this could backfire and be bad for business. I suppose I should have weighed that possibility, considering the scandal he's going through. I'd thought LC Consolidated was bulletproof, though. At least Sora thought so.

Now I know it's all a matter of perception, and our clients and potential clients aren't perceiving this as a good thing for them. What the hell was I thinking? I can't date Brandon, pretend or not. It was a ludicrous idea in the first place, and I let his God-damned dimples sway my decision-making process in his favor. Getting involved with him will ruin everything my dad built up. It'll get me caught up in the web of Brandon's trading scandal, which could sink our company and my dad's legacy. I need to fix this.

I turn my phone back on momentarily to send Brandon a text. I ignore all of the alerts that go off and start typing. He'll understand my change of heart. Shit, he probably won't care. It was all a game for him.

> ME: *I'm sorry, but I can't go through with this. I need to call off our agreement. I hope you understand. I wish you the best. -Normandy*

Shutting my phone off again, I turn to Chelsie. "Right. We need damage control."

She sits up and nods. "I'll grab Bianca."

Chapter 15

Do I Wanna Know?

Brandon

The text from Normandy calling our agreement off is not what I wanted to see this morning. I try calling her, and it goes straight to voicemail. Of course, she's probably got her phone off. I call Mischief Motors directly and get an answering service. I leave a message, but I can't leave this as it is. I need to talk to her.

Things went so sideways last night with the paparazzi showing up; I feel as though I'm leaving her to deal with all of this on her own. I would help her with all of this if she returned my call. I *want* to help her through this. She may think this is all fake, but this is my life.

Dealing with the press is what I have to do daily. It's the main ingredient in our fake dating plan, after all. I hate that it's overwhelming her. That is the last thing I want to do.

I have Diane postpone my morning meetings and coerce Taylor to ride with me to Mischief Motors. He's not happy with the plan, but he's learning that I don't like to be constrained by my security, and if he wants to keep me safe, he needs to keep up with me when I go off the rails.

This adventure allows me to drive Betty again, much to Taylor's dismay. There are no blackout or bulletproof windows, no anti-roll cage, no run-flat tires, no reinforced gas tank, just a plain old car. Emphasis on the '*old*.' There is absolutely nothing safe about this car, *and I love it*.

"I'd like to reiterate my strong objection to this activity, sir. For the record." He glowers as he watches his men clear a path on the other side of the gate for me to drive through and get on the road. "Especially since we don't know anything more about Ms. Blake's potential involvement with the criminal underworld of Vegas."

"You really think Normandy is actively involved with the mob?" I can't believe he thinks that could be the case.

"I can't say one way or the other at this point, which is the problem."

"Well, your objection is noted. And ignored. But I think we know that by now."

Once we're clear, I gun it, and the highly fuel-inefficient engine doesn't disappoint. We take off like a rocket. I see the paparazzi in the rearview mirror scrambling to get to their cars to give chase, and I can't contain my smile. They'll never catch us. Unless I were to hit all the red lights on Tropicana Avenue, which of course, I do.

"Smile for the cameras, Taylor," I say, nodding my head toward the car next to us, where the driver is pointing a colossal camera lens right at us. Taylor doesn't smile but keeps his eyes intently on the surroundings. I smile and wave, then take off again as the light changes. I beat them to the next light, and they get stuck. It's ridiculous how little things like that can entertain me. Vegas in the daytime can feel like a ghost town on some streets, so the lack of cars in front of me is enticing.

"Sir."

I reluctantly let off the gas and ease down to the speed limit. "Fine. Any updates on what we discussed last night?" I didn't get much sleep, thinking about the possibility of Normandy being in danger. I can't help but wonder if she knew about her father's troubles with Calnetta. It also makes me wonder if those troubles contributed to why the business is in such a state. It would make sense.

"Nothing yet, sir. But I'm still following up."

"I've said this before, you don't have to call me, 'sir.'" I can't help but cringe a little inside every time he says it. It makes me feel old. I appreciate the respect it conveys but hearing it so often in one conversation borders on annoying.

He nods at me, but I can tell he's thinking, '*Yes, sir.*'

We pull up to Mischief Motors, and the gate is unsurprisingly shut, with a group of paparazzi milling around in front. Hopefully, that means I was correct in coming here instead of Normandy's house to find her. I push the button on the intercom, ignoring the cameras being shoved in my face and the questions being thrown at me. After a beat with no response, Taylor pulls out his phone.

"Let me get someone inside." He finds a contact and starts a call. "Wayne? Taylor Moore from Citadel Security here. Mr. Carmichael is outside the gate and would like entry to the depot. Can you assist?" There's a pause as he listens to the reply. "Very good. Thank you." He disconnects the call and turns to me. "It'll just be a minute."

"Who is Wayne?" I don't recall meeting anyone here by that name. The jealous tone in my voice takes Taylor by surprise. It kind of shocks me too.

"He's the head mechanic...?"

"And you have his number?"

"I have everyone here's number, sir."

"Of course, you do." I think I see Taylor's lip twitch into a smile out of the corner of my eye. "Too bad you don't have the code to this gate."

He glances at me in question as if I'd actually want him to get it. "Sir?"

"Taylor, come on. I'm joking." I lift an eyebrow at him, curious now. "Could you get it, though?"

He only smiles in return, and I guess I have my answer. There isn't much Taylor can't find out, given enough time.

An older man in coveralls appears as the tall gate slides open. He steps aside to let us through, yelling colorful profanities at the paparazzi. Okay, I like this

Wayne guy.

We park and enter the main garage, where there doesn't appear to be anybody working. The lights are on, but it's deathly silent. I glance at Taylor, but he just shrugs a shoulder.

"Hello?" I call out, and my voice echoes in the cavernous space.

A head peeks out of one of the office doors. Chelsie's eyes widen as she sees us.

"Oh, hi Brandon--" She quickly disappears as if being yanked away from the door. A flurry of whispering that I can't decipher follows and goes on for a few minutes.

Taylor and I stay awkwardly silent, unsure what to do now. They've seen that we're here, but no movement has been made to address or greet us outside Chelsie's brief appearance.

Wayne enters behind us, stares at us, standing by ourselves quizzically for a minute, but shrugs without a word and walks to the back of the garage. This is getting absurd now and a little rude.

When it's gone on for an unreasonable amount of time, I head toward the office Chelsie appeared from.

"Well, that's not your decision to make," an angry whisper reaches me, but I can't tell whose it is. If I had to guess from the context, I would say Normandy.

As I step into the doorway, Normandy and Chelsie jump at the sight of me as if caught with their hands in the cookie jar. Nervous smiles are plastered on both of their faces, and standing side by side like this, the resemblance to each other is evident. Even though they are entirely different, their similarities are more distinct than I previously thought.

"My apologies, ladies, for intruding on your discussion, but could I possibly speak to Normandy in private?"

They glance at each other briefly, Chelsie maintaining her smile, which now looks authentic, and Normandy, with panic and fear, hinted at in hers. She reaches out for Chelsie as she steps away toward the door to keep her in place. I'd almost be amused if I wasn't concerned about why she'd be afraid to talk to me.

"Of course," Chelsie smoothly evades Normandy's reach. "You two have a good talk." She winks at me before closing the door behind her. I have no clue what that was all about, and I'm not sure I want to know.

"Normandy--" I start but don't get to say anything else as she interrupts me.

"Mr. Carmichael, I sent you a message this morning; perhaps you didn't get it, letting you know I will not be able to proceed with our agreement. I hope you understand. I seem to have bitten off more than I can chew when it comes to the press and publicity surrounding us, and it's starting to reflect poorly on the business, which is unacceptable and not something I anticipated, though I'm sure I should have...."

I step up and place my hands on her shoulders, forcing her to look at me. She's wound so tightly, spinning herself into knots over this. I can't stand to see her so upset, especially since I feel like I caused it, *because I did*.

"Deep breath." I take a long drag of air, waiting for her to copy me. When she finally does, I exhale slowly along with her, giving her a small smile. She relaxes a little, and I step back, giving her space. "Better?"

Nodding, she runs her hands through her hair. "Yes. Thank you." She falls into one of the office chairs, and I lean back against the desk. "The past 24 hours have been way too crazy for me. I can't function like this. I know I should have, but I didn't realize what exactly I was signing up for."

"Normandy, as soon as we went out in public, this was going to happen. I should have warned you, but I have a bad habit of assuming that everyone knows what my life is like since it's so public. Case in point, what happened last night and today." I reach down and take both of her hands in mine, a jolt of electricity rushing through me as our skin meets. She doesn't pull away like I thought she would, which is encouraging. "So, yeah, my life is crazy, and the internet is disgusting, the paparazzi are assholes, and the general public, believe it or not, is kind of tolerable. Most days."

"Did you know I was a stripper and a backup dancer for Celine Dion and Britney Spears?"

Her expression is so serious that I honestly don't know if she's pulling my leg or telling the truth. If it's true, it's a random thing to burst out in the middle of a conversation. It's got to be something that the tabloids falsely reported, but damn, my mind can't help but imagine all of those scenarios, particularly the stripper idea....

She must sense my thoughts because she starts to turn pink and clears her throat, pulling her hands away and crossing her arms. Bashful Normandy is adorable. So, we have hot and skeptical, and sweet and bashful Normandy as our favorites so far. I have a feeling that list is going to grow exponentially over time.

"I did not know that about you, no. I guess I should have done a more thorough background check."

She laughs but stops just as quickly, giving me a dirty look. And not the good kind of dirty.

"You ran a background check on me?"

Shit. I've stepped into it again. I can't win. And I really can't seem to say the right thing around her. *Ever.*

I shrug as though it's not a big deal. "Sure. If I'm going to spend any time with anyone, at least a cursory check is done, so one was completed for almost everyone attending the funeral." It's not a lie. One was completed. I just skimmed over the fact that I had one performed before that too.

She still looks a little upset at this, so I try to lighten the mood.

"Why? Is there something we missed I should worry about? The stripping job, maybe?"

God-damn. The blush deepens but then morphs into anger, her entire body tensing and her expression turning to steel. The Ice Queen is back in full force.

Chapter 16

Seize the Power

Normandy

My anxiety since meeting this man has been at red flag levels, but there is still this unreasonable pull toward him that is driving me crazy. Sometimes, when Brandon speaks, I don't know whether to laugh or scream. Or, in some cases, kiss him. Like right now, I would like to do all three, but my anger is winning out. This situation isn't funny. Nothing has been the least bit amusing since I met him.

"Brandon, I don't think you understand the gravity of what is happening. What has happened to me due to one dinner with you. What you've done to my life in a matter of minutes. And I don't think it's fixable. It won't ever go back to how it was. This will now follow me for the rest of my life. Whatever the hell this is." Angry tears are threatening, and I need to shift my eyes away from him to gather myself.

"Let's go grab some breakfast and talk this out."

I turn back to him, and he's smiling at me, his stupid dimples on display and his eyes full of compassion. Again, I'm not sure which of the insane emotions flowing through me in this instant makes the most sense because none of them do.

"Did you not hear what I just said?" I can't believe that is his response. Does he honestly think going for breakfast is going to solve anything? "Did you not see the mob of paparazzi at the gate? Do you hear the business phones ringing in here? Do you see anyone working?"

"I saw Wayne...."

"Besides Wayne. He came with the building and never left."

His eyes widen in amusement, and he laughs. "Really?"

"That's what my dad always said. I don't know." He's starting to derail me and distract me from my anger. *Damn him.*

"C'mon. Breakfast." He holds a hand out to me with a grin. "I'll even treat."

That makes my mouth twitch, the idea of a billionaire offering to pay for breakfast, but I keep myself from laughing. I narrow my eyes at him, still unsure how I feel about this. "You'll need to convince me better than that. Other than you'll scrape your pockets and pay."

He folds his arms and rubs his chin, pretending to look pensive as he considers his answer.

"Convince you, huh? Let's see. First, there's the obvious; you get to spend time with me." He checks my reaction and, seeing I'm not impressed, continues. "Okay, interesting. That's a first, but I'm up to the challenge. What else? Well, you yourself admitted that things can't go back to how they were, so perhaps instead of dwelling on that, we should talk about what you *can* do from here on out. Believe it or not, this isn't my first rodeo in this arena, and I might be able to help."

The words sound like those I should be offended by or that I've been condescended to, but his delivery wasn't that way at all. Instead, it appears that he genuinely cares and he thinks he can help. I can only hesitate, though. The last 24 hours have done a number on my decision-making, causing me to doubt every single thought in my head. I hate it.

"Normandy, I got you into this. At least let me try to help get you through it if I can." He pushes off the desk and again holds a hand out to me. "Tell you what, I'll count this as one of our two dates to sweeten the deal. Final offer."

"Oh, really? Do you think our agreement is still valid? I thought I canceled that."

"I didn't accept. And sorry, no refunds, exchanges, or cancellations. You should have read the fine print." He leans down and grabs my hand, pulling me out of my chair. "And remember, you're free to trigger that kissing clause anytime."

He hasn't moved, and we stand so close to each other

that I swear I can sense his body heat. I can't breathe without taking in his spicy cologne, and he's still holding my hand, now interlocking his fingers with mine. Being at eye level with his mouth since he's so tall, I can't avoid noticing his lips and wondering what they would taste like if I ever did kiss him. The thought of it twists something inside of me, but in the best of ways.

When I glance up and into his eyes, I'm surprised to see they're actually hazel. They were darker the other day, but today they're light and sparking with an intensity so compelling, it's hard to look away, but I do. I have to somehow keep my composure around him. Just because I find him physically attractive, like any woman would, doesn't mean I like him. Quite the opposite. His whole "that's a first" about my needing to be convinced to go with him rubbed me the wrong way. He's trying to sound confident, but it's coming off as arrogant to me.

He is right about one thing, though. There is no going back in time to reverse what's already happening with the press, so I need to figure out how to navigate this now that I'm knee-deep in it. It would be foolish of me not to at least talk about it with him and get some help in that regard. He's had to deal with the tabloids and paparazzi for years and is probably an expert on handling it. Plus, he's conceded to count this against our agreement dates, so there will only need to be one more after this before the gala. That's a bonus.

He's still looking down at me as if he's expecting some sort of reaction about the kiss comment. I need to disabuse him of the notion that I will be doing any such thing.

"I do realize that I'm free to kiss you, and as you can see, I'm not availing myself of that option. Shall we go?" I smile wide and tilt my head in question.

His grin grows wider at my response, making the corners of his eyes crinkle. He does like a challenge, doesn't he? He has no idea who he's up against.

"We'll need to coordinate with Taylor for security if we're going to be in public for any amount of time. Let me go find him."

He squeezes my fingers before stepping outside my office and waving Taylor over. They have a hushed conversation for a few minutes, and his head of security is not happy with whatever Brandon tells him. He apparently has a short time to arrange the outing as he looks at his watch, and I can tell he internally swears. The poor guy. I feel like this is my fault for causing all of this trouble. If I'd followed my instincts in the first place and never gone out with Brandon, none of us would be in this position. Taylor reluctantly nods and walks away.

"A plan is in motion." Brandon swings his arms and claps his hands together to a strange internal rhythm as he paces the office and talks. He's anxiously fidgeting, obviously not a fan of waiting for things to happen. I'm sure he's used to the snapping-fingers speed of his requests being filled.

A few minutes later, Taylor is back with another security guard, and this time Chelsie is tagging along with them, an excited smile on her face. Bianca follows a second later, crossing her arms and leaning against the door frame. Her smile is amused, but she twists a long dark curl nervously as she assesses the situation. I need to find out what that's all about.

"We're going to run a decoy with Chelsie and Mike here pretending to be you and Brandon," Taylor says. "They'll head west toward Mr. Carmichael's home while we go north to the restaurant a few minutes later. Additional security is en route to meet us there. The restaurant has been alerted to expect us. This won't eliminate all of the paparazzi, but it should fool most of them for a little while."

"Are you okay with doing this, Chelsie?" I don't want her to think this will be a regular thing because it most definitely will not. Our lives will not be full of body doubles and cloak and dagger maneuvers. That is not how I want to live the rest of my life. Surely, after this initial buzz dies down and Brandon returns to his life, the press will leave me alone, and we won't have to worry about things like this. "It will be just this once."

"Are you kidding? This is the most excitement I've had since Phil Helton threw his chips at me during the World Series of Poker three years ago. I'm more than okay doing this."

I can only shake my head at her. My stomach is starting to do flips in anticipation of this crazy ruse, and her kinetic energy is feeding my anxiety.

"All you two have to do is to pretend to hide your faces under these jackets." Taylor hands them each a Mischief Motors jacket I didn't even know we had. "There will still be privacy glass, but silhouettes are still visible to a camera, so do your best to avoid a clear profile shot in case it gets scrutinized later. Alright?" He includes Bianca in the question, and she nods her understanding. "Let them chase until they hear about the true location and abandon their efforts. Then you can come back here."

"Right, then." Brandon sighs, but his mouth twitches up into a half-smile, flashing a single dimple. It's still devastatingly handsome. "Let's go eat some breakfast in public."

Chapter 17

Hunted Down

Brandon

The deception works for the most part. We arrive at the restaurant in a strip mall, with a back patio where we find a table with a little bit of cover from some large leaf foliage in planters. The space heaters are full blast since it's still a bit chilly. Normandy eyes them curiously.

"Is there a reason we're not sitting inside the restaurant like normal people in the middle of January?" She wraps her Mischief Motors jacket around herself snugly.

"That's precisely why we're out here. Normal is boring."

"So, you're abnormal. Got it." She nods to herself, confirming an internal thought, but she smirks. *God, she's even gorgeous when sarcastic. I might be in love.*

I glance down at my watch and do a quick calculation in my head.

"In about ten minutes, give or take, paparazzi will show up to take pictures of us sitting here, talking and eating." She looks a little shocked, but I go on. "The key to dealing with all of this is not something you're going to want to hear."

"Oh?" She shifts in her seat and bites her bottom lip, obviously anxious. "What is it?"

I absolutely know she's not going to like this. When we were negotiating this whole thing, she made a point to leave the press out of every counteroffer she came up with. Unfortunately, it's a fact of my life I need to deal with daily. I probably should have explained that much to her better than I have.

"The way to deal with the paparazzi is to give them what they want." I can tell by the grimace now shadowing her face she's not happy about this. I predicted as much. "They only chase when they don't get what they want, a picture they can sell. If you give them that, they will mostly leave you alone."

"It can't be that simple...." She's dubious, and I don't blame her. She's not wrong; it may not be that simple.

"It might not be. You're an unknown quantity. They could be more aggressive with you and me since they know nothing about you. Once they know more, it should be easier. But the press is a monster that needs to be fed fairly regularly. It's just the way things are."

"So, what am I supposed to do after the gala, when our agreement is over, and you're gone, but they're still hounding me? Will it ever end?" The worry clouding her features floods me with guilt. She's in this position because of my selfishness in wanting to be with her. It's not enough for me to stop, though. My want for her is greater than my guilt. *Much* greater.

"What makes you so sure we won't go beyond our agreement?" I lean back as the waiter places our food on the table. Once he steps away, I go on. "In the immortal words of Rick Blaine in Casablanca, *'I think this is the beginning of a beautiful friendship.'* You disagree?" I know I'm poking the bear, but I can't help myself. Something about Normandy brings out this spirited side of myself I've not visited in years. I've not allowed myself to explore this part since college, which seems like forever ago.

"You do realize Rick said that to the police Captain *after* Ilsa leaves him and gets on a plane, never to be heard from again, right?" Her eyes dance with mirth; she's enjoying the banter. *Good. Progress.*

"I do, but the point is relationships go on, even after endings." It's weak, and I know it, but what the hell. I didn't expect her to call me on the damn movie quote.

"I'm serious. How am I supposed to deal with all of this craziness when you're not here? I don't have security guards 24/7." The lip biting is back, and the crease between her brows deepens. I guess I didn't account for how much this would upset her. I really am an asshole.

"Ah, but you do."

"Oh? This is news to me." Her eyes dart to a

commotion that starts behind me on the other side of the wrought iron fence across the patio from us. "Shit. Your ten minutes were generous."

I turn and find a bunch of photographers jostling with my security guards, trying to take our picture.

"You want to run and hide? Or face it and maybe have some peace during our meal?" It's a challenge, and Normandy searches my eyes. I try to express confidence and comfort simultaneously and don't know if I succeed, but she swallows hard and nods.

"Do I have to speak? Or can you do all that?" She's twisting the napkin in her hand nervously. Seeing her so anxious is weaving threads of doubt into my mind. I didn't expect her to be so damned vulnerable. She was so self-possessed last night at the restaurant, so sure of herself. Now, she's so fragile she could break with a touch. I dare it, though, and reach over to pull one of her fidgeting hands into mine.

"I'll try to deflect back to me, but they'll direct everything to you anyway. Just know that. It's up to you whether you answer or not."

"What's our story? We need a story. We should have worked this all out before. Now they're going to know we're faking it." She's working herself up and starting to come unglued.

"I'll take care of everything. Don't worry." I pull her with me toward the gaggle of photographers at the fence, trying to keep my manner as relaxed and confident as possible. Taylor sees what I'm planning to do and rushes over to interrupt us.

"Sir, I advise you not to approach with the limited number of people I have here. I can't guarantee...."

"It's fine, Taylor. We'll only be a minute." I pat his shoulder, appreciating his concern. "I promise to keep it as brief as possible, and we'll keep a safe distance away."

He practically glares at me, which I *don't* appreciate, but steps aside to let us approach the fence. Taylor directs his men to move away but stay close. All the while, the photogs are snapping away, hurling questions at us, or more specifically, at Normandy.

"Normandy, what's it like to date a billionaire?"

"Is it true you two got married at an Elvis chapel? And is there a prenup?"

"Are you the next Eve Cromwell?"

That's enough of that shit.

"Guys, c'mon. Have some respect. Please." I put an arm around Normandy's shoulders and pull her close to me. She leans against me and puts a palm on my chest, and for a second, I forget what the hell I'm doing. I wasn't expecting her to respond to me so easily. I thought she'd be stiff and resistant, but I'm pleasantly surprised. "We're okay with you guys taking our picture here and now, but we'd like to eat in peace if you don't mind. This is technically our first date, and you guys are kind of cramping my style." This gets a round of chuckles, at least. "Is that cool with you?"

I can hear the camera shutters clicking and whirring like mad, and I squeeze Normandy's shoulder quickly, encouraging her to hang in there a little bit longer while the vultures get their pound of flesh. Nobody responds to my request for peace immediately, but they start to break off from the group after a minute. A few even thank us for giving them time, which is rare. When there's only a couple left, I give them a wave and turn Normandy with me to head to our table.

Taylor gives me a reluctant nod as we pass, and I shrug at him. It won't always be this simple. Sometimes you have to take risks to get the rewards. I know that better than most. Luckily, it worked this time.

Normandy is back to her icy self when we return to the table, and it appears all the photographers have dispersed.

"So, is that the great wisdom you were going to impart on me on how to deal with this? Just give in, let them take my picture, and throw stupid and offensive questions at me?" Her lips press into a slash, and her jaw clenches.

"That was lesson number one." I sigh. She's not going to make anything easy. "Lesson number two is never assuming there's not a camera on you every second. Just because the photographers left the sidewalk doesn't mean they're not sitting in their cars right now with telephoto lenses trained on us." I flash her a quick smile, though its sincerity at this moment is questionable. I'm still reeling from the about-face between her leaning into me only a few minutes ago and this subsequent cold shoulder. It's dizzying.

Her eyes widen briefly as she takes in the implications of what I just said, but then she smiles back at me. It's about as genuine as my own but would fool any photographer. Only I can see the disdain in her eyes since it's pointed right at me. I can't blame her for being irritated. The paparazzi are the absolute worst. But it's what we both wanted out of this, so we can't complain too much.

"So, am I the next Eve Cromwell?" Her tone is sickly sweet and dripping with sarcasm. "Whatever that means?"

I cringe inwardly, recalling the question that was thrown at her. It was so out of line, but typical of what happens.

"I was going to ask what you thought of the Elvis ceremony, actually."

We stare at each other, glaring through our smiles, and the utter ridiculousness of the entire situation must hit us both at the same time because we can't help but break out in laughter. Seeing Normandy genuinely cheerful isn't something I've seen until now, and it's her best version yet. I want to see this one all the damned time.

Chapter 18

Willow Tree

Normandy

Well, at least we found some humor in all this madness. I was beginning to think the horribleness of this situation would be permanent. Luckily, it's not.

When I get home that evening after work, I can't help but reconsider my feelings toward Brandon. Aside from the obvious physical attraction, he's turning out to be quite the charmer. But as charming as he is, I have to remind myself almost hourly he *did* offer me money to date him once upon a time. I don't know if he meant it, but the fact sticks with me more than it should. I can't help it.

There were a bunch of photographers outside the house when I got home, as was expected. I'm starting to get the hang of this thing. It sucks I can't go about my daily business like I'm used to. I can't go to the store. I can't go to visit Chelsie at her apartment. I can't drive anywhere. I definitely can't go anywhere on the strip. I am like an animal in a cage.

Brandon said the press will ease off once they get to know me, but I don't *want* the press to get to know me. I don't want anyone to get to know me. I want my life to be my life. The whole point was to get my father's business on the map, not me. I am not a fame chaser and definitely not the next Eve Cromwell. I don't want to be the next anything for Brandon Carmichael other than a memory.

We only have a few days to fit in our second date in our agreement, and I've been racking my brain trying to think of something appropriate but not too date-like for us to do. It's a little tricky because I don't know Brandon at all. And, I don't know what billionaires do in their free time outside of counting their money.

The local entertainment changes so often I don't know what would be fun to do. Vegas reinvents itself every three to six months, so figuring out an event or venue will take some research on my part. I find a local variety show that looks interesting, but who knows if Brandon will like it. The exciting thing is the purpose of the show is to raise money for charities and do so in a short amount of time. I'm curious what Mr. Billionaire will do when faced with public charity demands.

When I propose this venue to Brandon, he's unaffected and eager to check it out. I may or may not have told him about the fundraising aspect of the evening, so this will be a test.

The event is called *Dark Mondays* since it's based on the premise of Broadway shows being dark on Mondays, and when we arrive, Brandon's team has already made sure we can enter and leave as inconspicuously as possible, though even that level is uncomfortable. We again stop for photos with the paparazzi. However, we controlled the narrative this time and alerted them to our outing, so I was at least prepared. Brandon showed up in a suit and looks more delicious than any man has a right to, and I need to remind myself I don't like him. And it's not only that he's attractive, obviously, he is attractive physically, but the way he protects me when we're out in public is so comforting, I could get used to it quickly. And his sense of humor is just dark enough to match mine, and I find myself laughing involuntarily at his jokes.

When we arranged tonight's outing via text messages, he had me rolling my eyes so hard I thought they would fall out of my head. But then, I was laughing so hard my stomach started hurting. This is both endearing and infuriating because I don't want to like him. I don't want to feel anything for him other than animosity, but he's making that very, very difficult.

> BRANDON: *How many billionaires does*
>   *it take to make a superhero?*
> ME: *I don't know, tell me.*
> BRANDON: *Three. Two to die and one*
>   *to never get over it.*
> ME: *That's horrible.*

> BRANDON: *But wait, there's more. I*
> *even have one-liners.*
> ME: *Oh no...*
> BRANDON: *A guy walks into a bar.*
> *He's immediately disqualified from*
> *the limbo contest.*
> ME: *You need to stop. I'm trying to work.*
> BRANDON: *You're perfectly capable of*
> *turning your phone off and ignoring*
> *me, you know.* 😊

So, after another hour of texts, I finally did. And now, he's in this suit, with an open collar just inviting kisses on the neck, that's going to be the only thing I think about all night. *Great.* Maybe he was right about me being the one to instigate a kiss between us. Damn him if he's right about that.

We wear our fake personas impeccably throughout the evening, holding hands, leaning our heads together to talk, and whispering into each other's ears during the show. I'd think we were a real couple if I didn't know better. There are moments when I forget we're not and have to check myself. It would be so easy to let myself fall into that trap. Too easy.

I don't want this life. I don't want to live in the spotlight. I don't want to be chased by the paparazzi. I don't want my life on display. I want my life back. And to live it in private. And I want my father's business to thrive. I don't know if I can get to that now after all this. But I'll do what I have to to get there.

When we arrived at the venue, there were listings for

silent auction items in the lobby, and one thing of interest to Brandon caught his eye; a signed hockey stick by one of the stars of the local NHL team. He was nonplussed at the charity theme of the evening, and I think he made quite a large bid on that particular item. And I believe the amount was more than the entire monetary goal for the evening. So, that cemented my appreciation of his generosity. And it was even more endearing because he made me walk away before making his bid so I wouldn't see. It lets me know he wasn't doing it for my benefit or to impress me, which is even better.

Toward the end of the show, while Brandon and I are holding hands, he starts rubbing the top of my knuckles with his thumb, and I can't help my physical reaction to his touch. We've been holding hands all night, but this elevates it to an entirely new level. I don't understand it because I think he's done this before, but something in the way he's doing it now is driving me crazy. I have to put my free hand on his to stop him, but leave my hand there as if I only wanted to hold his hand with both of mine. He studies me for a second but then goes back to watching the show.

I can't deny my attraction to him, but I have to. I have to find a way to keep myself in line. It's almost a challenge for me not to be the one to instigate a kiss like he said I would. I have this unnerving need to prove him wrong, and I don't know why. Everything about Brandon is a challenge for me; to my libido, to my mind, to my spirit, to my goals, and a challenge to my way of life. It's exhilarating and exhausting. But it's also addicting.

Out of the corner of my eye, I examine his profile. His

powerful features exemplify his personality. His strong jaw shows his confidence. His smile and those god-damned dimples display his humor. And his eyes, which can go from light to dark in a heartbeat, show his intensity. He is the entire package, physically, at least.

When the show is over, we meet with the performers on our way out, and Brandon is gracious in his compliments and gratitude, and something in my heart stirs as I watch him interact with them. It's just a tiny bit, but I can sense a little of the chill I have towards him thaw. I don't get to see him interact with other people outside of his security team, and I'm almost surprised at how it amplifies his humanity for me. He's always on the go and wasn't human to me until now. I don't know why I thought he was almost a machine.

When he finishes his conversation, he turns to me and grabs my hand to leave, and it's so natural, our fingers sliding together. He notices this, too, and catches my eye. Something passes between us. Some sort of understanding that we both had the same thought at the same time. I shift my gaze away as fast as I can, not wanting him to know I felt it too.

"Have I told you how beautiful you look this evening?" He's helping me into the limousine waiting for us behind the venue, and once we're inside, I give him a wry smile.

"Actually, you've told me several times. And I have thanked you each time. Are you fishing for me to compliment you back? Because that's not going to happen. I'm sure you don't need me to tell you how attractive you are. You probably pay people to do that for you." I cringe a little at my words, but it's been said, and I can't take it back. *Is that what I wanted to say?*

He pretends to act offended, and the gesture only makes him more attractive as it shows how playful he can be when he wants to. And it seems like he can be *very* playful.

"You know, just because I offered you money *once* to date me doesn't mean I pay everybody off. There are a few people in the world who like me for me, believe it or not."

"I don't think immediate family counts or your employees. As a matter of fact, I think employees should be specifically excluded since they fall under the 'paid for' category."

"OK, then you're right. Outside of immediate family, there aren't many people." A shadow covers his eyes as he says this, even though he's smiling, and I think I glimpsed a vulnerability of his. Who would have thought the great Brandon Carmichael had vulnerabilities? But I think about his words, and I'm overcome with sadness for him. It must be lonely in his position. So disconnected from the world, from people. Never knowing if the people in your world are there because they want to be or because you have money. That's got to be the loneliest feeling, and it occurs to me that his offer to pay me for the date may not have been so strange to him. He most likely equates money with emotions, either friendship or love. I can't imagine living like that. It's got to be so isolating for him.

That thing inside of me that melted a little while ago when he talked to the performers melts a little more, and I can't help but feel a wave of attraction for him. A wave so strong I can't stop myself from leaning over and kissing his cheek lightly.

He's shocked by my actions as much as I am. I couldn't say what came over me. Concern for him and how hard his life must be. People probably think he couldn't be unhappy because he has so much money, but I've seen unhappiness in his eyes. He covers it up but not completely. Not to me, anyway.

"What was that for?" He leans back, studying me, the surprise still lingering in his eyes.

I shrug, unsure what to say and how to explain myself without sounding like a weirdo.

"That was for whatever your donation was because I'm sure it was above and beyond. I could tell your bid for the hockey stick put the night's donation goal way over the top."

He hasn't stopped staring at me. His eyes are dancing and bright, with a confident amusement.

"Well, if that's what I get for buying a hockey stick, I'm curious what I need to do for something more." Again, with the challenges. His smile is devious, and I can't stop myself from smiling back. I wonder if everything is a game to him.

"Well, you'll need to keep wondering because that was a one-time-only experience and will not be repeated."

His eyes narrow so seductively as though he knows better; that was not a one-time thing. I have to squirm a little. If he can turn me on by a look like that, then I am in major trouble. Because he is correct, and that will absolutely be repeated, built upon, and left in the desert dust of Vegas.

"So, is that how you became a billionaire? By challenging everything and everyone?" I'm honestly curious if he's always been like this. It doesn't seem like a personality trait you would grow into. It's one you would have been born with.

He cocks his head at me slightly; his eyes are suddenly curious yet still intense. But then he turns serious.

"I suppose it had something to do with how I got where I am. But, so many factors that went into me getting where I am today have nothing to do with me; it's hard to say I deserve any of it."

"What do you mean? Aren't you a self-made billionaire? You didn't inherit anything, right?"

He takes my hand into his and starts rubbing my knuckles again, but this time I ignore how it's making me feel. He wants to divulge something to me that's important to him.

"While I admittedly did work my ass off to get where I am today, I didn't do it alone. I had a fantastic team who are still around me today. I've had great mentors from other industries advising me along the way. And I've had a hell of a lot of luck. Anyone who thinks luck isn't a factor in success doesn't understand how the universe works. You need to be in the right place at the right time, no matter your situation. That's what happened to me. I was in the right place at the right time, in the right market, and with the right people. And, here I am today sitting with you in the back of this limousine because I was lucky enough to know your father, be at his funeral, and meet you."

The ice around my heart melts. Completely. And as he puts a hand around the back of my neck and pulls me to him, I go willingly. When his lips meet mine, I savor the sensation as a tingling starts where his hand is on my neck and travels down the length of my spine, causing me to arch into him. My hand automatically reaches for his neck and pulls him to me in an echo of his movements. The kiss is sweet but passionate. A promise of something more lacing its edges. When we pull away, each of us trying to catch our breath, I know if I let it, my life will never be the same after this kiss.

We stare at each other for an inordinate amount of time. Not saying a word. Feeling the rolling of the road beneath the tires.

"Would you like to come to my house for a drink?" There is more to this question than his words, and I can see it in his eyes. Again, I'm left debating my intentions in this relationship, not just because the attraction to him is growing beyond physical. I need to consider the long-term repercussions of anything I do with him. After the gala, he'll be gone. He'll go back to his life in New York, and that will be the end of that. This is a fun little game for him while he's in town for his company's meeting. I'm a convenient tool to use in his public relations resurrection, and probably just another distraction for the billionaire who can have anything and anyone. LC Consolidated's stock is on the rise now that he's done the public flirting thing with me his business needed. I'm a toy or another number in a long line of women. I'm the next Eve Cromwell. But so much of me craves to accept his invitation. To ignore any barrier between us, throw caution out the limo window and release this incredible sexual tension between us. It could be worth the heartache, or it could be devastating. Most likely the latter.

"No, thank you. I think I'll just go home." I inch away from him and stare out the window at the casino lights that are garishly happy, contrasting with my darkening mood. That's the thing about Vegas, it is a bright and shiny mask covering some of the most tragic and sad people, and I am now one of them. I can feel Brandon's eyes on me, so I turn to him, put on my own mask, and smile.

Chapter 19

Your Touch

Brandon

I knew it. I knew she would be the one to instigate our first kiss. I just had no idea how absolutely fucking amazing that kiss would be. And it was fucking amazing. I can still taste her lips on my ride home. Her demeanor after the kiss, though, is bothering me. I could tell she was upset, but I knew better than to ask her about it. She doesn't trust me enough to talk to me yet, which is fine. This is new to both of us. I can't expect instant affection or mutual understanding so early. While the physical side of things is definitely there, the intellectual side will need patience, something I've not been known to have much of. But I'll have to work on that if I want this to be more than just a fling. And I think I do want that because I want all of Normandy, not just her body. And the thought scares the shit out of me.

I haven't been this captivated by someone since Eve, which is the cause of most of my hesitation. Knowing what Eve has done, not only to herself but to my company and my reputation, all in the name of her fucking greed, puts me off from attempting anything substantial now with anyone until I met Normandy. And I still have reservations, although I'm starting to not care about them so much. Is that fair to her? No, it's not, but life isn't fair, and people have baggage. I don't know what Normandy's baggage is or how heavy it might be. Taylor's documentation on her previous boyfriends is sparse. There were boyfriends in college, but nothing of consequence since. This makes me wonder how I will ever get through to her if no one in her past ever has. There's got to be a reason for her avoiding a significant relationship; I need to figure out what it is. I am dying to know how someone as spectacular as her hasn't already been snatched up by someone.

Over the next few days, Taylor discovers more information about Victor's autopsy and the cause of death, and unfortunately, we were right; the Medical Examiner now suspects foul play. Victor's latest toxicology screen appears to display a common heart medication that, at toxic levels, induces severe bradycardia and sudden death. The amount in his bloodstream was four times the normal level and was not one that was prescribed to him. And while I'm not crazy about it, Taylor convinced the M.E. to keep the results quiet while we coordinate with local law enforcement and not tell the Blake sisters until there is something definitive.

We also discovered Victor had been paying protection money to another local family for protection against Louis Calnetta. He had marked those payments as alimony to his ex-wives, but every penny went to the protection of his business and, indirectly, to his daughters.

I'm debating whether or not to tell Normandy any of this. It won't change anything for her, and I don't want her to think poorly of her father. Victor did what he felt he had to do, and you can't blame a man for following his heart and trying to protect his livelihood. Especially against someone like Calnetta, who has zero respect for any of those things.

If I tell Normandy, it will only be to confirm something she asks of me. I won't be the one offering this information to her freely. I owe my friend Victor that much.

I have had Taylor increase the security around Normandy and Mischief Motors in light of the new information we've received. I can't get through an hour of the day without wondering about her safety, and I'm constantly checking in with the team to confirm that she is OK.

Taylor has half-heartedly suggested perhaps making an offer to Calnetta to pay him off and get him out of

Normandy's life for good. But I am well aware people like him aren't bought off so easily. There will always be strings attached. There will always be a tail to that comet heading straight to Earth. Nothing is ever final with them. If I thought for a second it would work, I would hand the money over personally and with a smile. Snakes like Calnetta enjoy the game and lifestyle that comes with it too much. They bask in the power that they hold.

So, for now, I do nothing. I will wait and consider. And debate internally. And work myself up. And get nothing done because I seem to be stuck. I'm stuck in a crisis of conscience. Better angels would have me tell her everything, but I can't do it. I can't be the one to break Normandy's heart. Not now that I have the sense I'm getting close to it.

The night of the gala comes, and Normandy is beyond words. There are literally no adjectives strong enough to convey the beauty she possesses. Stunning is the closest I can get because I am genuinely stunned when I see her for the first time.

She is wearing a smokey grey evening gown that shows off every single delectable curve she has. And her hair is curled and loose and even looks a little wild but still elegant, classic, and totally Normandy.

Also in typical Normandy fashion, she had refused to allow me to buy anything for her for the evening. She can be too stubborn for her own good, but in this case, I don't mind because she is gorgeous.

It's near impossible for me to keep my hands off her on the way to the venue. I have to physically sit on my hands, so I don't accost her in the back of the limousine. I think she senses my distress and enjoys it a little too much because she makes a point to lean over provocatively as we talk on the way. *Damn her*. She knows what she's doing and what it's doing to me, and this is only the beginning of the evening. I will have to touch her repeatedly for the next few hours and simultaneously restrain myself. It's going to be an excruciatingly impossible mission.

When we get to the venue, we are directed along the red carpet while having questions thrown at us as our picture is taken. The questions range from benign to malignant. Innocently asking about Normandy's dress, to not so innocently asking about our sex life. If only we had a sex life. She handles the questions in stride, though she flushes a little at the more risqué ones, and that heat on her cheeks combined with her elegantly tousled hair makes me picture her blushing for so many other reasons. All of them pleasurable for her and caused by me. *I am not going to make it through this night*.

When we enter the ballroom, the event is in full swing. The band is playing, people are dancing, groups are congregating, and everyone seems to be having a good time.

Sophie finds us and gives Normandy and me big hugs, thanking us for attending the event, which is amusing since I'm the one throwing this shindig. Sophie gives Normandy a strange once over.

"What a lovely dress. Do you mind if I ask where you got it or who the designer is?"

Normandy appears surprised at the question but happily answers. "I don't know who the designer is as there was no label, but the dress belonged to my mother. I couldn't say where she got it either."

Several emotions ripple through Sophie, but she smiles and says, "Well, it's lovely on *you*."

I catch a hint of an emphasis on the word 'you,' and give Sophie a discrete questioning look, but she looks away without responding. I have no clue what that was all about.

While I know generalities about Sophie's history with the nightclub she owned, I don't know any details. I suspect there are a *lot* of details and perhaps a lot more I don't want to know. Her reaction makes me curious if I should find out those details now. For God's sake, I'm suspecting everyone and their motives so readily anymore, it's ridiculous. Sophie's been with me for years, she doesn't have an agenda.

I excuse us to Sophie and place a hand on Normandy's bare back to guide her to the dance floor. I don't really want to dance. What I want to do is feel her skin beneath my fingers. It's exactly as smooth as I imagined it to be, and the experience of touching it, touching *her*. Only makes me want more.

She effortlessly fits in my arms as we dance smoothly to the orchestra. It feels as though she's finally comfortable with me. That's something I didn't expect. She seems to be responding to me the same way I am to her, and the thought she might reciprocate my feelings, whatever they are, makes me bolder to explore more, so we dance on, oblivious to everyone around us.

I glide a hand down the bumps of her spine, feeling a tremor run through her as she shudders and melts into me a little more. Her breath catches as my fingers teasingly savor the softness of her exposed skin

Pulling her tighter against me, it has to be evident that I'm having a physical reaction to her, but she doesn't pull away. Instead, she curves into me and wraps her arms tighter around my neck, pressing her chest into mine.

I lean down with my lips caressing her ear and whisper a statement mixed with a question. "Do you want me as much as I want you right now?" I let my breath linger, feeling her shiver in my hands.

She tilts her head up, placing her mouth near my ear, her warm breath tickling the fine hairs.

"And what if I do?"

She leans back slightly, her eyes meeting mine as if in a challenge. Is she daring me to do something about it? Because if she is, she does not know me very well.

I tilt in again; this time, my voice is thick with gravel. "Well, if you do, we need to do something about it. And you should know better than to dare me because I usually get what I want."

This time I lean back with a devious grin, and I can tell by the return flush in her cheeks and neck it's working. And now I need to find a room with a lock on the fucking door as soon as humanly possible.

I grab Normandy's hand and pull her through the crowd of people, most of whom are vying for my attention. But I only wave politely, nod, smile, and keep my course steady for the exit to the main lobby. Once there, we practically run to a side room. The closest room. Any fucking room. And once inside, we only make it as far as the other side of the door. I make sure to engage the lock.

Our mouths crash together. Our hands are mad to find purchase on the other. Raking through each other's hair, lifting dresses, unbuckling pants. We're doing everything we can to get closer to the other person. All the while, our lips never falter from the other. My hands discover she's not wearing anything under the dress, and my fingers find she does, in fact, want me as much as I want her.

She groans into my mouth as I touch her, tease her, and explore every inch of her. A gasp escapes her lips when my fingers slide into her sex, and she shudders against me as she shatters. Her hands wrap around my length firmly, and I'm not going to last much longer. I have imagined this scene in my head for nearly two weeks straight, and the mere thought that it's actually happening is pushing me over the edge.

I fumble for my wallet and pull out a condom, quickly sheathing myself, and still, our mouths don't falter. I reach around, grab her ass, and grind her against me. The exquisite pain that flies through me as I strain against her is almost too much. The anticipation of burying myself inside her is overpowering.

I pull away from her briefly, searching her eyes to ensure we both want this, and it's clear we do. So, I lift her up and guide her onto me, her back against the door.

As I thrust into her slowly and deeply, our eyes are still trained on each other. Watching the pleasure roll through her increases the intensity of my own as our touches become more desperate and greedier. An energy is passing between us that is beyond carnal and way beyond physical. This feeling transcends all of that, taking this to another level I've never seen or felt before. And I can see in her eyes that she's feeling the exact same way.

Our breathing is ragged as our pace increases, and just as I'm sure she's about to climax, the knob to the door we're fucking against starts to turn. We both hear it and stop moving. Even though we've stopped, the thought of being caught must be enough for Normandy because I suddenly feel her pulsating around me, and her eyes shut as she arches her back and bites her lip hard to keep from crying out. It has to be the hottest fucking thing I've ever seen, and the sight of it does me in. I have to swallow my own groan as I come, throbbing silently, my body stiffening as the sexual tension finally releases.

Whoever was attempting to open the door knocks, but Normandy and I ignore it, still trying to catch our breath. I lean my forehead against hers, and her eyes meet mine with a mix of satisfaction and amusement. It's hard to know what she's thinking since she can sometimes be so hard to read. I just wish one of those times was not now.

"Mr. Carmichael, are you in there?" *Shit, it's Taylor.* He probably thinks we've been kidnapped or something and has called out the cavalry to find us. I should have known better than to think we could have a private moment.

"It's fine, Taylor. We're both fine," I call through the door. Normandy giggles at this a little as she runs her fingers hesitantly through my hair. "We're both more than fine if you get my drift?"

He doesn't respond right away. And when he does, his voice has a bit of a laugh in it. "Excellent, Sir."

I reluctantly slide out of her and find a box of tissues for us to clean up with. As I glance around, I notice this must be a small lounge next to the ballroom. There are couches, some comfortable chairs, and a drink station. I find a bottle of water and, after opening it, hand it to Normandy, who still leans against the door, trying to gather herself. As she takes a drink, I place my hands on the door on each side of her and blaze a trail of kisses down the tender length of her neck, brushing my lips against her skin until goosebumps appear.

She shivers and squirms her way out from under my arm, moving away from me, and I get the sense whatever spell we were just under has been broken. I don't know what I did to break it, if I did anything, but the air in the room seems to have definitely chilled.

"Normandy? Is there something wrong?" When I turn to her, she avoids my gaze, seemingly interested in the label on the bottle of water.

"No, nothing's wrong. That was perfectly fine."

"Perfectly fine? I think that was a little bit more than just perfectly fine." I don't understand why she's acting like this. Why she's making this out to be nothing when it was definitely more. I take a step toward her, but she takes a step back. "You can't tell me you didn't feel something there besides a fantastic orgasm. You can't honestly believe that was just a fuck. I felt it, and I know you felt it too."

She still hasn't lifted her eyes from the water bottle, and I can feel her shutting down. Shutting the doors and windows to her emotions completely. Shutting me out. Something inside me splinters, and the sharp edges are scratching at my soul as I watch her turn what happened between us into something inconsequential.

I need to know what the fuck is going on here. Because I did not just imagine it.

Chapter 20

It's Not Your Fault

Normandy

I can't believe that just happened. That was freaking amazing. I can't believe I let myself do that. I can't. I don't know what to do. That was incredible, but... I don't know how to react. My emotions are so muddled right now and so scattered. And the way Brandon talks, you would think he was in love with me or something, which can't be the case.

The look he just had in his eyes fills me with so much guilt, and I don't know why. It's not like this relationship was ever going to go anywhere. This is the end of the road today. It was always supposed to be the final stop for this crazy train. But he's acting like I'm breaking his heart, which makes no sense. Yes, the sex was incredible. It was beyond incredible. And what he's saying is true, I did feel something more. But I can't believe he did too. That's not how this works. How this works, is I show an inkling of my soul to someone, and they use it against me. Or they crush my spirit for the fun of it. That's how this goes. Or, used to go. I know better than to get attached anymore.

I can't believe for a minute, not a single second, that Brandon Carmichael could ever feel more for me than lust. Someone like him doesn't do that with someone like me. I know this from experience. If I allow myself to think his words are true in any way, it will be the beginning of the end for me. Because that's all they ever are. Words.

So, why did I let myself get put into this position if I knew that? Why did I allow him to break down my barriers? Why did I allow myself to start to feel things for him? And why did I just let that happen?

Because the heart wants what the heart wants. A heart doesn't have the sense to know what's best for you. And the heart doesn't have a mind to change. A heart can't see the cliff you're about to fall over.

I finally glance up from the water bottle to meet Brandon's eyes, and it takes everything in my being to not crumble in front of him like I want to. I know I'm being cold. I know I'm being a bitch. I know there is the slightest of possibilities I might be hurting him. But I can't stop myself. This is how I protect my stupid heart from getting crushed by him.

"Brandon let's not make a big deal out of this. You

and I knew this was the final date, and I think this was a great way to end it." He raises an eyebrow at me, scoffing at my words, but I go on. "We've fulfilled our agreement, and you are no longer obligated to me for anything. You're free to go."

His mouth drops open, and his eyes widen in surprise. "I'm free to go? Did you really just say I'm free to go? How can you be so callous right now?" He rushes over to me and puts his hands on my shoulders, and I swear I'm going to buckle. I'm going to cave. I'm going to give in. I compose myself and harden my features, steeling my eyes against the pleading he's showing in his.

"Brandon, it would never work between us. Our lives are so different. I could never function in your world, and you could never survive in mine, and that's just how it is. This was nice. I had fun against my better judgment, but this is where it has to end."

Each word coming out of my mouth stabs at me with 1,000 little needles. Every syllable pounds into my chest, trying to get to my heart, but I don't let them. I have to make him understand this situation is untenable. He's basically a genius; he should have figured this out already. Any relationship between us couldn't work.

The weight of his hands on my shoulders is almost too much for me to take. I can feel the warmth in his palms, and that only makes me remember his fingers moments ago gliding over my skin, running down my spine, raking through my hair, and I have to step away from him again before I give in and do something I'll regret later.

"We barely started this relationship, there's no way

we can know one way or the other if this will work. We can't know if we don't try. Believe it or not, I have resources available to me. I can be in your life if you'll let me. But you need to let me."

The determination and intensity in his eyes are so powerful that I want to believe him. I want to believe he would actually try. But that's all I can do, is want.

"I'm sorry if I gave you the impression things would go farther than they have today, but they can't. Hopefully, you've gotten what you needed from me. And I think our fake relationship was enough to distract from your former relationship with Eve. I'm fairly confident my dad's business will be able to grow again now that the name Mischief Motors is in the public eye. And, thank you for that."

"This was not a fake relationship, and you know it. Not for me and not for you. I'm not even talking about what happened tonight. You know our kiss in the limo the other day was more than just a kiss."

Now I have to turn away from him because, of course, he's right. It was more than a kiss. But I caught myself then, and I'm trying to catch myself again now before I go any deeper. But this is so hard. My dumb heart just wants to throw my arms around him and say yes, let's do this. Let's throw caution to the wind and try to beat the house's odds. I know more than most the house always wins.

I step further back from him and cross my arms so I don't do that, and his hands drop to his sides, his eyes dark with defeat. And the little flame that burned with blind hope in my chest for him burns the bridge between us, and goes out completely.

"I'm sorry." I rush past him and out the lounge door into the lobby. I realize then I can't go back into the gala. I can only imagine how awful I look right now. And with our fake relationship now over, there's no point in me being here. I notice Randall not too far away, so I approach him.

"Randall, I need a ride home right away. Can you please have the car pulled around as soon as possible?"

The expression of concern in his eyes breaks something in me, and I have to choke back tears. Once these tears start, I know they won't stop.

"Right away, Ms. Blake. Let's get you somewhere quiet to wait." He puts a hand under my elbow lightly and guides me down the hall to a private restroom, where I attempt to clean myself up, but I can't look myself in the mirror. I can't face what I've just done, even though I know it was the right thing to do. A few minutes later, there's a light tapping on the door, and Randall calls out, "Your car is waiting, Ms. Blake. Whenever you're ready."

I sigh deeply and exit the restroom. Randall is there waiting for me, but I can see over his shoulder. Brandon is watching us with his hands shoved in his pockets. No expression on his face. He doesn't nod. He doesn't smile. He doesn't wave. He just stands there and watches me leave.

I'm able to withhold my tears until I'm inside my own house. That was a feat I didn't think possible. And I was right; once they start, I can't stop.

I know deep down I've done the right thing. I've done the responsible thing for both of us. That doesn't give me any comfort, and as I try to fall asleep, I'm haunted by the pain in Brandon's eyes as I left. Those eyes are going to haunt me for the rest of my life.

Chapter 21

That's Us

Brandon

I return to the gala without Normandy because I don't have a choice. I can't up and leave like she did, even though I want nothing more than to follow her. I'm the event host, and not attending isn't an option. When anyone asks, and almost everybody does, I claim that Normandy has taken ill and needed to leave. Every time I tell the lie, I die a little inside, knowing she just didn't want anything to do with me. Knowing she got what she wanted from me and is done.

Never mind the fact that the entire agreement scenario was my idea in the first place. I understood what I was getting into, and I knew the risks. I always know the risks. I just didn't think this outcome would hurt this badly. I didn't count on catching real feelings for Normandy. I didn't count on any of this.

Every single relationship I've had since Eve has been strictly physical. And up until now, I was okay with that. If I'm honest with myself, I probably expected that from Normandy as well. But somewhere along the way in these last few weeks, I've fallen for her. And I've fallen far and hard.

I honestly don't know what I thought or expected to happen, but it definitely wasn't this. This excruciating pain was not on the menu at all.

I finish the night going through the motions, a plastic smile on my face to hide my real feelings. As far as I can tell, no one notices my fake party persona. But, of course, I'm wrong in that assumption. When I arrive home, I find Sophie in the kitchen making tea, waiting for me.

"Sophie, what are you doing here? It's way too late for you to be working. Is everything OK?" I pull my tie off from around my neck with a frustrated snap and drape it over one of the bar stools.

She still hasn't acknowledged me entering the room, but surprisingly, she says, "Have a seat, Brandon. We need to have a little chat."

I study her for a moment as she busies herself around the kitchen, trying to figure out what she could need to talk about at one o'clock in the morning. I wonder if she's OK. Is it her health?

"Sophie, you're starting to worry me. What is going on with you?"

She grabs her own drink and sits beside me at the

counter, and I still can't read her face. Whatever she needs to talk about is serious, I can tell that much. She stares at her mug before speaking for a solid minute, tapping the sides anxiously.

"You are aware of most of my past. Particularly my nightclub. But you don't know everything, Brandon. And, with Normandy now in the picture, I think perhaps it's time you did know everything."

I am bewildered. I have no idea what Normandy could have to do with Sophie and her nightclub. I instantly want to ask a million questions, and I want to tell her that Normandy removed herself from the picture a few hours ago, but I force myself to be quiet and listen.

"Normandy is a charming girl, and the two of you make such a handsome couple. You remind me of another couple I knew a long time ago."

"Oh? Who would that be?" This is going in a bizarre direction. I did not expect Normandy and me to be the topic of conversation, especially since it's been made clear to me, we're not a couple.

"You two remind me a lot of Victor and his first wife, Joan. As a matter of fact, Normandy could be Joan's twin, they look so much alike. And when I saw her in Joan's dress tonight, I knew immediately who she was."

I raise an eyebrow at her but don't interrupt. How could I not know Sophie knew Victor? But then, why would I know that? It had nothing to do with anything. At least, I thought it didn't. I have a feeling that's about to be disproven.

"Normandy's mother was a dancer at my club for several years until she met Victor. Once she met him, she was so smitten, and he was so protective of her that it wasn't long before she quit, and the two of them were married. And the next thing I know, Normandy came along."

"That doesn't sound too bad."

"No, that wasn't bad at all. I was very happy for Joan and for Victor. They both deserved happiness. And they were both so in love with each other. But, with that love, Victor overextended himself and made some bad business decisions, let's say, to put it nicely. Though it was much more than that."

"I have since learned of Victor's possible... connections to some nefarious people. Is that what you're referring to?"

She looks a little surprised I would know anything about that part of Victor's life, but I shrug a little, indicating to her it's kind of what I do; learning about people. She nods and goes on.

"In his effort to make Joan happy, he was so blind with love for her and for Normandy...It started with loans, and then instead of robbing Peter to pay Paul, he ended up paying Peter to protect him from Paul."

"Louie Calnetta is Peter in this situation, isn't he?"

"I think so. I never got involved with names. He and Joan were careful not to get anyone else mixed up with their troubles, but there were always grumblings on the grapevine here in Vegas. It got to the point where Joan was threatened and kidnapped for a short time, which was her last straw. She wasn't hurt or anything, and it was brief, but when she was released, she immediately filed for divorce and moved herself and Normandy to North

Las Vegas. Not entirely out of harm's way, but close enough so Victor could still see his daughter and vice versa. Where it was relatively safe.

Victor tried to find love a couple more times after that. But I don't think he ever got over Joan. None of those women were from my club, though. And I know for a fact the money he paid was to continue to protect Joan and Normandy."

The last part grabs my attention. "With Victor gone now, does that mean Normandy and her mother are back in danger?" I remember Normandy telling me about the incident with Calnetta the day of the funeral, and something in my spine tingles sharply. This information is not what I wanted to hear tonight.

Sophie glances down at her mug, twisting it on the countertop nervously. "That I don't know, Brandon. I wish I did." She raises her eyes to meet mine, and a sense of deep sadness in them hurts to see. "You're a good man, Brandon. I wanted you to know what you were getting involved with in Normandy. Like I said, I don't think she's aware of any of this, but you should be."

Is Sophie trying to warn me off of Normandy? Or is she trying to get me to help out with the situation? I can't tell by the sadness in her eyes. Maybe it's both, and she's sad the problem exists.

"So, do you have any advice for someone who might want to be involved with Normandy?"

Remarkably, the sadness in her eyes deepens further, and my hands holding the hot mug of tea, suddenly go ice cold.

"I can't tell you what to do, Brandon. Lord knows,

even if I tried, you wouldn't listen." That makes me chuckle, but I nod for her to continue. "My only advice is to be careful. Your money and security can only go so far, and you're only one man. If you were to pursue Normandy, you'll need to be ten different men." She tilts her head, questioning if I understand.

"I get it, Sophie. Thank you for letting me know."

She nods and stands, going to clean her mug. After she dries it and puts it away, she gives me a weak smile before leaving, not saying anything else. Leaving me with my thoughts, the silence, and the loneliness I've become comfortable with. Well, it was comfortable until today. Now it's more like isolation.

Chapter 22

20,000 Seconds

Normandy

Throughout the following week, I try to keep myself busy, so I don't have to think about Brandon. It gets harder each day instead of easier, and I don't know how that's even possible. While I don't regret how things ended between us at the gala, I also can't stop thinking about what an incredible connection we had, both physically and mentally. Thoughts of his hands on me pop up unbidden without warning when I least expect it, and it's taking more and more effort to push those thoughts away.

The tabloids have caught on to the fact that we've not been together since the gala, and the rumor mill is churning with gossip about what could have happened between us. According to one website, our twins are deathly ill, and Brandon's now a deadbeat dad. That at least makes me smile. I've avoided answering questions since I don't go anywhere but work, and the press only yells at me through the car windows.

Brandon's company had its annual meeting, and the last I saw, he's gone back to his life in New York. Our plan worked, and his reputation is back on the plus side, and business at Mischief Motors is on the rise too. It was a win-win after all. I try my best not to pay attention to the internet, but it's really damned hard.

To further distract myself, I take time on the weekend to start going through my father's things to clear them out. I've put it off long enough and have given up on waiting for Chelsie to help me with it. Whenever I bring it up, she finds an excuse to avoid it. So, lucky me gets to handle something else entirely on my own. No problem.

While going through his files at his home office, I come across a plain white envelope with my name on it. I don't know how long this envelope has been here, but it's yellowed around the edges with age. I hold it for a moment before opening it, anxiety taking over, and I search the folder I found it in to check if there is one for Chelsie, but there isn't. I pace the room for a minute staring at the envelope and my father's crooked handwriting. Finally, I give in and open it, my fingers shaking and the paper tearing roughly. Inside is a letter written with choppy writing that can't be anybody else's but my dad's.

Dear Normandy,

If you are reading this, I am no longer of this world and have moved on to the next. That sounds ominous, huh? I hope I went quickly and painlessly because you know what a wuss your father is.

If you haven't already, you're about to find out some things about your dad that aren't great, and I'm sorry for that.

Just know that I loved you and your mother with everything I have. Or had, I guess. The things you're going to learn about me will probably be hard for you to understand, and that includes Chelsie too.

I can only hope my death takes my debts with me, but if it doesn't, I am very sorry. Know that I never intended to involve you in any of it. Please believe that if you believe nothing else.

You know how I always say, 'Vegas is not for the faint of heart,' that couldn't be more true.

Please tell your mother that I'm still sorry. She'll know what it's about. I continue to be sorry for everything and that I loved her till the end. Sometimes people just do stupid things when they're in love, and I was very in love, so I did very stupid things. It's no excuse, but it's an explanation if you need one, which, if you're like your mother at all, and I know you are, you need one.

To give you more of an explanation for this letter, there is a man who has been after me, after your mother, and after my business for years. His name is Louie Calnetta, and he should be avoided at all costs. Him and his business are only the tip of the iceberg of what I've gotten myself into, but I think he's the one that will show up first. I don't know what he'll do once I'm gone, but if I know

Louie, he will at least try to take the company from you or eliminate you as competition once and for all.

While I have no right to ask you for anything, please do not let that happen. I have fought too hard and lost too much in my life for him to win.

I'm sorry the only things I have left are my house and my business to give you to continue this fight. I fought alone, but you have Chelsie. Get to know her. Learn to love her like a real sister, even though I think you already do. You will need each other's strength.

I am sorry, Normandy. From the bottom of my heart, I'm sorry.

Love,

Dad

I stare at his words in disbelief. Even with everything he said, I still don't understand what he meant by any of it.

I reread the letter three more times, trying to analyze what my dad was trying to say. What he was trying to warn me about. I've already met Louie and instantly had a bad vibe from him, so I know my dad isn't lying there. But what debts is he talking about? Nothing in the accounting I went through mentioned Louie Calnetta or his company.

I suddenly remember the business card that Bianca gave me from some Consultant at Calnetta Cars and I rush to the kitchen to find the card again. Hopefully, I didn't throw it out. I find the card on the desk and reread the name: Frank Santangelo. The words "CALL ME" are etched across the back of the card. A chill runs through me. I have a feeling that Louie and Frank are picking up where they left off with my dad. I could be in trouble.

Finding my phone, I do a quick internet search for Frank Santangelo but come up with absolutely nothing. It's almost as if he's a ghost. I guess that's how people like him operate, completely under the radar.

My fingers itch to dial his number, to find out what the hell is going on and what my father got himself into with Calnetta Cars. I can't work up the nerve to do it, though. An ominous feeling of dread slithers up my spine just thinking about it.

Instead, I call Chelsie to come over for lunch, telling her I found something of Dad's I need to talk with her about. I have the letter open and waiting on the kitchen island when she shows up. She glances at it, then at me with a questioning look.

"Can I assume you expect me to read this?" She picks up the letter and starts scanning it.

"Yeah, that's for you to read too, even though it's addressed to me."

As Chelsie reads, she slowly sinks into a seat at the kitchen table, her eyes wide and never leaving the letter. After she finishes reading, she lowers it to the table and stares at me, her mouth hanging open in surprise.

"What the fuck, Norm? What the hell did Dad get into?"

"I don't know, but I intend to find out." I sit across from her and slide Frank Santangelo's card across the table to her. She picks it up, reads it, and then throws it back on the table.

I witness several emotions roll through her, ranging from intrigue to anger and confusion to resolve.

"So, are we going to call this Frank Santangelo person?"

"To be honest, I'm not sure what to do. But Louie Calnetta is already a problem." I tell her about the incident on the day of our dad's funeral, and then Frank coming to the depot and leaving his card.

I'm relieved to have someone else know what's going on, but I'm concerned for Chelsie's safety at the same time. She can be impulsive and headstrong, and her mouth has gotten her into trouble more than a few times. I need to keep her as far away from this as much as possible.

"I'm going to see if Taylor can spare some extra security for us. I don't think you should be going around town alone. I'll find the money somewhere to pay for it."

"Norm, wait a minute. I don't need bodyguards 24/7. There's no reason he'd come after me. I have nothing to give him."

"Just until we figure out how to deal with this permanently. It'll only be for a little while."

She scowls and sits back with a huff, almost pouting like a little girl, and it just proves her impulsiveness. I can't take a chance that she won't say or do something to get herself hurt.

"I need to talk to my mom about this. I have a feeling she knows more from what Dad said in the letter."

"So, what am I supposed to do in the meantime while you're figuring out what's going on?"

"Just be careful until we get security for you. Don't go

out anywhere by yourself. Make sure you're always with a group of friends. Or, if you can stay here with me at least for a few days, there's security here for the press, so I'm assuming they'll be here as long as the press is."

It's the only thing I can think of doing at the moment. There aren't many options for us until we have more information. My primary goal is to keep Chelsie safe for now.

She nods her agreement, which I'm surprised at, but I don't say anything because I don't want her to change her mind.

"Let me see if Bianca can take you to get some things from your apartment, OK?"

She doesn't respond but picks up the letter and begins to reread it. I guess that's answer enough.

I head back to my father's office to call Bianca, but before I can pull up her number, my phone buzzes with an incoming call. It's Frank Santangelo.

Are you kidding me? The back of my neck prickles with foreboding. I stare at the phone in my hand, a heated debate going on inside my head. *You were about to call him, he just beat you to it. Answer it and find out what Calnetta is up to. Let it go to voicemail. You don't want to get mixed up in this.* Curiosity wins.

"Hello?" This is a horrible idea. My voice shakes so much I barely recognize it. I should hang up now before I say anything else.

"Normandy Blake?" He sounds normal, like a regular guy. I thought somehow he'd sound like an evil villain or something. It feels like a trap.

I don't respond. I don't know why not precisely, but I

can't make words come out of my mouth, and I'm gripping the phone way too tightly.

"My name is Frank Santangelo. I knew your father."

Still nothing from me.

"My condolences to your family."

I wait silently for him to go on.

"Would it be possible to meet somewhere to talk privately? Phones aren't secure. I'm with --"

"Norm, maybe we should see if Taylor or one of his guys can take me to pick up stuff from my apartment instead."

I quickly disconnect the call and whirl around to find Chelsie leaning in the doorway. I don't know what the hell I was thinking, answering that call. I don't think I was thinking at all. Curiosity just got to me.

"Are you okay? You're looking a little pale."

"Yeah, I'm fine. Great idea about the security. Let me make a call."

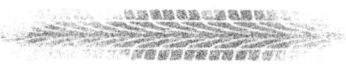

That evening after dinner, Taylor comes by to take Chelsie to her apartment to grab some things to tide her over while she stays here. When he arrives, I'm astonished to find Brandon with him. Seeing him startles me, and my breath catches in my throat. With everything going on, this was the first day I didn't think about Brandon every minute of every hour. It was maybe every minute of every *two* hours. It was still too much.

Taylor nods and walks past me into the house while Brandon stays on the doorstep. Our eyes are locked in an intense staring contest. His eyes are tired, and the shadows on his face seem deeper than usual. I want to run into his arms and slam the door on his face at the same time. It's irrational. I've spent this time away from him trying to organize my feelings about us, and each time I try, I just end up confusing myself. There is definitely something special about him, and I could probably fall in love with him in a heartbeat if I let myself, but the chaos that surrounds him is too much for me. Only now, the chaos I'm afraid of is surrounding *me*, not him, so my rationale falls flat.

"I thought you went back to New York."

"I did." He looks away for only a moment, then back at me, his intensity ramping up. "But I had to come back after I heard...." His voice trails off, not finishing his sentence. I know exactly what he's referring to.

After a minute of heavy silence, he steps up and wraps me in his arms, his hard body and strong muscles enveloping me, protecting me, and comforting me. I can't help but lean my head onto his chest and allow myself to be weak, comforted, and protected. I have needed this all day and didn't know it.

"Taylor told me about the letter you found from your dad. I wish you would have called me." His voice is low, and his warm breath on my ear makes me shiver.

"Why would I call you? What could you do about any of it? I thought you were in New York."

"I could do what I'm doing right now. I could get more security for you. I could leave everything in New York behind and be here for you. I *am* here for you."

I tilt my head up and search his face for some kind of

catch. Some sign that this is a quid pro quo and I'll owe him something, but I don't see it. All I see are concern, worry, and anxiety. And I don't think he's faking it. It's hard for me to tell.

"Brandon, you know I would never ask you for anything."

"I do know that, which is why I'm here offering. There is a time to be stubborn and do things yourself. This is not one of those times. You were absolutely right to reach out to Taylor to get someone to watch over Chelsie. And I love that you also offered whatever security was protecting you to be transferred to protect her instead. That's not happening, but I appreciate the thought." He chuckles, and I can feel his chest rumble against me.

"I need to take care of my tribe. What can I say?"

"Well, in doing so, you have made yourself even more irresistible than you were. Which, to be honest, was near impossible to do."

Chelsie and Taylor walk past us to leave, and she raises an eyebrow at Brandon and me.

"You kids have fun, but not *too* much. I *will* be back."

I smile at her and wave, but I don't laugh. Too much is happening to think about what she's insinuating. I pull away from Brandon and head into the kitchen, knowing I have to let him read the letter.

Something in my gut tells me my dad was determined to see Brandon and me together, even though he never told me they were friends. Maybe the dark cloud hanging over him kept him from telling me. My dad the hopeless romantic. At least the hopeless part is accurate.

Chapter 23

Be There

Brandon

Seeing Normandy again for the first time since the gala and knowing she is possibly in danger makes me want to just grab her and take her away from here. If I thought she would let me for a second, I would, and I still plan on trying to convince her to return to New York with me.

Being able to hold her again after thinking of her nonstop for the past week chips away at something in me. The wall I put up when she left the gala after being together is having a hard time standing now that she's been in my arms again. I can't forget the feel of her skin so easily. How my body reacts to her when I'm in her presence is hard to ignore.

She shows me her father's letter and the business card, and I examine them both carefully. It's hard to say how old this letter is, but it doesn't look like it was written recently. It's clear that Victor loved his ex-wife and his daughters, but it's also clear he knew he was in over his head. So, he had been living with this threat hanging over him and his family for God knows how many years.

"So, what do you think? Any ideas about what kind of trouble my dad could have been in? What those debts he's talking about in the letter are?" Normandy's eyes are tight with anxiety, and her body seems to vibrate with restlessness. She keeps shifting in her seat as though she can't get comfortable and won't stop biting her lower lip.

"Actually, there are a few things I need to tell you that coincide with this letter." I should have confided this information to her before, but I could never find the right time. And it's not like we've been on speaking terms, either.

She looks curious, but the concern in her eyes deepens. I don't want to be the one to put more stress on her than she already has, but I don't have a choice.

"Have you talked to your mother yet about this letter?"

"No, I haven't been able to reach her. Why?"

"I've learned some things that involve your mother that you should know about. I had hoped she would be the one to tell you these things, but I guess that hasn't happened."

"Brandon, what are you talking about? What does

any of this have to do with my mother? Other than my dad really loving her?"

"Apparently, during your parents' marriage, your mother was kidnapped by Louie Calnetta. And that was what prompted her to file for divorce from your dad."

Normandy freezes in astonishment, her dark eyes wide in surprise. "You can't be serious. I would have known if my mother had been kidnapped."

"I don't know when it happened or how it resolved. I just know that it happened. I assume you were very young at the time."

"How could you possibly know any of this?" She shakes her head in disbelief at me, doubt and certainty coming and going in her features.

"My house manager here in Vegas, Sophie, owned a nightclub years ago where your mother used to dance and where she met your father. She recognized your dress at the gala belonging to your mother, Joan?"

My words solidify the thoughts in her head, and I can see when the realization of the truth of it all hits her. It's a visceral reaction, almost like she's been punched in the gut. I jump out of my seat and go to her, pulling her hands into mine, but she can't look at me. Her eyes stare off to somewhere behind me, as I'm sure her imagination fills in all the blanks.

"This is all insanity. I can't believe this is happening. What the hell was my father involved with? Kidnapped? By Calnetta?"

"There's more, Normandy." Her back stiffens, and her eyes snap to mine, and I can see the dread forming there. I have debated whether to tell her this, but in light of this letter, she needs to know. "There's a chance that your father didn't die of natural causes. The police are looking into your father's toxicology, which may lead them to investigate his possible murder."

I can sense her hands begin to shake even though I'm holding them tightly; her entire body seems to flinch at the word 'murder.' Her shoulders start to curl in, and it looks as though she's about to fold in on herself under the weight of the news. I let go of her hands and pull her to me carefully, wanting to take away all her distress and suffer in her place so she doesn't feel this pain.

She pulls away from me, and her face is so pale she looks like she's going to be sick. Jumping out of her seat, she starts pacing around the kitchen, her breathing ragged, and I'm afraid she might hyperventilate.

"Normandy, you need to calm down. We're going to figure this out, I promise."

"How can you say that? My dad had years to figure this out and couldn't do it. And now he's dead. They fucking killed him." She runs a shaky hand through her hair. "Can you call Taylor and check on them to make sure Chelsie is OK? I need to know that she's OK. I need to call my mother again."

She's rambling and about to lose it, so I pull my phone out of my pocket. "Fine. I will call Taylor to check on them, but I can almost guarantee they're perfectly fine." I briefly cringe inwardly at the phrase 'perfectly fine,' but push it just as quickly out of my brain. I dial Taylor with the speakerphone active, and he answers on the first ring.

"Sir?"

"Taylor, I'm calling to confirm that you and Chelsie are, in fact, fine."

"Yes, Sir. We are OK and on the way back."

"Thank you, Taylor. See you soon." I disconnect the call and shove the phone into my back pocket. "There. As you heard, they are unharmed."

As I glance up at her, I notice she has stopped pacing. She's standing in the middle of the kitchen with her arms crossed and the crease between her brows deepening.

"How long have you known all of this, Brandon?" The ice in her tone sends a chill racing down my spine.

I can't help but swallow hard. I know she's not going to like my answer.

"Since before the gala."

"How could you keep something like this from me? Don't I deserve to know something like this?"

"I didn't want to worry you until I had all the facts. And I still don't have them all. The police are still investigating. "

"Why wouldn't the police talk to me about this? I would think law enforcement would keep the next of kin informed of a potential murderer on the loose. Did you pay them to keep quiet? Is that why nobody's talked to me about this? Would being with someone like me ruin your reputation? Is my family now suddenly a disgrace to you? A social media optics risk?"

"What? What the fuck are you talking about? Of course, I didn't pay anybody, and this has nothing to do with me. As I said, I didn't want to upset you like you obviously are until the police finished their investigation." I can't believe she just accused me of paying off the police to be quiet. "Is that really what you think of me? That I would bribe law enforcement to keep quiet? Or that I'm somehow ashamed to be connected with you? Really, Normandy?"

She doesn't meet my eyes and starts pacing again.

"I don't know what to think, and that includes about you. Excuse me if I'm not reacting *correctly*, but I'm currently processing a lot of information. In a matter of a few hours, I discovered that my father got himself into a shit load of trouble, then at some point in my life, my mother was kidnapped, and now my father was most likely murdered, and Chelsie and I could be next."

"I understand. And this is precisely why I didn't want to tell you anything until I had the facts."

"Yeah, well, so much for not getting me upset." She throws her hands up in exasperation and leans against the counter. I close the distance between us and try to pull her into a hug, but she yanks her hands away.

"Normandy...."

"Just don't, Brandon. I don't need to be babied right now."

I hold my hands up and step away. "Whatever you need me to do, I'm here for you."

The following 20 minutes are awkward as we wait for Taylor and Chelsie to return. Normandy can barely look at me, let alone be in the same room, and she definitely doesn't want to be near me. That has been made abundantly clear. She practically leaps away if I even step in her general direction. I know she is processing a lot of devastating news, and everyone does that differently. Apparently, Normandy needs space to do that, so I give it to her. Whatever she needs right now from me, she will get.

When Taylor and Chelsie arrive back at the house, it's clear to at least Chelsie that the mood has changed between Normandy and me, and she gives me a questioning glance. I don't know how to respond because I don't know what's happening either.

"I think the two of you should come with me back to New York, at least for the time being, until the police have finished their investigation." This time Taylor gives me a questioning look, but I ignore him. This is the only proactive thing I can do right now, so I at least have to put the option out there for the two of them.

The sisters gaze at each other and have a silent conversation, at the end of which Chelsie shrugs her shoulders, and Normandy scowls.

I'll take that as a yes. "Right. So, Chelsie, I assume all of your things are already packed, which leaves Normandy to get some things together before we go."

"I didn't say I was going anywhere." She glares at Chelsie. "We do have a business to run, remember?"

"Norm, I don't know if I feel safe here or at the depot. I do know that I'll feel safer in New York. Besides, Bianca can handle things for a few days."

Chelsie is now my favorite person outside of Normandy in this room. Like an asshole, I hadn't considered their business, and what Chelsie says does make sense to me, at least. The question is still whether it makes sense to her sister or not. Normandy chews on her bottom lip as she considers it, and that habit of hers will drive me to distraction.

"It feels like we're running away. Like we are hiding, and I'm not comfortable with that," she sighs deeply and continues, "but I also know it's probably the right thing to do at the moment." She turns to me. "We will accept your offer to go to New York, but I insist that we pay for our accommodations at the very least."

I take a deep breath and release the air slowly, relieved that calmer heads have prevailed in at least one instance. The fact that Normandy and her sister will be safer puts my mind at ease. Having Normandy so close, on the other hand, is putting my nerves on edge. This can either be incredibly great or an incredible disaster. Right now, it's too close to call.

Chapter 24

Wild Flowers

Normandy

After throwing a quick bag together and knowing I'm most likely forgetting everything necessary I'll need while out of town, we get to the airport and, well, avoid the airport altogether. We're driven to an open tarmac where Brandon's private jet is waiting, ready to go. The awe on Chelsie's face when she first glimpses it is priceless. I reach over and gently lift her jaw that's dropped. I should be laughing at her about it, but I can't manifest that emotion within myself.

"Chelsie, don't tell me you've never been on a plane before." Brandon's amused tone matches the glint in his eye as he watches her react.

"Well, no, actually. I've never flown before." She doesn't sound nervous, though, only excited. I'm sure a lot of that has to do with her first flight being on a private jet.

"Unfortunately, this is going to ruin it for every other plane you board." His laugh is infectious, and I can't help but join in a little.

"I'm totally okay with that. Ruin away."

When we pull up to the plane, she jumps out of the car and runs up the steps and inside. She doesn't act phased at all by what's hanging over our heads right now. We filled her in on the ride about Brandon's discoveries, and while she's concerned, she didn't seem overly so. Not like me, who can't help but overreact and overthink everything.

Brandon helps me out of the car, and the cool evening air whips around me, causing me to shiver. I realize we're in the middle of winter, and New York City will not be this mild. I didn't bring a winter coat. I wasn't thinking about the weather.

"Shit. I forgot my coat. Should we go back and grab it?" I start turning to get back into the car, my mind overflowing with things I've forgotten.

"We'll buy you a new coat in New York. Don't worry about it." He tucks me under his arm, shielding me from most of the wind, and walks me slowly toward the plane. "Whatever you need, I'll take care of."

His words hit my brain but don't reach my heart. That path is blocked off and under construction right now. Besides, it's my head needing calming at the moment. I can't stop picturing my mother kidnapped and hurt and my father writhing in pain as he died alone. It's gruesome and traumatizing, and I'm making up all the pictures of it in my imagination, but there's nothing I can do about it. My thoughts are on a runaway train.

We board the plane, and I take the seat Brandon points me to, moving robotically and not noticing my surroundings. I'm sure they're lovely. I assume we're in a flying palace from the sound of Chelsie's chatter. I take her word for it and fasten my seatbelt, staring out the window at the mountains in the distance, pale and dark purple in the late sunset. *They really are pretty....*

"Norm!" Chelsie's voice is annoyed, and I snap my attention to her across from me. I barely acknowledge Brandon sitting on my right, holding my hand. I don't remember him sitting there or taking it.

"What, Chelsie? Stop yelling at me." The ice in my words lashes out, and everyone around me freezes, but I hardly notice. Chelsie's exuberance and upbeat mood are so contradictory to how she should be acting that I can't take it anymore. "What the hell are you so excited about? This isn't a god-damned field trip we're going on. We're running away to hide so we're not fucking killed like our father was. Don't you get that?"

She rears back as though I've slapped her, the smile on her face instantly crumbling, and her eyes fill with sudden tears. My hand flies to cover my mouth in shock at what I've said. That is so unlike me to yell like that. I immediately regret my outburst.

"I'm so sorry. I didn't mean to yell at you like that, Chels." I reach out to her, but she pulls herself out of my reach. "I didn't mean to take all this out on you."

"It's okay," she sniffles, wiping her wet cheeks. "I get it."

I squeeze my eyes shut, trying to force my mind to clear the tornado of negative thoughts whirling through it, but it's not working. Nothing I do makes me feel any better. Brandon carefully takes my hand in both of his again, and the solidness of them surrounding mine makes me feel small and weak in comparison. It's supposed to be a comforting gesture, but instead, it reminds me how vulnerable I truly am. Despite this, I can't pull away from him. I'm not even strong enough to do that.

"I am sorry, Chelsie," I whisper.

"I know, Norm. And I *am* worried and scared. I guess I'm still processing all of it, I don't know." I can sense her shrug without even seeing it.

"Look, the two of you are now under my protection. I won't let anything happen to either of you. I promise you that." Brandon's voice is so severe and full of emotion I need to open my eyes. "Every single resource I have is now at your disposal. And if you need something I don't have, I will find it for you without question. We will resolve this."

I can't help but stare at him, taking in his passion as he speaks. I see now why he's so successful. He makes me want to believe every single word he says. I would follow him anywhere and join his cult in a hot minute. It's not just that he's charismatic; it's beyond that. He's earnest. You can tell he believes what he says, which makes you believe it too. It's incredible. It's like being covered with a security blanket during a storm, precisely what I needed to hear.

Chelsie must feel the same way because she's staring at him like I am. Neither of us says anything in response. I think our reaction is response enough. We are both amazed, and rightfully so.

He blushes a little under our intense gazes and lets go of my hand. If I somehow didn't think he was attractive before, that look solidified it.

"Let me see when we're taking off." He stands and makes his way to the front of the plane.

Chelsie and I turn our attention back to each other, our eyes meeting briefly, then looking away.

"That right there, sis, is what we call the whole package." Her voice is back to being excited but is more restrained now. I can't help but smile at her comment about Brandon.

"He's almost too good to be true." I sigh inwardly, considering the idea. "He's probably a mama's boy or has some other fatal flaw I've yet to discover. It'll rear its ugly head when it's exactly too late."

Her expression sobers. "Norm. Don't you know anything about his family?" She seems surprised.

"No. He hasn't talked about his family yet." The deepening concern in her features has me worried now. "Why? What should I know about his family?" I hadn't thought much about it since we discussed so many other things during our few outings. And now I feel like an asshole for not asking him about his family because I know absolutely nothing about them.

She cranes her neck to check the area for Brandon, but he's not back yet.

"His mother went on some talk shows in England a

few years ago and talked total shit about him. I think they paid her for her sob story. She dragged him through the mud, saying he wouldn't care for her financially and she was basically destitute, but you could tell she was lying through her teeth. Eventually, it spun back on her, exposing her as a bold-faced liar, but I don't think they have a relationship."

"That's horrible." I couldn't imagine having your own mother do that to you in public, especially over money. That had to be awful.

"She's a real piece of work. His dad left when he and his brothers were young, and they never heard from him again. I'd bet he ran far away from her, but still shitty to do to the rest of the family."

I didn't know this either, but I never paid attention or asked. "How many brothers does he have?"

She makes a face at me, scowling at my ignorance. "You didn't know any of this? What kind of girlfriend are you? Two brothers."

"What? I don't interrogate people when I go on dates." I shift in my seat, knowing she's at least partially correct. I should have asked Brandon about his family or at least ran a quick internet search. I'm sure it's all public knowledge. Just not the public I'm a part of, apparently.

Once we're in the air and at cruising altitude, Brandon disappears into the back. The next thing I know, a glass of white wine is hovering in front of my face, and I happily take it, no questions asked. When I glance up, I see him smiling at me, his hazel eyes light and entertained.

"You know, there is a bed in the back." The

suggestive tone of his voice is squirm-worthy, but before I can respond, Chelsie is up and out of her seat, heading toward the back of the plane.

"Thanks, Brandon. Let me know when we're close to landing." She pats his shoulder lightly as she passes with a huge yawn.

I shrug at him and take a sip of the outstanding wine. *That's Chelsie.*

He stares at me, his face drawn and exhausted but still gorgeous. It's not fair he can be so handsome when tired. I can only imagine how horrible I look now. I swear I feel the shadows under my eyes. Not that how I look matters anyway.

"Come sit with me in the lounge area." He holds a hand out to me, curling his fingers to beckon me to join him.

His tone is no longer suggestive, and the invitation seems innocent enough, so I follow him to an area of the plane with a comfortable couch and large TV.

"You're not expecting Netflix and chill or anything, are you?" I fall onto the couch, careful not to spill the wine, kick off my shoes, and pull my legs up under me, getting comfortable.

"It can be..." he grins wickedly and again with the squirming. I need to stop. Or he does. One of us does.

Chapter 25

Angel

Brandon

I swear it wasn't my intention to get Normandy drunk, but the night and the wine got away from us. I thought for sure she would be an angry or sad drunk, but instead, she's giggling like she doesn't have a care in the world. Her laugh is so infectious that I can't help but laugh along with her, and each time I do, my heart surges with emotion in my chest. Seriousness overtakes her momentarily from time to time, but it's fleeting. During those moments, I can tell that the heaviness of the day's events overtakes her briefly. The superhero wannabe inside me wants to move heaven and earth to make everything better for her. Perfect, if I could.

But regular me knows I'm walking on thin ice around the Ice Queen, and a wrong move could prove fatal for any relationship we might have.

She's also become more and more affectionate as the evening goes on, which I am not complaining about in the least. On the contrary, I wholeheartedly encourage this kind of behavior, at least from her I do. Her touching me so casually on occasion triggers feelings I don't know what to do with, and not just physical ones. Knowing that she feels comfortable enough with me to be so warm makes me think she might be passed the whole "I'm an asshole billionaire" mindset. At least, I hope that's the case.

She's allowing me to sit with my arm around her shoulders, and it feels natural, like we do this all the time. I *wish* we did this all the time and things between us weren't so tenuous. I haven't wanted to bring up anything related to our relationship, whatever it may be, with everything she has going on. I'm sure it's not a priority for her right now, and I don't blame her.

"So, how much?" She's leaning back to meet my eyes with a challenging expression.

"I beg your pardon?" I have no clue what she's referring to. "How much is what?" My first thought is she's wondering how much the plane cost, but I'm not going to tell her the price under any circumstances. Even I can't stand how rich I am sometimes. It's obscene.

"Me." From the hardness in her eyes, I know that I need to be very careful with how I tread here. The challenge is even stronger now, and my spidey senses go into full-blown red alert. My mind announces to the rest of my body that we are at Defcon level one, and I can feel a sweat start to break out on my forehead.

"I...still don't understand the question." I half-laugh, but it's full of nervous energy, betraying my anxiety. "Please explain."

She shifts to pull away from my arm around her and slides a little down the couch, obviously putting distance between us. I don't like this.

"Once upon a time, you offered me money to date you." The smirk on her lips is growing, and the sarcasm thickens. "I'm curious what you would have paid."

There it is. The minefield laid out before me. *Shit.* I will never be able to live down that one rambling mistake, will I? How interesting that her intoxicated mind goes to the topic, though. She must either be very bothered by it or intrigued. I'm afraid to ask which.

"I get the feeling that you're a very stubborn person, is that correct?"

"Don't change the subject." She wags a finger at me. "But yes. I can be a little stubborn sometimes."

"You've been chewing on that particular bone for a few weeks now."

"And?"

"And nothing. Just making an observation."

"Well then, answer the question, and maybe I can let it go."

Giggling and carefree Normandy has jumped off the plane and been replaced by her super-serious alter ego. The change is jarring, but I suppose it can happen when alcohol is involved. You'd think I'd be used to this side of her by now, but it still intimidates me for some reason.

I've never reacted like this to a woman, and it's unsettling. And admitting that to myself is pretty crazy.

"Despite my countless apologies and retraction of said comment, you'll recall that I said you could name your price." I look her straight in the eye, meeting her challenge. If she wants to know, I've got no problem telling her how it is. I say what I mean and mean what I say. Any other way wastes time, and my time is precious.

"And if I said I would charge every penny you have?" The smirk turns into a devious smile, which looks damned sexy with her cheeks a little flush from the wine. Add that one to the fucking list.

"Then you would get every penny."

Suspicion takes over, and she eyes me warily, unsure if I'm joking or not. "Seriously?"

"Yup. If that's what I offered, and you accepted, it would be yours in a heartbeat." I match her sly smile as I lean over and twist a lock of her hair around a finger. "I'm a man of my word."

Of course, I know in my head she's referring to cash, which not many people know; rich people don't technically have a lot of. Most of our wealth is dumped into various assets and tax-safe havens. Cash on hand isn't something I keep stuffed in the mattress. But she doesn't know that. I know within myself I would still pay whatever price she demanded. That's not a lie. It's just a little bit more complicated than she most likely expects.

A burst of giggles erupts from her, and she covers her mouth, trying to contain her laughter. I don't know what exactly is so funny, but I can't help but laugh along with her. But the harder she laughs, the more I start thinking I'm the joke.

Once she gets control of her laughter, she sighs. "I'm sorry, you were just so damn serious it struck me as hilarious." She places a hand on my thigh, squeezing lightly, and my mind pivots and dives straight into the gutter.

"I'm glad I amuse you," I manage to say, trying desperately to refocus on the conversation. The wine is getting to my head, too, it seems. The combination of alcohol and Normandy's presence is enough to intoxicate me.

"No, you're taking it all wrong." She sighs deeply again and returns to snuggle against me, wrapping my arm around herself and intertwining her fingers with mine. "I would never ask you for money."

"I know."

With her head on my shoulder, and her body secure in my arms, I know I did the right thing in coming to get her and Chelsie out of Vegas. I wouldn't have been able to function knowing they were in danger. I still don't know what *type* of threat surrounds them, how deep it goes, or how far it reaches. I can only hope that New York is far enough away to keep them safe.

Next, I need to work on locating Normandy's mother, Joan, and getting her to the city to join her daughter. While I don't think she's in danger, I can't guarantee it. Not that I can ensure anyone's safety, really. If someone is determined to hurt someone else, they will find a way to do it. But if I can increase the odds of avoiding that by even the slightest margin, I will do whatever I need to achieve that.

This entire week apart from Normandy just about wrecked me. I barely made it through the annual meeting the day after the gala; I was such a fucking mess. It's a miracle I still have a company after being so distracted with everything Normandy. Memories of her cold stare after our 'perfectly fine' time together warred with echoes of her warm body rocking into mine, leaving me aching to touch her again to prove I didn't imagine the whole thing.

And now, holding her like this, it's clear I didn't imagine a damn thing. Patience with her is going to be critical. I still don't know much about her dating history and why she's not had a serious relationship. At least, nothing that I've been able to find. Like everything else about her, I suspect the answer to that question is more complicated than what's showing on the surface.

She shifts next to me, making a slight contented noise in her throat, and I notice her breathing has become deep and steady. She's fallen asleep in my arms. While it's probably a consequence of the wine, I want to believe it's because she feels safe with me.

Since learning of Calnetta and his evil intentions, protecting her and her family has become my only goal. I've never been this concerned about someone else's welfare before in my life. I don't know how, but somewhere along the way in the last few weeks, Normandy Blake has become the center of my universe.

Chapter 26

Dear August

Normandy

"Good morning," a deep voice rumbles next to my ear, pulling me slowly out of a dream. I feel an object digging sharply into my cheek as I open my eyes. I realize that I'm lying with my head on Brandon's chest on the couch, a button of his shirt leaving a small and round divot on my face. I must have been sleeping a little *too* soundly. My sleep has been filled with bad dreams lately, but it appears for the last few hours at least, I made it through without a nightmare.

I sit up quickly with my eyes still shut, and the blood drains out of my head, making me dizzy, and I sway a little.

"Whoa, easy there, Quick Draw." Brandon's voice is soft and comforting, and I want to curl back up and listen to it so it can ease my pounding head. "Hangovers and changes in air pressure can be a real doozy." He rubs my back gently, making me want to go back to sleep.

I squint, examining the too-bright interior of the plane. "It's dark out. You said morning," I grumble. My mouth is so dry it feels like I swallowed the entire desert before leaving Vegas.

"It's about 5 AM, so technically, it's morning. We're landing soon." He sounds completely normal and looks no worse for wear. He's somehow even more attractive when he wakes up. Really not fair. And I guess he can handle his wine better than I can. "Water?" He can also read minds now, too. Awesome.

"Water." I nod because I don't think my talking made any noise, at least not that I could hear. He comes back with a bottle of water and some pain relievers. Cool. So, he's an adorable mind-reading angel. "Thanks," I croak and take the pills, gulping half the bottle of water in the process.

He's watching my every move, and I'm becoming self-conscious. I may have gotten too comfortable and friendly with him last night while we talked. I let my guard down again around him, which is so not what I want to do. I can't let him slide his way into my heart and life. Right now, I'm dependent on him for safety, but this is an extreme situation. I don't have a lot of options at the moment. Getting drunk and muddling up my mind isn't going to help. That was not my brightest move.

I stand up when he sits next to me and puts an arm

around my shoulders. I panicked when he got close, and now I need to look like I had a reason for standing. I have not had enough sleep to think straight. *Okay, we're landing...Chelsie! I need to wake her up.* I swear I'm losing it.

"Normandy? Are you okay?" The concern in his tone claws at me, making me even more confused. I want to give in, but the wall around my heart tells me no. Nobody gets in.

"I'm fine. Thanks." I avoid meeting his eyes as I glance around, reorienting myself to the plane. Once I figure out which way Chelsie is, I head that way. "I need to wake up Chelsie."

Before I get too far, Brandon reaches me and grabs my arms gently, turning me to him. I'm ultra-aware of his body so close to me. You'd think I'd be too hungover to notice stuff like his solid muscles, sharp jawline, or damn, those bedroom eyes that are so captivating. But no, these things about him are so damned obvious, I'd have to be blind not to see them. Anybody would. I am not unique in these observations, and I know it.

"What is wrong?" He's trying to catch my eye, but I avoid it, looking everywhere but at him. I know in my soul if I meet his eyes right now, I'll lose myself in them. "And why won't you look at me?"

I try to twist out of his grasp, but he holds me firmly in place. I stop struggling and silently stare at his chest. Gazing intently at a button of his shirt, wondering if it was the one that left a mark on my cheek. *Is that mark still there?*

"Normandy, talk to me." The frustration in him is

growing; I can feel it. "You're not looking at me. You're not talking to me. You barely even said ten words to me since you woke up. What is going on with you?"

I don't have a good answer. Not one that he wants to hear anyway. *Sorry, I'm sending all these mixed messages. I'm just a little screwed up right now. Actually, all the time. I'm trying to save both of us from the inevitable heartache that comes with being in a relationship with me.*

I shrug weakly. "I'm just hungover. That's all. It's no big deal."

"You don't look at people when you're hungover?" He leans in again, forcing me to meet his gaze. And when I do, I can feel when it happens. When the blocks of ice around my heart melt into oceans. His hazel eyes capture mine, and I can see everything. His painful past, his chaotic present, and his hopeful future. It's all laid bare for me in that stare. He's always so open and honest with me in everything. Earnest. That was the word I thought to describe him once, and it was spot on. I know that he means every word he says.

But with that knowledge comes security I've not known in all my 31 years, and it scares me to death. How safety and security in a person can be so terrifying, I have no idea, but I don't always make sense.

"I'm looking."

"I won't pretend to know what you're going through right now, but I want you to know that I'm not going to rest until you and your family are safe. I gave you my word, and I meant it."

I study his face, looking for any sign of deception, even the tiniest hint that he might have ulterior motives, but I don't see anything. I am not used to guys being so honest with me.

Before I wised up after college, every single man in my life that I had a 'relationship' with went out of their way to do something to hurt me. They either left, cheated, or lied and, on one occasion, even hit me. That was the lowest point and the last time I let myself believe anyone who said they cared. It will take a lot more than words to prove otherwise to me. I'll give it to Brandon, though; he is trying very hard to convince me of his honesty. But then, who comes out and says they're a liar? Nobody.

He sees my hesitation and fear and shrouds me in his arms. I don't fight him. I don't have the will anymore, and my defenses are gone when it comes to him. He's become my port in this storm, and I need someone I trust to give a shit.

"I'm not used to...." I pat his chest, where his heart is beating strong, "this. I'm not used to anyone...." I can't finish my thought. He doesn't let me.

He puts a hand under my chin, tilting my face to his, and runs his thumb across my bottom lip slowly, stopping my words as he shakes his head silently. The sensation causes all the butterflies currently fluttering around in my stomach to fly free, and they take all of my common sense with them when they go.

I push up on tiptoe and press my lips to his, wrapping a hand around his neck and pulling him in to deepen the kiss. The sudden need to be as close to him as possible overtakes me, and I press against his body, and he echoes my movements. Drawing me closer for a moment, he pulls away, tearing apart our kiss, leaving us both gasping for breath.

"Sorry..." I don't know what came over me just then. Something about how he was touching me, looking at me, propelled me to want to be closer. To see if he was real.

"Don't ever apologize." He smooths my hair, probably mussed from sleep and our kiss. "I only stopped because we're about to land. We need to wake up Chelsie. Otherwise, believe me, we'd be doing a hell of a lot more than that."

I nod. Of course, I've completely forgotten what we're doing and why we're on the plane in the first place. How could I let myself do that? I must be more hungover than I thought. I cringe, trying to remember if I did or said anything incriminating last night while we talked. I don't think I did, but then I haven't had that much wine in one sitting in a very long time. Who knows what came out of my mouth. Brandon doesn't seem too concerned, so it must have been fine.

"Right. Sorry." I flinch at the apology. "Sorry for the sorry... you know what I mean."

He chuckles and caresses my cheek. "Go wake your sister. We'll need to be seated and buckled up in a few."

When he turns back to head to the seating area, I watch as he walks away, admiring the rear view, as it were. I still feel woefully inadequate around him for some reason that I can't explain, but that kiss proved he's sincere about me, at least. He might just honestly like me, for me. Crazy.

I wake up Chelsie, who is almost as horrible as I am first thing upon waking, and we land safely in New York.

Before we deplane, a drop-dead gorgeous redheaded woman comes on board with winter coats for me and Chelsie. She has a bit of an attitude toward us but is nothing but smiles for Brandon. Her name is Diane, and she's his assistant. Lovely. Not jealous of her at all. Nope. But it looks like the feeling is mutual.

She glares daggers at me as Brandon helps me into the coat and puts a hand on my lower back as he escorts me off the plane. I give Diane a tight smile as we pass, but I don't see her reaction as the wind whips my hair into my face, temporarily blocking my view of her. If I were to bet, I'd put my money on her not liking me. It's okay. I'm not here to be liked. I'm just here to survive for a few more days. That seems to be a little more important at the moment.

Chapter 27

Please Forgive Me

Brandon

The trip to my penthouse on 57th Street takes longer than usual due to the incessant snow that keeps falling. Chelsie looked out the car's window once and fell back asleep. At least we could get back to the city without issue despite the weather. Flying to Vegas and back in 24 hours, plus the emotional roller coaster of everything surrounding Normandy, I'm left beyond physically exhausted. This kind of tiredness hits you in your soul.

If I'm being honest with myself, a lot of my soul-crushing tiredness comes from my relationship with Normandy, if I can even call it a relationship. Whenever

I think we're getting somewhere on the communication front, she suddenly pulls the rug out from under me. I can't keep doing this and expect to maintain my sanity. Volatility isn't something I tolerate well. Things seem to be on the upswing, but I feel it can change in the blink of an eye. I like to count on patterns and be able to predict outcomes. This has been impossible to do with her, and it feels like I'm trying to balance on shifting sands whenever we're together.

Everything between us has progressed so quickly that it's hard to believe I've only known her for a few weeks. At times it feels like we've known each other forever, and other times it's like I don't know her at all. I suppose we're really in the middle, but having to guess where I stand with someone isn't how I like to do things. I need to know where I fit in someone else's life, if I fit at all. I want to believe I fit somewhere in her life, but where that is still is up in the air, along with everything else surrounding her. Maybe we'll figure things out while she's staying with me.

She glances around with a confused frown when we pull into the garage beneath my building.

"I thought we were staying at a hotel?"

"No. You're going to stay with me." I never agreed to her demand to pay for their stay somewhere. And I wouldn't. Not when I have too many bedrooms as it is. I can only sleep in one at a time last time I checked.

"But I said...."

"And I never agreed or disagreed." I can't help but smile at the incredulous expression on her face. "Taylor had to leave some personnel in Vegas, so we're spread a little thin here for a while with protection. It's better if you stay close and with me. I've got plenty of room for the both of you, don't worry."

"But... Brandon, no." She sees the finality of the decision in my eyes and deflates; her shoulders sag as she accepts her immediate fate. "Fine. Remind me to have a conversation with you later about respecting boundaries."

"Sure thing." I force myself to maintain the smile to keep things light since I can see I've crossed yet another line with her. So, there is no doing for her. Everything needs to be done with approval or not at all. I don't know if I can operate that way. It's not like I have bad intentions and made these arrangements to purposely go against her wishes. On the contrary, given the information regarding the shortage of security, I did the only prudent thing: to do what I needed to keep her and Chelsie safe. Nothing nefarious about that.

After finally coaxing Chelsie awake, we make our way up to my penthouse. I brace myself for what I know is coming.

"Oh my God. This is your apartment?" Chelsie's eyes are as wide as saucers as she takes off her coat.

And there it is. The response I was expecting from Chelsie. She seems as though she'd be easily impressed with the view. Normandy, at least, is keeping herself reserved as usual. I can see a bit of intimidation in her tense expression, though. I'll admit, it can be a bit much on first viewing. Seeing the entire New York City skyline across Central Park from the floor-to-ceiling windows as soon as you enter the apartment was a central selling point for me when I bought the place.

Even in the middle of a snowstorm, it's still a breathtaking view.

"Well, this is part of it. There's this entire floor and the floor above where the living quarters are." I beckon them both to follow me further into the apartment instead of standing in the foyer, gawking out the windows. Though, to be honest, I still do that sometimes when I'm alone.

"Pfft. Living quarters. Good Lord." Chelsie scoffs, rolling her eyes at Normandy, who shrugs back at her. "Are there servant's quarters too?"

I sarcastically deadpan a look at her indicating, *of course, there are.*

"Seriously?" I think her jaw may actually hit the floor.

Now I can't help but laugh. She's too easy to mess with.

"Of course not. The servants have their own apartments...I assume." I continue the sarcasm and pretend I don't care, turning to head into the kitchen, signaling them to keep following me. I don't get to play the 'asshole billionaire' very often, and it can be fun. Normandy snickers, but when I hear Chelsie gasp behind me, I glance over my shoulder at her. "I was kidding, Chelsie. I don't have servants. I'm not royalty."

"Tell that to your decorator," she mumbles behind me. And that's fair. My décor isn't that of a typical bachelor. Apart from the windows, it's not all glass, metal, or leather. I don't like modern. I prefer layers. Rugs, tapestries, and plush couches and chairs. Real art on the wall, not crazy abstract pieces. Art is so subjective, though. What I call "real" someone else could just as quickly call crazy.

"Next time I see him, I will." And I'm serious. I'm sure Dennis, the designer who decorated the apartment, will get a real kick out of that comment.

I lead them into the kitchen, glancing at the clock on the wall and seeing it's still super early, say, "Do you want anything to eat? or a drink? Coffee? Or do you want to get some more sleep?"

They both say, "Sleep," and give each other a look and a nod of agreement that the other is correct. It's amusing to watch these two interact like real sisters. You'd never know they didn't grow up together.

"Right. Sleep it is then. Follow me one more time." I lead them to the internal elevator that leads to the floor above and the bedrooms. I show Chelsie to the first bedroom and then lead Normandy to the next one down the hall closest to mine. I could have given her the room across from Chelsie's but selfishly want her close to me, even if it's not in the same bed.

She enters the room and throws her bag on the bed, but I stay in the doorway, not wanting to cross more boundaries with her than I already have by assuming anything. I know I'm the last thing on her mind, as I should be. Even though we kissed on the plane, she's been reticent since we landed, barely speaking in the car, and almost not at all since we arrived at the penthouse. She's had a death grip on her phone ever since she woke up and is constantly checking it, I assume, for word from her mother.

"Are you okay?" I give in and go to her, take her

phone and toss it next to her bag, then rest my hands on her waist. "You're worried about your mother, aren't you?"

She bites her lip and nods, her eyes filling with tears. I wipe them away as quickly as they fall, but it's hard to keep up.

"She's not one to go radio silent like this. And with everything going on, and the letter...." She doesn't finish. She doesn't need to. If I had that kind of relationship with my mother, I'd be beside myself with worry too. Just the thought of my mother starts to fill my mind with hatred, and I have to push those thoughts away. Now is not the time for my own mother issues.

"We'll find her. Don't worry." I pull her into a hug, savoring the feel of her against me and wanting to pour all my strength into her. I want to give her everything she needs to feel safe. For all of her outer bravado, I can tell that she can also be fragile and delicate and needs to be handled with extreme care. People with the toughest exteriors sometimes only hold them up with a bit of duct tape and a wish. "Try to get some sleep if you can. I'll be right next door if you need me."

She nods against my chest with a sniffle, and it almost breaks me to turn and go to my own bedroom. The last thing I want to do is leave her alone. What I want to do, is hold her and never let go.

Chapter 28

You Should Know Where I'm Coming From

Normandy

I'm waking up slowly, and I'm crying. I can feel my tears sliding back into my hair, but I don't want to open my eyes. If I open my eyes, I'll see that I'm not at home; neither in my apartment in Sacramento nor my father's house, and I don't want to recognize how truly lost I am.

Echoes of the nightmare that woke me replay on the screen in my mind, my mother hurt, Chelsie, bleeding and not responding, Brandon.... A sob breaks free from my chest, and I turn on my side and pull the covers closer, trying to keep quiet as I hide my face in the pillow.

"Hey.... None of that." Brandon's low voice is almost

a whisper, and I sense the bed dip slightly as he crawls under the covers with me. A warm hand glides around my waist, and he pulls me back against him, holding me tightly as I cry, the tears unstoppable now as they flow freely. "I heard you...Did you have a bad dream?" His breath skims my neck as he speaks, and then his lips brush my shoulder with light kisses.

I can't help but turn over and bury myself in the refuge of his arms around me. Allowing myself to feel protected in the safe haven that he represents in a way I've never felt before in my life. I've never been able to trust anyone with my vulnerability like this, and it scares the shit out of me.

"I did have a bad dream, but that's not all...." Yes, the nightmare was distressing, but I need to clear the air. *I can't believe I want to talk to him about this.* I need to let him know what he's getting into with me. If this is going to go anywhere between us, all of this needs to be laid out in the open. It's always buyer beware, but he's looking at damaged goods when it comes to me. It's only fair.

"What else is there?" The concern in his words and the solidness of his body against me give me a little more courage to open up.

"You scare me, Brandon." I swallow hard and wipe the tears off my cheeks before he can get to them. "I can't.... I don't.... My previous relationships have been...." I can't bring myself to finish a sentence. There isn't an adjective strong enough to describe how painful my history has been and why I've learned to be the one to leave first. I glance up and get stuck in an intense stare with him, trying to express all this hurt without words.

The tears continue to fall, and I give up trying to catch them all.

"You can talk to me." He brushes the hair out of my face, removing the strands stuck to my tears carefully.

And for the first time in my life, I tell someone about my pain. I trust someone with my heart.

"I've been hurt so many times and in so many different ways. Emotionally and... So, I don't put my trust in anyone. And I don't get close. And I hurt everyone first now. Well, I break things off before they can get serious. ...." I drift off, not wanting to relive all the horrors I've experienced in any detail. I've never revealed this to anyone, and I feel so vulnerable right now. I do not like this feeling.

He reads my eyes carefully, taking it all in. After a while, his expression morphs from concerned to enraged, and I can feel his body tense against me. "Who the fuck could do this to you?" His nostrils flare as he growls, and he squeezes me tighter. "I'm not kidding when I say I want names. Please tell me it wasn't physical."

It's my turn to tense up as I hesitate before I answer. I wasn't expecting such a visceral reaction from him, and telling him the truth might push him over the edge. I don't want to describe any of this, so I just nod slightly but clarify, "That was only once and wasn't sexual...." I'm not proud of letting myself get into that kind of relationship, and I've told nobody about it until this minute.

"Jesus, Normandy. Once is too many." He pulls me against him, and his strong arms and solid chest become a sanctuary I didn't know existed in this world. I never knew that just the act of being held by someone who knows your truth would be so comforting and healing.

He pulls away from me sharply, framing my face with his hands, ensuring he has my attention.

"I would never." He's so stern his voice cracks with the passion behind his words. "Fuck. I would never. I can't believe anyone would.... For fuck's sake, no wonder...."

"I know." I nod and reach up to stroke his cheek. The protectiveness for me that he just displayed moved something inside of me. Any ice that may have lingered around my heart because of my past was just melted by his emotions. "I figured you should know what you're...."

His lips gently steal the end of my sentence as his kiss consumes me, instantly chasing all negative thoughts out of my head. As the kiss and his touch change from lingering to greedy, all thoughts are replaced by a desire that shoots from my core to my brain and back, leaving my spine tingling in its wake.

He slowly shifts and covers me with his body, nudging my legs apart with his knee and settling over me. The sensation of his rigid erection rubbing firmly against my center through his pajama bottoms leaves me aching for more. I slide my hand between us, stroking his silky length, and his breath catches against my mouth.

Pushing up as he grinds into my hand, his biceps and shoulders flexing with the movement, he groans softly on an exhale, "I want you, Normandy. No, I *need* you."

Something in me stirs at his words, and I wrap my fingers around the back of his neck, pulling him down to whisper in his ear, "Then take me." His rhythmic movements falter for a moment, but he composes himself quickly, drawing back to study me. A small smile plays on his lips, but it's controlled. Everything about him is so controlled and deliberate and always decisive. *My* brain seems to spin when I'm around him, and I lose control of my senses.

He leans to the side, deftly opens the nightstand drawer, and pulls out a condom. I take the opportunity to admire his smooth bare chest and drag a finger along his rib cage, making him flinch but flash a dimple. *So, he's ticklish, good to know....*

He sheaths himself swiftly and makes quick work of my underwear, and then he's sinking into me completely, and I melt underneath him. Every single muscle in my body becomes pliant and taut at the same time under his gossamer touch, driving my hunger for him to levels I've never known. The throbbing that starts at my core sings through my blood, and I cling to him as he kisses and licks the spot where my neck and shoulder meet.

Our breathing becomes ragged even though we're moving so slowly as the intensity between us becomes overpowering. The craving for more of him echoes in my bones as I rise to meet every one of his gentle thrusts, and it finally builds and builds until I can feel the euphoria about to crest.

I dig my nails into his back as I arch against him, letting the thundering vibration spike and flow throughout my body. I can't help but bite down on his shoulder to stifle my release. My bliss erupts around him as he plunges into me with searing shudders of his own.

We lay simmering in each other's heat silently for a minute while we recover our breath.

Eventually, he lifts his head to gaze at me, stroking my hair. His eyes are bright and almost look like they're full of wonder.

"You are stunning in every fucking way." He kisses me so sweetly and tenderly that I feel tears prick at the backs of my eyes, but I force them away. "Simply stunning."

That does it. I can't hold the tears back, and I try to turn my head to hide them because I don't want him to think what we just did is making me cry. It isn't that at all.

"I'm sorry...." I choke out a half laugh, mostly out of embarrassment. God, what a mess I am. What we just shared was so much more than just sex, and the mere knowledge of it is crisscrossing my wires. I should be elated, but instead, I'm full of a mixture of fear of leaving myself exposed to him and a desire to give him every part of me.

He gently grabs my chin and turns me to him, his brows furrowed with concern but edged with empathy.

"I get it." He meets my gaze, and I can tell he's telling the truth instantly. It was more for him too. He nods to reinforce his words. "Believe me, I get it." He brushes my shoulder with a kiss as he gets up to go to the bathroom.

While he's gone, I let my mind go blank of anything else other than what just happened between us. Things are different now. We've crossed some invisible relationship threshold of trust, and I've never been here before. I'm still unsure what I'm doing or if everything I do is wrong, but I need to learn to trust myself for a change. I have to believe that I can choose a man correctly for once in my life. Not every man is only out for themselves. Statistically, that's impossible. Maybe I can allow myself to hope my trust is earned in Brandon's case. *Maybe.*

Chapter 29
What Went Down

Brandon

As much as I would love nothing more than to lay in bed with Normandy all day and repeat what happened this morning until fatigue sets in, there is way too much happening outside of us to lose focus on any of it. I need to remind myself every other minute to keep my mind on the matters at hand and not my hands on Normandy, let alone what any of it means.

Normandy still hasn't heard from her mother and is convinced she's dead in a ditch or the desert by now. I need to get my ass in gear.

After a quick shower, I have to attend a few corporate

meetings that really could have been emails, and then I call Taylor for an update on his multiple investigations. It still strikes me as insane that the simple act of me attending a friend's funeral would lead to all this.

"I've got my men split into teams for each problem, one for Ms. Blake's mother and one for Calnetta's involvement with Victor's death. I've even called in some favors with a friend's security company here in the southwest to help with the extra load." Taylor is being as efficient as ever.

"Okay, that's great, but what is happening? Have you found out anything at all on either problem?" While I'm happy to know things are in motion, I need answers. Yesterday. Seeing Normandy so worried rips my soul to shreds every time I see it.

"We may have a lead on the Frank Santangelo involvement, but it's looking like it's a red herring."

I sigh. More rabbit holes. "Taylor. Tell me what you have." I wait for a beat and go on when he doesn't speak right away. "Even if it's just preliminary." I can feel myself turning into an asshole, and I hate being that guy.

"Yes, sir." He pauses, and I wait him out this time. "We think that he might be a plant, but we're not sure for who yet. It could be another family using him as an informant, or it could be government. Just like people ghost and disappear without a trace, he did the opposite and ghosted in out of nowhere."

"No record of him from anywhere?" That can't be right. Something is definitely off about that.

"No, there are records of him, but they're too clean. Too neat. To the untrained eye, they probably look fine, but I can just tell they're not right. I can prove nothing, so I need to confirm some things before making judgments."

Now that makes sense to me. I've almost always trusted Taylor's gut instinct on things in the short time I've known him, and it has yet to disappoint. The only thing I disagreed with him on was Normandy, and I know he was just being careful there.

"So, what's next then?"

"We keep digging. We're getting pressure from Clark County to move on Louie, but even they know they'll need something more solid to act on before doing anything. Right now, it's all just suspicion and finger-pointing."

"And Normandy's mother?"

Again, a pause, but this one feels weighted. "Unfortunately, nothing. She hasn't been at her house since we started monitoring it, so we have no idea how long she's not been there."

"You're positive she's not in the house at all?" I try not to imagine her dead inside all this time.

"Yes, sir. We ran a recon sweep late last night so as not to draw attention and didn't find anything. Doors and windows were locked, nothing seemed in disarray, and there was no sign of struggle. Also, her vehicle is gone from the garage."

I'm reminded of our conversation at the gate of Mischief Motors. "Can you locate her phone?" *He can do anything, right?*

"Theoretically, yes. If the phone is on and has location services enabled, but the legality of doing that...."

"Good. Do that. Keep me updated."

We disconnect, and I feel only slightly better now that I know what's happening, even if it's very little. Something is better than nothing.

I update Normandy on her mother's empty house during lunch, and the news seems to increase her anxiety and not lessen it like I hoped it would. Before I can tell her anything else that Taylor and I discussed, her phone rings, and the screen shows the name 'Frank Santangelo.' She's about to deny the call, but I grab her arm to stop her before she can.

"I'm calling Taylor on my phone. Answer that on speaker once I have him on the line."

"What? What's going on?"

I don't have time to answer and just hold up a finger for her. Taylor answers after one ring.

"Stand by, Taylor," I say quickly, setting my phone on the table near hers, and nod for her to answer. Chelsie stares at us with wide eyes, clearly confused by everything happening.

Normandy shakes her head at me like I'm crazy but answers the call.

"Hello?" She's trying to sound confident, but the nerves are leaking through.

There's a slight hesitation, and then a deep voice asks, "Is this Normandy Blake?"

"Yes, and I'm not alone, just an FYI."

"I know. You and your sister are with Brandon Carmichael in New York."

Her eyes snap up to mine, fear jolting through her.

"Where is my mother? What have you done with her? I swear to God if you've harmed her...."

"Your mother is currently in Lake Tahoe in a very swanky safe house."

Well, that confirms Taylor's suspicion. This guy must be government of some kind.

Before Normandy can ask anything else, I jump in.

"What exactly is she being kept safe from, Mr. Santangelo? And who are you with?"

"I'm pretty sure you know who we're keeping her safe from, and technically I'm with the FBI."

That sounds sketchy to me. "What do you mean, *'technically'*?"

"It's a Special Operations Division focusing on transnational organized crime."

"Louie Calnetta is involved in transnational organized crime?" Not that I know a damned thing about this guy's division or organized crime, but seriously, Louie feels more like a petty criminal, all things considered. "He doesn't seem like that big of a fish."

"Oh, he's not a big fish, but he's on the same line, so to speak, of the fishes we want."

"So, what do you want with Normandy?"

"Are you her keeper? Or can I actually talk to her?" The irritation is understandable since I just jumped into the conversation, but I still don't appreciate it.

"I'm still here." Normandy is hesitant, anxiety written all over her face, and when her eyes meet mine, I see total fear.

"Ms. Blake, a situation involving you has arisen, and

I'd like to set up an in-person meeting to discuss cooperation, if possible."

Her terror intensifies. "What kind of situation?" Now she's looking between Chelsie and me as if we have the answers somehow. I wish to God that I did.

I see a text from Taylor flash on my phone screen.

> TAYLOR: *Set meeting up on Mischief Motors property. OR yours. NOT neutral or theirs.*

"It's one I can't discuss on the phone right now and why we need to meet face to face. How soon can you be back in Vegas?"

"I don't know. Let me check." She mutes her phone. "How soon can I get home?" I swear she's going to jump out of her seat in a second.

"At the last minute, barring weather issues, it's about five hours. We can be there around four or five local time."

She just nods and unmutes her phone.

"We can be there late this afternoon." She's started wringing her hands, and Chelsie has started chewing on a lock of hair. These two are definitely related.

"Fine. I'll be at your depot at six o'clock." He pauses briefly. "I shouldn't have to say this, but you'd do well to keep this conversation private."

"Understood," I say and hang up on him. We don't need lectures on confidentiality. "Taylor, what are you thinking?"

"It's as I thought. I knew something was off with him." He still doesn't sound happy. "But at least it's in a good way, and not another family."

"So, what's bugging you?"

"I don't understand what they would need Ms. Blake's cooperation with. Unless it somehow relates to her selling the company to Calnetta, that doesn't make much sense. I can't think of a scenario where that could be turned on him."

Normandy finally does jump out of her chair and starts pacing the length of the room, every muscle tense.

"Okay, we'll see you in a few hours."

After I hang up, I go to Normandy and pull her hands apart to wrap them around my waist to ground her in the here and now. I can tell her mind is racing with imaginary scenarios she's creating, and I don't know how to help her.

"We'll go. See what he has to say. And go from there. You're not obligated to do anything for the government. There will not be a problem if you refuse to help them out. They need you more than you need them."

"But if Calnetta killed my father, he needs to pay." A bit of anger now edges her tone. Good. Anger is better than fear.

"True, but there are always options on how to do that. You don't have to take the first one presented to you."

"No, but it sounds like it's the only one I'll get help from the FBI with."

She has a point, and I can't argue with that, even though I want to. I don't know what it is, but something about this isn't sitting right with me. My gut is telling me this is a bad idea, but if I can't say precisely why I can't convince Normandy of it either. Superstition and gut feelings don't fly in a court of law. Just the court in my head.

Chapter 30

Call Me A Saint

Normandy

The flight out of New York is delayed for about a half hour due to snow, but we still make it back to Vegas in time to meet with Frank at the depot. We arrive with some time to spare, and luckily the paparazzi aren't camped out like they have been at the gate. We must be old news now. *Good.* Though I feel bad for whoever their next victim is.

I can't stop pacing. Even on the plane, I struggled to keep still and found myself walking around. Thank God it's a private jet, or I would seriously have annoyed the other passengers. Hell, I'm annoying myself at this point.

"I don't like this. I'm just going to keep repeating it

until somebody pays attention." Chelsie has already said this about ten times, which isn't helping my anxiety to know that everyone thinks this is a crappy idea. "This Frank guy seems like a real weasel, you know? I don't trust him."

"It only seems that way because he's already pretending to be a bad guy. It makes it feel like he's pretending to be a good guy too." That's how I've rationalized my distaste for the man in my head. I'm not sure how accurate it is. "I get it."

Brandon hasn't taken his eyes off me since we left New York. I don't know what he's expecting to happen to me, but there are times it's comforting to know he's watching out for me, and other times when it feels invasive. I know he's not trying to make me uncomfortable, but I can't help my hypersensitivity now either.

"We don't know that he's a good guy," Brandon says, checking his watch. "We don't know much of anything, so until we do, it doesn't make sense to worry about any of it. Let's wait to hear what he has to say. He should be here soon."

He sounds so calm. He even looks calm. Seeing him like this only makes me more unnerved since I'm apparently not reacting right. I've never been close to a situation like this, and the proper etiquette for dealing with the FBI wasn't in any book or magazine I've read. I can picture the clickbait article in my head, '*The Top Ten Must-Have Lipsticks to Wear at Your Next FBI Interrogation.*' And I'm officially losing my mind.

Before I can completely go off the deep end, Taylor opens the office door and peeks his head in.

"He's here. I'll bring him right in."

Brandon thanks him and gets up to lean against the desk, looking like the billionaire CEO that he is, controlled and commanding. I take the seat he just abandoned; my knees are getting wobbly.

"Normandy," Brandon calls my attention to him but doesn't say anything else. He holds my gaze, and I calm down almost instantly. I don't know how or why, but I'm not going to question it. I want to hold his hand so badly, grab onto him for dear life, but I also don't want to look like a complete weakling. I'll just take the comfort that look gave me and run with it.

The door flies open again, and a tall, heavyset man with dark hair and eyes comes in, with Taylor following behind and staying at the door.

"Frank, I'm Brandon. Nice to meet you." Brandon holds out a hand to the man, not moving from his perch against the desk. The man studies him and nods before taking his hand to shake. Brandon then introduces Chelsie and me before directing him to take a chair.

"I need to make this quick. I can't be gone for too long, or it'll raise suspicion." Frank seems almost more nervous than I am. That's not a great sign.

"So, what is it you need my cooperation with, Mr. Santangelo?" I ask, happy to get to the heart of the matter.

"Frank. Call me Frank." He shifts his massive frame to face me. "It actually will involve the two of you if I can convince you to participate."

"Go on. We're listening." I nod to include Brandon. I didn't know he would be a part of whatever this is.

"Here's the thing. Louie is already making these arrangements, so it's more that we want to get ahead of it and control the process and outcome."

"Arrangements for what?" Brandon's forehead creases with concern.

Frank swallows hard, avoiding my eyes, but looking directly at Brandon. "Kidnapping Ms. Blake for a large ransom from you. As soon as he saw the two of you get involved with each other, he started chomping at the bit to get this in motion. So, the FBI wants to turn this whole thing into a sting to nab Calnetta, if possible."

Brandon practically leaps off the desk, making me flinch. "What? Absolutely no fucking way." His face is stern, but I see the fear behind his eyes. I'm too stunned to even respond. All I can do is watch the two of them spar while my heart races.

"Mr. Carmichael, as I said, he's already got the gears moving on this, but we can control it and make sure that nobody gets hurt while finally getting Calnetta on the racketeering charges we've been building against him. I've been embedded with him for almost three years, and this is the only real chance I've seen to bring him down hard. This kind of charge will be the final nail in his coffin and send him away for the rest of his miserable life."

"Can you guarantee Normandy's safety?" Brandon asks, deftly avoiding the glare I throw his way.

"Excuse me?" I scoff. "I don't remember agreeing to

do this." I can't believe Brandon would be so quick to throw me to the wolves like this.

"Obviously, Normandy. That's why I asked if your safety could be guaranteed. Because if it can't, there's absolutely no way you'd even consider it. Right?" He turns back to Frank. "Can the FBI guarantee *anyone's* safety?"

Frank shifts uncomfortably in his chair as he eyes me cautiously. "Nobody could guarantee total safety. That's an impossible condition in any circumstance." He shakes his head in disappointment. "And here I thought you would want to see the man that killed your father pay for his crimes. I guess family really isn't what it used to be." He shrugs his shoulders to accentuate his guilt trip.

"Now that's just fucking low, and you know it." Brandon steps up to Frank, and I can feel Taylor behind me move in closer. "Is that how the FBI recruits people? By shaming them into it? You've been hanging with Calnetta too long. There's no way Normandy is going to do anything if that's how she's treated."

I glance at Chelsie to see how she's responding to all of this, and she's just as pale with her eyes wide, taking it all in. Not too unlike myself. Though, I don't like being talked about like I'm not even in the room like Brandon is doing right now. I didn't give him authority to speak for me, and his assuming he can rubs me the very wrong way.

"Mr. Santangelo, how about you tell me exactly what you're asking *me* to do, and *I'll* make the decision based on that information, okay?" I flash him a syrupy sweet smile, letting him know I don't mean any of its assumed joy.

He lifts a brow at me, examining me closer, and it's some kind of test. I cross my arms, waiting for him to go on, and ignore Brandon running a hand through his hair in frustration in the corner of my eye. I'm not sure what kind of woman he thought I was, but it's apparent that I've surprised him somehow. Maybe because I was initially quiet when he came in, he wasn't expecting me to speak up for myself. *Well, surprise, shithead. Deal with it.*

He clears his throat. "Fine. To give you a basic summary, we'd like you to allow yourself to be kidnapped, where you'll be under my protection at all times. If there's even an inkling of funny business, we pull the pin, blow up the plan, and get you out. A ransom demand will be made to Mr. Carmichael, which I'm assuming you'll agree to pay, so have your bank account ready with a large amount of cash...."

"Doesn't the FBI provide that? Like fake bills or something?" I can't believe Brandon's reaction now is to the need for him to put up money to save me. I stare at him, incredulous.

"That's what you're worried about now?" I can't keep the shock out of my voice.

"What? Of course not. The money is absolutely nothing." His jaw tightens, and a dimple pulses briefly. "I just figured there was another way since this is a setup." I can tell he senses that he's digging a deeper hole for himself. "I have no problem with arranging for cash. Please continue."

Wow. I've never seen Brandon so upended before.

This really is getting to him. *Good.* Because it's been getting to me for a while now. I refocus on Frank.

"This is the twentieth century, Mr. Carmichael. We're not talking about a suitcase full of cash money in bills. Everything is real streamlined nowadays. It will all be done electronically to some untraceable offshore accounts. Well, mostly untraceable if we can keep the government's big nose out of it. Everything leaves a fingerprint, even things without fingers." He chuckles at his own lame joke. "Anyway, it's that simple. You pay the money, he hands over Ms. Blake, we take him down for good, nobody gets hurt."

"Why can't you just arrest him for our dad's murder if you know he did it?" Chelsie chimes in. It's something I've been wondering about too.

"No proof. I wasn't around when he made the order. And he went off campus to order it, too, since none of our surveillance picked it up. I've only been there a few short years. I'm not part of his inner circle yet, so he doesn't totally confide in me. That takes years, if not decades. Something we don't have."

I gaze at Brandon, and I imagine him getting hurt for the simple reason he started dating me, and my stomach churns at the thought. It's because of my father that he's involved in this, and it isn't fair to him. He shouldn't have to risk anything for me, even if he doesn't care about the money. I do. I care about all of it. The best I can do is cooperate and get Calnetta out of our lives for good.

"So, if Victor was paying Calnetta protection money, who was he protecting him from?" Taylor pipes up from behind me. I'd almost forgotten he was there; he's been so quiet.

Frank, too, must have forgotten him because he starts a little at his question.

"The Mamana family. He wants to use this money to buy his way in with them and merge power. Otherwise, he'd never come up with this kind of cash, and he's about bled dry paying them off too." He shrugs. "Honestly, if we don't get him now, the Mamana's might take him out before we do."

"Don't the Mamana's own the Bliss casino on the strip?" Taylor asks.

"They do indeed." Frank starts counting on his fingers. "They also own two casinos in Reno, one in Biloxi, and a few in Atlantic City. And now they're getting into real estate in New York of all places since the money laundering is harder and harder to cover up in the casinos nowadays."

Brandon turns away from us, leaning his hands on the desk, his head down. He's deep in thought, but I think he's coming around to seeing that this is the best course of action for us to take if we want to see Calnetta gone from our lives.

"Isn't this entrapment?" Brandon asks, not lifting his head or turning to face us.

I hadn't thought of that. Of course, I don't know much about this kind of thing anyway.

"No, sir." Frank is confident in this. "This was all his idea, and he has no clue I know about it. Otherwise, we wouldn't be able to do any of this. Like I said, the gears are in motion already. I'm just letting you in on it."

The realization of it dawns on me. *Holy shit.*

"So, you don't even need my cooperation, do you? This is going to happen to me whether I agree to it or not, isn't it?" Terror shoots through me, pinning me in place. I grip the arms of my chair so tightly that I might break them.

Frank goes pale but nods his head from side to side. "More or less, yeah." He at least has the decency to look ashamed about it, but that doesn't appease me. "But bringing you in on it is cooperation in the eyes of the government."

"And, what? You wouldn't *'guarantee my safety'* if I didn't cooperate?"

"I didn't say that...."

"You didn't have to." I look to Brandon, still leaning away from us, his head down. He's not saying anything. *Why isn't he saying anything? This affects him too, doesn't it? Does he not have the money or something?* "When is this happening? And where? Who is going to do it? How long will they have me? What are they going to do with me?" The words rush out of my mouth before I think about what I'm saying. With every beat of my heart, another question pops up. My throat is tight, and I'm getting a bit dizzy.

"Breathe, Ms. Blake," Taylor says softly, putting a hand on my shoulder. It's enough to ground me and pull me out of my downward spiral. For now, at least. It also pulls Brandon out of his, and he turns around to face us.

The violent storm of outrage in his eyes is something I don't ever want to see again. And I most certainly don't ever want it directed at me. He looks downright unhinged. Frank physically cringes beneath the weight of Brandon's fury.

"Answer her fucking questions." The muscles in his jaw tremble as the words are forced out. He is not taking any shit from this man.

"Day after tomorrow. Here in the morning, since you come in by yourself way before everyone else. I'll be on the team, so don't worry about that. Nothing will happen to you. The ransom demand will come a little later after some fear sets in for you, with payment arrangements made for that afternoon, so prepare for several hours of roughing it." He meets my eyes for what feels like the first time, though I know it's not. "It's not like I'm a lone wolf here, the entire FBI is behind this, and there will be other agents ready to move in when the time comes."

The words feel hollow to my ears, even though I know they should be comforting. Nothing about this is comforting.

Brandon is staring daggers at Taylor for some reason, practically seething, and I have no clue what that could be about. There's no way Taylor could have known about any of this, is there? Maybe it's just a safe place to direct his rage.

Frank works himself out of his chair and glances around at us.

"I'm not the bad guy here." He takes another business card out of his pocket and hands it to Taylor for some reason. "I have a feeling you're the guy who'll need this."

He only nods as he takes it, his eyes tight with frustration.

Once Frank leaves, we sit in heavy silence. Each of us

ruminating on what just happened and trying to sort our scattered thoughts.

I'm going to be kidnapped. I'm going to let myself be fucking kidnapped. What the hell is wrong with me?

I actually came back to Vegas to put my life in danger. I should have stayed in New York, where it was safe. Away from all of this insanity. There is no guaranteeing my safety, but that can be true anywhere at any time. And like Frank said, this would happen if I knew about it ahead of time or not. At least now I can prepare myself for it.

How do you prepare yourself to be kidnapped?

Chapter 31

Bound

Brandon

I bring everyone back to my estate after the so-called "meeting" with Frank. That was less of a meeting and more of an information dump. There was no discussion, no exchange of ideas. We were just told what would happen, when, and where, and there is absolutely nothing we can do about it. That is not a fucking meeting.

Normandy is still trying to be brave but is failing miserably. The entire ride to my estate, she gripped my hand so tightly I lost feeling in my fingers. I didn't pull away, though. I can't imagine what she's going through right now. She's the one taking the brunt of this. She's the one risking everything. I just need to show up and pay the money to set her free. I have the easy part.

When I think about the risks, I can't help but think of everything that could possibly go wrong because that is what happens; things go wrong. And when they do, it's not usually on a small scale. No, it's typically catastrophic. The idea of Normandy hurt, or worse, hasn't left my imagination since this came up, and I don't see myself having a moment of peace until this is over. If something were to happen, I couldn't live with myself.

Sophie has prepared the house for all of us and has dinner ready when we show up. "It's so good to see you again, Normandy." Sophie pulls her into one of her big hugs, leaving her flustered. It would be cute if storm clouds weren't hanging over our heads. "And you must be Chelsie. How nice to meet you." She shakes her hand warmly. "I've set up a buffet-style spread for you in the kitchen, so it's a bit informal since it's last minute. I hope that's okay."

"It's perfect." Normandy is gracious as always, and I can't help but feel a pang of pride. "Thank you for going to all the trouble."

"I tried to call Brandon to confirm the number of guests and any dietary restrictions, but I couldn't get through to him, so I had to guess what everyone would like." She gives me a fake glare but winks.

I'd warned everyone not to talk about the upcoming events in front of Sophie, making things incredibly awkward once greetings are finished. It's evident to everyone in the house that something tense is going on, but nothing is being said about it, and we're all looking at each other sideways to make sure we're not giving anything away. It's worse than if we just talked about it in front of her.

Eventually, Sophie disappears somewhere as she always does and leaves us to our own devices. Taylor vanishes, too, leaving me with the sisters.

"Why couldn't she reach you?" Chelsie asks as though I should be reachable all the time or something.

"My phone has been off since we left New York and during our meeting, and I haven't turned it back on yet." I shrug. Someone could have reached me through Taylor if something important needed my attention.

"Won't world markets crumble or something?" Her tone is chiding, and I'm reminded of when we all first met in person at their father's funeral, where I said something similar. It makes me laugh, which I haven't done at all yet today. It feels good.

"Fair enough," I say, pulling out my phone and switching it on. I'm surprised at all the voicemails and text message alerts that pop up as soon as it comes to life. *Whoa. What the hell?*

I skim the texts from various members of my legal team, and if I'm reading them correctly, things have found a way to get worse. I go to my voicemails and listen to the first one from my personal attorney.

> *ABBEY*: Hi Brandon, this is Abbey
> Killian. We have ourselves a bit of a
> situation. We've just been served a
> subpoena on your behalf to appear
> here in New York before a Special

Grand Jury the day after tomorrow.
Special Grand Jury usually means
organized crime. Because these
things are so secretive, there is no
caption, but we think this somehow
relates to Eve Cromwell. We've
heard rumblings that they might be
going after her for something more
than the SEC thing. Call me as soon
as you get this.

You have got to be fucking kidding me.

I rush out of the kitchen, dialing Abbey as I go. I
need to get away from Normandy. If she hears this right
now, she will freak out. And rightfully so. Shit, *I'm*
freaking out. There has got to be a way to get out of
this.

"Brandon, you're alive. I take it you got one of my
many voicemails."

"What the fuck is going on?" How can she be so calm
about this? "We've got to find a way to make this go away.
I cannot be in New York in two days. It's impossible."

"Okay, first, take it down a notch, please." She draws
in a deep breath. "Second, there is no getting out of a
Special Grand Jury summons. If there were, I would have
done it so we could figure out what this is all about and
prepare for it."

"Fuck." This came out of nowhere. I know I should
apologize to Abbey, but I'm having a hard time thinking
straight.

"We're pretty sure this is about your personal

relationship and dealings with Eve because they haven't asked to see any documents. It's testimony only."

"Well, how long is testimony like that going to take? I need to be back here in Nevada the same day. That's non-negotiable."

"Brandon. There's no negotiating here. Like I told you, you need to comply with the subpoena. If you don't, you *will* be arrested for contempt of court. It's not a maybe."

"God damn it."

"Is there anything we should know about your personal dealings with Eve?" She sounds suspicious, which annoys me even more. "This came out of left field for us."

"What? No. Of course not. I gave you the run down of everything between us when the SEC indicted her. That's all there is. I have no fucking idea what else they can possibly want."

"And what about any organized crime?"

I hesitate at that, thinking of Calnetta and Frank's FBI connections. Could all of this be related somehow? Wouldn't Frank have told me about this since he would know about it, right?

"I have no clue." It's not entirely a lie.

"Have you ever testified before a grand jury before?"

"No. I don't usually deal with criminals."

"Well, you're going to be on your own in there. It's not like a deposition. Attorneys aren't allowed in the room. We'll be out in the hallway if you have questions."

"Great. Looking forward to it." I want to believe there's some sort of legal Hail Mary we can throw at this to make it go away. "You're absolutely positive there's no way I can get out of this?"

"I'm sure, Brandon. I'm sorry. I'll be in touch tomorrow with details."

I sigh. Defeat washing over me. "Thanks, Abbey."

Hanging up, I hurl my phone across the room. It doesn't travel far before shattering into mangled shards against the wall. A gasp sounds behind me, and when I turn, I find Normandy in the doorway to my office, a hand covering her mouth and confusion mixing with fear in her eyes as she stares at me. *Shit. How much did she hear?*

I watch her for a minute, waiting to see what she's reacting to. Was it just the phone throwing?

"I need to go back to New York. I've been subpoenaed by a Special Grand Jury to testify. If I don't go, I go to jail." I scrub my hands down my face and drop my hands to my sides. This could not have happened at a worse time.

Normandy's face drains of all blood, and she turns as white as a sheet. I rush over to her, fearing she'll faint on the spot, and help her into the office and a chair.

"You're leaving? When?" Something has shifted in her eyes. There's still fear, but it's got something else there that I hate even worse. Resignation. No, disappointment. Of course, she's going to feel like I'm abandoning her when she needs me most. It's how I feel too.

"I don't know yet. I need to talk to Taylor." I squat to be at her eye level and take her hands into mine. They're freezing and shaking.

I want to fix this.

I can't fix this.

"Okay...."

"We'll figure this out. I'll be able to be back here in time to do my part and get you. Don't even worry about that. I'll do whatever I have to to make that happen. It *will* happen. I promise you."

She searches my eyes, looking for the truth in them, and I hope she sees that I'm serious. I am not going to fuck this up for her. There's no way I will make her go through this alone.

"I promise. I won't let you down."

Chapter 32

Quiet Little Place

Normandy

"Brandon, I'm scared." I can't stop shaking. It started in my hands and has now spread to my entire body. I feel like one whole exposed nerve, raw and aching from sensory overload. I am usually a put-together businesswoman in my own right, but now, with all this craziness around me, I feel weak and vulnerable. I don't like feeling this way at all.

He rubs my hands between his, trying to warm them up and get the circulation going, but I can barely feel it. I'm going to be alone. I'm going to be kidnapped and alone. And there's no guarantee that he will make it out of court on time to pay my ransom. What if he doesn't make it out in time?

"I know. I know." He kisses the palms of my hands, his breath warm against my skin. It's the only warmth I feel at the moment. "I will make this work somehow. I'll be out on time, I swear. I promise you. Don't worry about anything. We'll get through this."

He sounds more like he's trying to convince himself than me. And he can't promise those things. There's no way he can promise anything.

"Please don't do that."

"Do what?" he glances up at me, his brow furrowed in confusion.

"Don't promise me things you can't follow through with. Or, at least, things we don't know you can come through on. What if you don't make it out of there in time?"

"I *will* be out in time."

"But you have no way of knowing that. We don't know what time they'll demand. And you don't know how long your testimony will take. It could take days, couldn't it? What if I don't have days?"

"I'll be ready." His voice rises, and his grip on my hands tightens, almost painfully. His eyes are such a dark green right now, the amber flecks in them sparkling sharply in the light of the office. He's willing me to believe him, but I can't. "I will be out and ready to get you back."

I can only shake my head at him. He may as well ask me to believe in unicorns or the Loch Ness monster. Those would be more likely.

He puts his weight on one knee and pulls me closer, surrounding me with his body, and I lay my head on his shoulder. I know he's trying to say the right thing to keep me calm, but I don't need platitudes. The only comforting thing right now is the truth. And the truth is, we don't know what the future will hold in the next few days. We could have only one day left together. And if that's the case, I don't want to spend our last night together like this, all stressed out and worried.

Whatever fate is going to do to us is already planned. All I can do is hold on for the ride, so I'll hold on to Brandon while I can. Considering our rocky start, I don't know how it happened, but I have fallen hard for this man. I've allowed myself to be vulnerable with him and given him my truth freely. I've never done that with anyone before, and if I make it through this, I'll never do it again with anyone else. He's it.

I can't bring myself to say it, though. It feels way too soon. And maybe I'm just feeling this way because of the craziness surrounding us this whole time. If we were an average couple, it would probably take months to fall in love, right? How long does it usually take?

"You okay?" he whispers, and I notice he's pulled back and is studying me.

"Huh? Yeah. I'm fine."

"You looked like you checked out for a minute there." A smile spreads from his lips, up to his cheeks, and into his eyes. Those damned dimples making an appearance. I can't help but give my own small smile in return. It's the best I can do.

"I'm okay. Really. Just tired, I guess."

He stands and pulls me up with him, resting his hands on my shoulders.

"We should try to get some sleep. I have a feeling neither of us will find it easily tonight."

This time I just go straight to bed with Brandon, not even trying to keep up the appearance of separation between us for Chelsie's sake. If I tried to sleep alone, I would have zero chance. At least lying here with Brandon, with his arms around me, I might get at least a little sleep.

I'm curled up with my back against his chest, and he hasn't stopped tracing lazy circles on my exposed shoulder. It's both mesmerizing and unnerving at the same time. It could lull me to sleep if I didn't know that he was deep in serious thought, just like me.

"What are you thinking about?" I whisper to the dark of the room, wanting to know but not wanting to disrupt his attempts at sleep.

His fingers hesitate for a second at my question but then go back to their design dance on my skin.

"You."

"What about me, exactly?" I'm trying to keep my tone light, though I don't feel it. My mood is anything but light. Maybe I'm hoping that a bit of banter between us will lift the atmosphere in the room.

He doesn't answer for a long while, and if it weren't for the constant swirls he's drawing on me, I'd think he fell asleep.

"I care about you, Normandy," he finally says. "Probably more than I've cared for anyone."

I don't say anything. I get the feeling that he has more to say but is figuring out how to say it. I know how that goes, so I give him time to go on.

"It doesn't make sense since we haven't known each other very long, but I kind of fell for you before we even met."

"Before we met? How is that possible?" That makes me laugh, and I squeeze the hand I'm holding under my pillow.

His chest rumbles against my back as he laughs with me. "I saw your picture. You were in an intense conversation with someone, and I just knew that you were different somehow. You were the most beautiful woman I'd ever seen, but your beauty went deeper than that, too. I don't know how to explain it."

I can picture him blushing behind me as he speaks, and the butterflies are back, fluttering around my rib cage, flying into each other. This is good. This is distracting and comforting.

"Well, I thought you were the most drop-dead gorgeous asshole I'd ever laid eyes on at my dad's funeral."

The next thing I know, my side is being pinched hard, tickling me and making me squirm with a yelp.

"Asshole, huh?" he growls into my ear. "Not all of us billionaires are assholes. But I guess I deserved that. I didn't exactly put my best foot forward with you, that's for sure."

"Yeah, no. You didn't."

"And accidentally offering to pay you to date me didn't help my cause either."

"Accidentally? How do you accidentally proposition someone?" This ought to be good.

He squeezes me tight against him, taking a deep breath. His body is warm, and the solidness of him next to me is a sensation I could get used to. "You know what I mean. I was a babbling idiot. I would have said anything to get you to say 'yes.' And I did."

I let him off the hook. "I know. You're just cute when you're awkward."

We grow silent as the air in the room gets heavy again. The weight of our circumstances presses down on us as we lie here, both of us avoiding the metaphorical Sword of Damocles hanging over our heads, held aloft by the slimmest of threads.

"I won't let anything happen to you, Normandy. I swear." His voice is barely a whisper, and there's so much emotion in it my heart constricts in my chest.

I pull his arm tighter around my waist, twining my fingers with his as I kiss his knuckles. I can't make words, or sentences, let alone thoughts. I want to believe him, that he has the power to make this all okay somehow, but I don't know that he does. We both have no way of knowing that he can control any of this. I know with all of my heart that he will do everything in his power to try, but I don't know if it will be enough. All I can do is trust him, something I'm not used to doing with anyone.

With the way that Frank basically tricked us into thinking we were somehow cooperating when in reality, we had no choice in any of this, I don't have a lot of faith in any of the reassurances that he gave us. I have a feeling the FBI is more interested in getting Louie Calnetta as a trophy than they are in keeping Brandon or me safe. I feel like an afterthought in the whole scenario, which doesn't boost my confidence when it comes to any of this going smoothly.

Eventually, sleep takes me, but it's restless and full of nightmares. Several times I'm awoken by Brandon holding me close and whispering in my ear that I'm okay. I lie awake for a while, definitely not okay until I drift off again.

I am not okay. I am far from okay.

Chapter 33

End of the Earth

Brandon

I've spent most of today on a shiny new replacement phone with my attorneys, trying to figure out what I could possibly have to testify about. We've repeatedly gone back into my history with Eve to see if there's anything we've missed that might raise a red flag, but we still came up with nothing. I'm hopeful that means that the time I'll be required to testify will be brief, and I can get back here to Vegas in time for Normandy.

I've already arranged with my bank to allow a large cash transfer tomorrow while I'm in New York, so the money will be ready when it needs to go. The bank president I dealt with directly asked me numerous times if everything was okay with me. Moving large amounts of cash is a surefire way to get the IRS curious about what you're doing, which is something I really don't need right now. I can only guess at the amount required to cover a ransom.

I'm reminded again of my foolishly asking Normandy how much it would cost for her to pretend to be dating me, and here I am, ready to spend any amount of money just to keep her alive.

It would be easy to say that money means nothing because I have it. To most people, it would be the most pretentious thing for me to say on the planet. But deep down, I know it's true. If I needed to give up every penny I had to keep her alive for whatever reason, I would do it in a heartbeat, no questions asked. That's what people do for those they love.

Shit.

There it is.

The "L" word.

Fuck, that snuck up on me. I was not ready for that word to pop into my head. Is it true? Do I love Normandy? I think all the signs are pointing to 'yes.' But why does that single word matter so damned much? Isn't it enough that the emotions are there? The actions that are supposed to speak louder than that word are there? Why is there always such a constant frenzy for people to say that word as soon as they think it? That's dangerous.

What if it's a fleeting thought? A momentary lapse in judgment? A fit of panic? A rush of endorphins? *What if it's only lust?*

Yes, I'm currently readying myself to lose millions of

dollars to save her, but I would like to think anyone in my position would be willing to do that to save anyone. Is that true? Who knows? All I know is that I don't know what I'll do if anything happens to her. I will not be able to live with myself if this somehow goes wrong because of me. Hell, even if it's not because of me, but still goes wrong. I can barely function just thinking about it.

Spending most of my day on the phone, Normandy spent hers at the depot pretending to work. It's been torture all day being apart from her. We can't do anything too out of the normal, or we might tip off to Calnetta that we know what's coming. This was Taylor's bright idea, though I suppose he's right. Still, Normandy and I text each other throughout the day, just checking in with each other to make sure we're each staying sane.

She gets back to my place in time for a quiet dinner together before I need to head back to New York. The conversation is stiff and awkward, and neither of us really eats our meal. It's pretty clear we're both nervous wrecks.

"Did you hear from Frank at all today?" she asks, pushing the food on her plate around with a fork.

"No. But I didn't expect to. Did you?"

She shakes her head, and more quiet settles between us, and the awkwardness only increases my anxiety. It's a vicious cycle of nerves, apprehension, and frustration thrown in for good measure, twisting around in my gut. I can't think of anything to say that will lighten the mood, and to be honest, I don't think trying is the way to go right now. Some things are too serious to try to change, like an impending kidnapping.

Once we've pushed our food around long enough to

be polite, it's time for me to leave for the airport. I don't want to go. I still can't believe that the government picked the absolute worst day for me to testify out of every other fucking one in the year. It better be a serious life or death matter that I'm being summoned for, or I'm going to blow a gasket. If it turns out to be some petty monetary thing that has no real impact on anyone, I'll seriously lose my shit in the fucking courtroom.

"I promise I will be back as soon as I can." I'm holding Normandy, who is burying her face into my chest and squeezing me so tightly I'm struggling to breathe, but I don't release her. I need to hold her just as much as she needs me now.

I have to make this quick. If I draw this out, it will only make it worse. I need to treat this like a bandage and rip it off quickly, or it will only hurt more. But I can't bring myself to let go. I need to take in every bit of her, the silk and scent of her hair, the smoothness of her skin, and even the sorrow and pain in her eyes. I need to memorize everything about her. I don't want to forget a single thing while we're apart. Regardless of what happens next for either of us, this moment of us together is now etched in my memory.

"Normandy." I pull back slightly to get a better look at her, and I almost say those three little words that I can't get out of my head. I catch those dangerous syllables in my throat before I can vocalize them, and I just stare at her like an idiot. I *want* to say it, and I don't know why I can't. So, I say what I think might be the next best thing. "It will be okay. I promise."

Her dark eyes, full of sadness and fear, search mine,

and I do my best to show the confidence I'm trying to feel. If anything, I know my determination must shine through because I've got tons of that. I'm resolved to see this through, no matter what I have to do.

"Come back to me as soon as you can." Her voice is small, weak, strained from her tears, and punches me right in the fucking heart. Her words only emphasize the fact that I'm abandoning her at this crucial moment. *Abandoning her.* There's no other way to put it. I'm basically leaving her on her own to deal with all of this by herself.

I frame her face with my hands, kiss her deeply, and show her how I feel about her without saying the words. When I pull away, I turn quickly to get into the waiting car because I can't stand seeing the hurt in her eyes for another second.

I'm a fucking coward.

I'm glad I didn't tell her I love her. I don't deserve to.

Chapter 34

Warflower

Normandy

A hand clamped over my mouth wakes me from my nightmare, and I have to double-check that I'm awake and not just in another bad dream, as happens sometimes. Cold metal presses hard against the back of my neck, and I know for sure that I'm awake. *What the hell is happening?*

"Nice and easy, now," a low voice hisses into my ear, sending a lightning strike of terror through me. "Slow and steady wins the race, and silence keeps you alive." The hand covering my mouth releases, and I'm roughly pulled out of the bed and shoved toward the exterior doors to the backyard. I try to open the door, but it's locked, and I have to fumble around to get it open. What I can only assume is a gun digs into the nape of my neck, causing my fingers to shake and falter even more.

Once it's open, I'm pushed into the cold night and almost lose my balance, but the strong hand again grabs my arm, keeping me steady and moving along the back of the house. I'm tempted to turn to see who the hand belongs to and if it's Frank, but the pressure on my neck tells me that's not a great idea.

I'm only wearing a tank top and pajama bottoms, and the night is freezing. My bare feet on the cold concrete of the patio are only further confirmation that it's still winter. The shivering starts with my teeth and travels through my whole body. It's not just the weather making me shake; I'm terrified. *Where is Brandon's security?*

This is not how any of this was supposed to go. This isn't the plan. I am only mentally prepared for this to happen tomorrow at work, not at Brandon's home in the middle of the night. A place that was supposed to be safe and secure. *Chelsie. Oh my God, I hope she's alright.* If whoever this is got through security to get to me, they could get to her too. I want to run and check on her, but I'm too scared to do anything but concentrate on not tripping over my frozen feet.

As we reach the end of the house, I'm held back with fingers digging into my arm painfully to stay in the shadows, but I'm kept facing forward so as not to see whoever is pushing me around. The sound of a car engine sparking to life nearby grabs my attention, and soon that car is pulling in front of us.

My instincts are screaming at me to run or yell for

help, punch or kick the person behind me, but I can't do any of it. I know the assignment, and as much as I hate all of this, I need to play my part. This is to catch and punish Louie Calnetta for killing my father. He needs to pay, and if this is how it happens, then I've got to do it. That means I need to ignore every cell in my being that is mounting a revolution against this plan. Fight or flight options aren't viable, so I'm trying desperately to suppress those urges.

The dark car stops, and as the back door opens, sudden sharp pain in the back of my head causes my vision to flash bright white for a split second before I crash to the ground. The side of my face hits the hard concrete driveway with a crack that reverberates through my bones. Before total blackness takes me, I see another pair of eyes staring back at me, though I can tell they are long from seeing anything. They are dead. *Randall.*

The smell hits me before anything else, and I barely keep from vomiting when I come to. Taking stock of myself, my skull feels like it's been cracked open with an ax, and I swear I can feel my head bleeding. Whoever hit me to knock me out did a damn good job. My wrists and ankles are tied to the arms of a wooden chair so tightly I can barely feel my hands and feet. My mouth is dry, but there's no gag, at least.

I don't hear anything or anyone around me, so I force myself to open my eyes. The first thing I see is an obnoxious carpet, but it doesn't give me any clue where I am. Vegas is the gaudy carpet capital of the world, so I could be anywhere. As my gaze lifts, it catches on a stain on the carpet, dark and brown. And then I see him, eyes held open by death, a small hole in his forehead. Frank. It's Frank Santangelo, and he's dead on the floor next to me.

There's no time for me to react as the door to the room I'm in flies open, and two men walk in. They're both young. A lot younger than I expected anyone involved in this to be. They can't be much older than me, if at all.

"Ah, sleeping beauty is finally awake," the taller one says, falling into a chair across from me. His dark hair is curly, and he's dressed like he's about to head to the gym. Since their features are similar, his companion could be his brother or some kind of relative. They have the same hooked nose and olive skin. That one looks nervous, and it makes me even *more* nervous. I'm already freaking out with a dead body on the floor next to me but haven't had time to process that fact yet.

"We really should wait…" the jumpy one says quietly, avoiding looking at the body next to my chair like I am.

"I'm tired of waiting. We need to get this show on the road." He eyes me up and down, and my skin crawls under his stare. "Things need to start moving already."

I try not to look directly at either of them, not wanting to provoke any interaction whatsoever. I shut my eyes tightly, then reopen them to find that this is, unfortunately, all too real. My thoughts are jumbled, and the terror flooding through me makes all of this seem like a nightmare. I wish I were still asleep in Brandon's bed, and I'll wake up any minute now, and this will all have been a bad dream.

He must notice my attempt at disbelief. "Oh, don't worry, darling, this is real. Probably not what you were expecting, though, is it?" He kicks at Frank's foot, making the body move unnaturally. I have to tear my eyes away. "You thought good old Frankie-boy was with the Feds, didn't you? He was going to make this easy for you, huh? Well, he made it easy for us, anyway." He leaves his chair and steps behind me where I can't see what he's doing, and my spine stiffens as I sense him lean closer. "We don't do things the easy way here. No, we like things hard. Frank was trying to loosen your ropes, which also isn't how we do things here. He thought he could take all the credit for this score but fuck him." A hand grabs my hair and yanks my head back, and I can't help but gasp at the shock of it. And now there's cold metal against my neck, sliding up my throat and stopping just under my chin. I don't think it's a gun this time.

"Vinny. Dad's gonna...." The other guy sounds almost as scared as I am right now, though I highly doubt that to be the case.

"What? What's daddy gonna do?" he chides, and his nostrils flare, but he doesn't look up. He keeps his eyes on me, watching my reaction. Almost like he's getting off on my fear.

The smell of his cheap cologne mixed with stale coffee hits me, and I almost gag. Again, the bile rises in my throat, but I force it down, careful not to move too much. My mind plays movies of me dead on the floor next to Frank. I don't know how long I was unconscious, but it still feels like everything is moving way too fast. My brain can't catch up between my fear and what's happening. The pounding of my heart is so hard I can feel it pulse against the blade at my neck.

I noticed no windows in this room, so I have no idea what time it is. I could have been out for hours, and I'm not clear what time it was when they took me from Brandon's house either. All I know is it was dark. Not helpful at all.

"We're going to give your boyfriend a call now. Get this ball rolling. Okay, sweetheart?" I'd cringe at the term of endearment if I didn't think he'd kill me for it. He pulls a phone out of his pants pocket with his free hand and dials a number while pressing the blade against my neck with the other. I assume he's calling Brandon. After what seems like forever, he must answer, but I only hear one side of the conversation. "Brandon Carmichael? No? Who is this, then? Well, Taylor, I need to talk to your boss. Pronto.... What do you mean he can't come to the phone? He does understand what's happening here, doesn't he?" He presses the metal harder, and I do my best not to make any noise but can't help a slight yelp of pain as the sharp edge digs in, breaking the skin. "Well, I don't care if he's having tea with the god damned Queen of England; here's what he's going to do if he wants to see Ms. Blake alive again.... I don't give a shit what he's doing. I think this is a little more important to him, don't you?" He pauses, listening to Taylor again for a minute, but he's growing more irritable by the second, the more he listens. "Anyway. Yada yada yada. Ten million. By 4:00, when the banks close. You'll get a text with the account numbers. If all goes well, you'll get another text with where to pick up your princess. If I don't have confirmation by 4:01, you'll get a call so you can watch her head being blown off. Understand?" He pauses again with a heavy sigh, growing impatient. "Like I said, I don't give a flying fuckity fuck if he's making fucking snowmen with the President on the White House lawn. Alright? 4:00."

He disconnects the call and finally lifts the blade from my neck. I can feel blood trickling slowly down my skin, and I catch the other guy staring at it. He's gone pale, and his eyes blink rapidly like he might faint. I think I might pass out right along with him.

The one named Vinny brushes past him and out the door. I guess he's done with me for now. "C'mon, Max. We've got a few last rides before we're millionaires."

Max halts in the doorway on his way out and glances back at me. I can't tell for sure, but I think I see pity in his eyes. His sympathy isn't going to help me. He doesn't say anything and shuts the door.

It sounded like there might be a problem with Taylor and Brandon, and I don't know what it could be. We didn't really discuss the possibility of anything going wrong. Brandon was adamant that everything would be fine, regardless of him being in New York. I'm realizing now that I was an idiot to believe him. I'm also surprised that I'm not a crying mess right now. I think I'm too frightened to cry. Too terrified. The only thing I can think of is telling myself not to look down at Frank's dead body on the floor next to me.

I start truly studying my bindings, which are

becoming extremely painful as they dig into my skin. It's a coarse rope, not smooth, so it's uncomfortable. I also realize that the entire left side of my face and shoulder hurts. I think I must have fallen when I was knocked out, but I'll be happy if that's the worst of my injuries. *Wait, I did fall, and I saw Randall. Or did I imagine that?*

The shock of everything is still running through me, and I'm not thinking straight. It's like I'm not feeling something I should be feeling, though I can't imagine what else to feel besides being frightened. I'm definitely frightened. No FBI is coming to save me and arrest these guys. That was all a setup. I have no rescue on the way. I am totally on my own. And with Vinny's argument with Taylor, I'm now worried that something will go wrong with the ransom. What am I going to do if something goes wrong?

Dear God, please let this go smoothly because I don't know what the hell to do if it doesn't.

Chapter 35

My Heart

Brandon

I spend the morning answering questions about my relationship with Eve Cromwell, as I figured would be the case. However, about halfway through the morning, the questions take a turn toward the weird, and I'm not sure what to make of it. The prosecutor is a no-holds-barred attorney who doesn't dance around what she's trying to find out. I'd admire her professionalism if I weren't so preoccupied with what's happening in Vegas right now.

"Mr. Carmichael, do you recall Eve ever talking about the Mamana family?"

I take a minute to consider my answer. The question

seems to come from out of nowhere and is a complete direction change from her last question. I'm trying hard not to give away that I'm stunned to hear the name Mamana in this line of questioning. Frank mentioned that Louie was trying to buy his way into their family. What the hell would Eve have to do with them now too?

"The name sounds familiar." It's not a lie.

"Well, you know the Mamana family owns the Bliss casino, don't you?"

"Yes, I believe I knew that." Again, not a lie.

"Are you aware they've started buying property here in New York?"

Jesus. Get to the point already. "Yes, I think I've heard that." Still not lying.

"Do you know Giuseppe Mamana?"

"No. I do not."

"Do you know *of* him?"

"No."

"Were you aware that Eve Cromwell and Giuseppe Mamana were married in Sicily in 2017?"

I'm stunned, and I think the jury is, too, since there's an electricity-filled shock spreading through the room. *Eve was married the whole time she was with me? To one of the Mamana family? What the hell?*

"Mr. Carmichael? Were you or were you not aware of Eve's marriage to Giuseppe Mamana?"

I snap out of my stupor. "No. I was not aware of that." *Why would she even bother with me? She didn't get anything out of the relationship I can think of that would have benefited her. How could I not know that? And why did this prosecutor wait all morning to bring this up?*

As I answer, the prosecutor studies me closely, but I know better than to perjure myself.

"Did you know they remained married during your relationship with Eve?"

Why do I feel like I'm the one being prosecuted here? I know that's not the case, but it sure as hell feels like it. These revelations, while shocking, don't mean a damned thing to me. And she's asking them in a way to almost provoke me into anger. What I'm getting angry about, or *angrier* is more like it, is that I even have to be here in the first place. There are more important things going on in my life than the fact that Eve had and has a husband. I couldn't care less.

"How could I know that if I didn't know they were married?" I ask. What a stupid question. My patience is growing very thin. Now she's just wasting my time.

The prosecutor realizes her mistake and shuffles some papers, trying to act like she'd meant for the dumb question to be asked. This is ridiculous.

I glance down at my watch, noticing that it's almost noon already, and we haven't taken a single break.

"Would it be possible for us to break for lunch?"

The prosecutor looks relieved that she can move on to something else, like food.

"Sure, let's reconvene at 1:30." She moves to speak with the court reporter, and I jump out of my seat, practically running to the hallway to find Taylor. I need to know what's going on in Vegas, if Normandy is okay.

Taylor finds me first as I exit the courtroom, his jaw clenched and eyes tight. "We've got a problem, sir. We need to talk."

"What's going on?" Panic hits me like a truck, but I keep my composure as we walk briskly toward the elevators.

"I'll tell you everything once we're out of the building, but I've discovered that Frank Santangelo is not with the FBI. He's actually with the Mamana family."

"What the fuck is going on with that family?" I hiss, trying to keep my voice low. The repercussions of what Taylor's said still haven't been processed yet. "I just discovered that my ex-girlfriend Eve has been married to Giuseppe Mamana since 2017."

"Do you think any of these items are related?"

"No. That's impossible. Calnetta's been milking Victor Blake for years. There's no way anyone would know that Normandy and I would get together like we have. It's just a creepy coincidence."

Once we're out of the building and in a private car, we can finally speak freely, but my head is still reeling from the last five minutes. What did I miss with Eve that I was so unaware of her being married? Was I that checked out of that relationship? I guess I was. But what was she doing with me then? It makes no sense.

"How the fuck did we not know that Frank Santangelo wasn't FBI?"

"Well, sir, the FBI never confirms or denies an agent's status. Second, my source there waited until the Mamana connection was confirmed before getting back to me, so we're working on a delay of information."

"Jesus Christ." This is why I want to be told things, even if they're preliminary, but now is not the time to get into that.

"I received a call from Calnetta's camp. I think it was one of his sons."

"How's Normandy? Is she okay?" My hands are balled into fists, and it feels like my blood pressure is through the roof. I can hear my pulse in my ears.

Taylor blanches slightly, not wanting to go on. He looks out the window as he hesitates, and I can't do this anymore.

"Taylor, tell me what the fuck is going on. What happened to Normandy?"

"I got a call from Chelsie just as you entered the courtroom. I guess Normandy was taken from your house in the middle of the night."

My blood chills. That was not the plan.

"And? I have the feeling there's more. Is she okay?" I repeat the question because he's not giving me a straight answer.

"I don't know for sure, sir. I received a call from a man, who I assume is one of Calnetta's sons; he has two, Vincent and Max. I'm not sure which one I spoke with. The demand is for ten million dollars by 4:00. And while we were talking, I heard what sounded like Ms. Blake cry out in pain. But it was brief." Like that makes a difference.

I bury my face in my hands. I am over two thousand miles away from Vegas, and I can't do a damn thing from here if Normandy is hurt. Fuck, if she's hurt, I'll never forgive myself. I should have risked it. I should have let them try to arrest me. I knew what would happen today, and like a fucking coward, I followed the law instead of my instincts.

I let out a long breath, trying to pull myself together. Trying to think straight, but it's difficult with my fucking imagination going wild with thoughts of an injured Normandy.

"Right. Well, can we get the money transferred? We need to do that while I'm on break." I wipe my sweaty palms on my pants. My nerves are shot, but I need to keep busy and do what I can instead of wishing I could do something else. That's not helpful. "They sent the information about where to transfer the funds to?"

Taylor glances out the window again with a scowl. Unbelievable.

"I reached out to the number that called me earlier to get that information, but the call wouldn't go through. Let me try calling again." He dials but then hangs up just as quickly. The call isn't going through. "It must have been a burner phone."

I'm speechless. We don't have any clue where to send the money, and we can't reach the assholes demanding it be paid? And Normandy's life depends on that money transfer? This is seven ways of fucked up.

"Call Calnetta Cars directly. Get Louie on the line." I stare out the window at the dirty grey New York landscape. Unless it's fresh snow, New York winters are not pretty.

Taylor nods and dials, and finds out Louie is unavailable, regardless of how important his call is. He hangs up and dials another number and hands me the phone.

I look at him quizzically but then take it. "Hello? Louie Calnetta?"

There's a pause, but then, "This is Louie. Who is this?" His tone is cautious.

"This is Brandon Carmichael."

"Ah, Mr. Carmichael. I believe we have a package of yours." Now he sounds friendly. *The asshole. Normandy isn't just a 'package.'*

"Yes, you do. And I need to know where to send the payment you requested for its safe return to me. Can I please get that from you now?" I even throw in the *'please'* to get this going.

"Of course, of course. I'll have one of my sons get it to you once they're back in the building." He doesn't seem eager to get this transaction completed at all. As if he's got all the time in the world.

I don't have time. I have maybe a half hour more before I need to be back in the courtroom.

"If it could be sooner rather than later, I'd appreciate it."

He chuckles. He actually fucking laughs. "I'll see what I can do. Goodbye." And he hangs up on me. I stare at the phone, incredulous at his brazenness to hang up on me.

Taylor glances at his watch. "He was keeping the call untrackable. He might not be in Vegas right now. He could be keeping a physical distance from the situation for an alibi."

All I can do now is wait.

We don't hear back by the time that I need to return to the courtroom, so I give Taylor all the instructions he needs to complete the transfer. He and Diane are coordinating to make sure it goes smoothly. I'm reasonably confident that it will, but there's still that niggling in my gut that something is utterly wrong about the entire thing. There's nothing I can do about it, though.

I spend the next two hours learning more about Eve's dealings with the Mamana family and her involvement in their real estate schemes, which actually are money laundering outlets for the crime family. I don't provide any valuable information since I was in the dark about all of it. I find myself repeating myself over and over and trying to find new ways to say the same fucking thing. *I knew nothing.*

Finally, a little after 3:30, I'm thanked for wasting my fucking time and let go. I doubt I was very helpful to their case against Eve, but personally, I hope they throw the book at her. But then, I also don't care what they do with her. She's no longer my concern.

Once I enter the hallway, I find Taylor in a panic, pacing while speaking quietly but forcefully into his phone. I've never seen him so upset. When he sees me heading toward him, his face falls, and his shoulders sag. I can't tell if it's in relief or defeat.

"I will call you right back. Mr. Carmichael just returned." He shuts off the phone and leads me to the end of the hall.

"Taylor, you're worrying the shit out of me. What's going on?"

He's sweating and almost looks like he's going to have a breakdown of some sort.

"The money transfer got flagged and stopped. I've been trying to convince them to let the money through, that it's for a critical business deal, but all of a sudden, they want documentation proving an international business transaction."

This can't be happening. This cannot be fucking happening.

"Who flagged it? Who have you been dealing with?"

"The Consumer Financial Protection Bureau, and your bank too. Every transaction over $10,000 is reported to the IRS, but it's not usually a big deal. I'm sure your company transfers large payments all the time. But when you called your bank directly yesterday and spoke to the bank president to ensure a smooth transaction, he apparently reported it to the U.S. Treasury as suspicious when the order came through today."

"Jesus fucking Christ. I can't believe this is happening. *That god-damned asshole!*" Other people in the hallway turn to stare at me, but I don't give a shit.

"Diane's trying to put together some sort of fake documentation, but...." He stalls, staring at me with the most miserable look I've ever seen.

"But what?"

"But I don't think we'll get this done in time, Mr. Carmichael. I'm sorry."

"No. No, that's not true. We can do this." I start to panic and rush to the elevators, pressing the button repeatedly as if it will make it arrive faster. "We can do this, Taylor. I just need to think." I check my watch, seventeen minutes. *Fuck.* "Call Diane, see where she's at with that fake paperwork." The elevator arrives, and Taylor follows me in, phone to his ear already. I have got to figure this out. I'm running out of time, and Normandy's life depends on it. She's counting on *me.*

We spend the next fifteen minutes calling everyone we know in the financial world to try to get this transfer through. Still, everyone's hands are tied by the regulations. My pleading only worsens everyone's suspicion of the large amount of money I want to transfer offshore. The money they demanded, and more is right fucking there in my account. Ready to go. And I can do nothing with it. At this point, I wouldn't care if I had to break the law to send it. I have to do this. I have got to find a way to do this.

It turns out I can't do this.

It's now 3:59. I've failed. All of my money. All of my connections. Useless. Fucking useless. It all means nothing because I'm about to lose Normandy, the one thing in my life outside my brothers that I truly hold dear to me. She came into my life from out of nowhere and turned my world upside down. And now, she's going to die because of me. Because I can't save her.

The plaza in front of the building we were in is bustling with people leaving work and heading for home. Home to their families and loved ones. The sky gets dark early now, and it starts snowing. Not fluffy, pretty flakes, but hard, wet, freezing snow. I don't feel it. I can't feel a damned thing. We take cover in the walkway under the building.

Four o'clock comes, and I can only stare at the people

passing by but see none of them either. Taylor's phone rings with a video call, and my stomach drops. I want to vomit. The dread overtaking me is paralyzing. He answers and holds the phone between us so we can both see the call, and when I see Normandy on the screen, in her pajamas, tied to a chair and gagged, with bruises on her face and dried blood on her neck, I want to reach through the phone and grab her. Pull her out of there. Hold her to me and tell her I love her. Say those three fucking words.

Her head is down, and she's not looking at the camera, but I can tell she's crying. Her shoulders are shaking with her silent sobs.

"We tried to send you the money. Believe me, I did everything I humanly could to get that money to you, but the government stopped it. It's not my fault. Give us more time. Just a little more time...I can have it for you tomorrow. I swear...."

"Too late, Mr. Billionaire. You had your chance. And you had plenty of time to work out the details. Besides, your so-called FBI friend over there gave you an early head's up, right?" The phone pans down next to Normandy, and I see the obviously dead body of Frank Santangelo.

Holy shit. They killed Frank. "But I didn't know the government was going to...."

He doesn't let me finish. "4:01." I see a gun raised into the frame and hear the shot, Normandy's muffled scream, but then there's some sort of a scuffle, and the call disconnects.

Taylor and I stare silently at the now dormant phone,

neither of us able to form words. I just witnessed them kill her, the woman I love, in cold blood. She died because she trusted me. She had faith in me to get her out of there, and I failed. I fucking failed.

I fall to my knees in the snow and bury my face in my hands in anguish. *I've lost her.*

Chapter 36
Black Holes (Solid Ground)

Normandy

B eeping. This incessant noise has haunted my dreams all night and doesn't ever stop. Maybe it's my alarm clock. I try to reach my nightstand but can't move my arm. Slowly opening my eyes, I discover I'm not at home or any place I've recently called home. I'm in the hospital, and my arm seems strapped to my side.

All at once, everything that happened rushes back to me. Frank's dead body at my feet, the dirty rag in my mouth, the phone call with Brandon, the Calnetta brothers fighting with each other, the gunshot, the excruciating pain. Then it all faded to black for me. I don't remember anything else. The beeping on the machine speeds up as I recall the entire series of events. The more I wake up, the more the right arm that is strapped down starts to hurt.

"Don't try to move it. You'll make it worse."

I turn toward the voice and find Chelsie sitting in a chair beside my bed. I hadn't noticed her until now. She looks exhausted. The dark windows behind her tell me it's late. Or early.

"What happened?" My voice is a cracked mess, full of pain and drowsiness.

"Well, you were shot, obviously." She indicates my bandaged arm. "And you kept flailing around while you were out, so they strapped it down to stop you from hurting yourself even more."

I glance down and see that she's holding my other hand tightly. Seeing it causes a mixture of relief, fear, and tension to release from my chest in a sob I can't hold back. She squeezes my fingers even tighter.

"Did they get Calnetta?" This all has to have been worth something. I need to know it wasn't for nothing.

"I think so, but I don't know for sure. The FBI isn't telling me anything." She rolls her eyes. "It's an 'ongoing investigation' or whatever. But they want to talk to you as soon as you wake up. We can put them off, though, if you're not up for it yet."

"Let me get my bearings first." I lay my head back on the pillow and close my eyes, but as soon as I do, my mind replays the horrific scene in that room, the flash of the gunfire, the searing pain as the bullet hit me.

"Normandy?" Chelsie's voice drifts back to me, and I

force my eyes open to look at her. "Brandon is on his way."

"No." I shake my head. "I don't want to see him."

"But...."

"But nothing." My voice is perfectly clear now and rising. "I said I don't want to see him. Do not let him near me, Chelsie. I mean it."

"Norm, why not?" her brow furrows in confusion. "He's been beside himself. He thought you were dead."

"Yeah, well, it's no thanks to him. I just got lucky." I can hear the machine beeps racing again, echoing my heartbeat. "I'm lucky that one of the stupid Calnetta brothers had a conscience. Otherwise, I would be dead."

She swallows hard and nods but presses on. "Norm, he had the money ready to go. He tried to send it. Brandon did everything he could to...."

"To what? Break his promise to me? Go back on his word that everything would be fine?" I let go of her hand and point to my wounded arm and bruised face. "Does this look fine to you? I am not fine, Chels. Not even close. I don't think I'll be 'fine' for a very long time, no thanks to Brandon Carmichael." She shrinks back from my outburst, and I feel bad for taking it all out on her. She's just the first person I saw that I could vent to. "Sorry. I didn't mean to yell at you."

"I get it. But...."

"Ms. Blake. I'm glad to see you're awake and alert," a deep bass voice says. We both look up to see two people in the doorway to my room; a tall black man with a goatee and a slightly shorter blonde woman with a ponytail. Both have on FBI windbreakers and have badges dangling around their necks. I instantly wonder if they're real FBI agents or just pretending to be. "Can we ask you a few questions?" They walk in further, and it's clear they're going to ask me whether I want them to or not.

"Sure."

They ask Chelsie to leave, and she reluctantly goes, letting me know she'll be just outside.

I spend the next half hour or so going over the events involving the Calnettas and Frank Santangelo from my dad's funeral through the present. By the end, my head is pounding, and I just want to sleep for weeks.

"So, Max Calnetta tackled his brother Vinny, who fired the gun?" the blonde asks, scribbling furiously in a notebook.

"Yes. If he hadn't, I'd be dead right now. I was looking straight down the barrel of that gun." I squeeze my eyes shut, trying to chase the picture out of my head. I can feel myself starting to shake again, just thinking about it. I've never been more terrified in my life, and I hope to God I never am again. "How did you guys get involved?"

"While you said Frank wasn't FBI, that's true, but we've been surveilling him since he left New York three years ago." The man, whose name is Agent Ross, has been quiet this whole time until now. "He's part of the Mamana crime family."

"He's a Mamana?"

"No, just part of their 'family.'" He rubs his goatee thoughtfully. "He was sent in to evaluate Calnetta. Kick the tires, as it were before they invited him into the fold. They do that with all prospective business partners."

"Well, didn't you know Frank was about to be killed?

Or that I was kidnapped?" They should have known that something was wrong if they were watching him. "How could you let this happen to us?"

"Frank would often go off the grid for days at a time." The woman is at least a little sympathetic. "So, it wasn't unusual to lose track of him from time to time. He'd always resurface, though."

"So, how did you find us?"

"Again, it was Max Calnetta," Agent Ross says, getting up from his chair, apparently ready to leave. "He turned everyone in, even his own father. We also just got word about some big money payout that was attempted but caught before it could go through."

"Well, you know they killed my father, right?" It's the whole reason I'm in this situation, to begin with. I at least want to make sure they get that in their stupid notebooks.

He nods. "We have been in touch with the Clark County police and will work with them on that case. We'll keep you updated."

"Thank you." Maybe something good will come out of all of this, and my father can finally rest in peace. And I can too. It's what I crave now, just some peace.

They leave with promises to keep in touch with news of their investigations, and I beg off a further visit with Chelsie. I just want to sleep. The nurses come in and give me some more of the strong stuff, and I'm finally able to close my eyes to just darkness, not memories. I eagerly let the comfortable blackness take me.

Chapter 37

Hollow Eyes

Brandon

Everything that possibly can go wrong today is going wrong. The blizzard that hits New York that evening keeps us grounded at the airport for hours before we can take off. The only good news that I've gotten is that Normandy is alive.

I had finally worked up the nerve to call Chelsie to tell her what happened when she called me instead, beside herself with the news that Normandy had been shot and was being taken to the hospital. She was bewildered at my elation until I told her what we had witnessed and what I assumed happened.

Now, in the hospital and at Normandy's bedside, holding her hand and watching her sleep, I feel like I can finally breathe for the first time in days. I'm hopeful that the whole Eve ordeal is behind me, and she'll get whatever she has coming to her. I still don't understand what she was doing with me while she was married. The only thing I can think of is that she needed to separate her name from theirs, and I was a secure way to do that publicly. It could have been any celebrity, I guess.

And now, with Calnetta out of Normandy's life, she can move on with her and Chelsie's business if that's what she wants to do. She no longer has that dark cloud over her, threatening their father's legacy. And speaking of Victor, they will now have closure on his murder once the Calnetta's are convicted. I think, all in all, things have resolved themselves pretty well. Not ideally, or how I'd like it to have gone, but I'll take it since Normandy is at least alive.

I must have dozed off at some point because I'm woken by Normandy shifting in the bed, pulling her hand out of mine.

I glance up and give her a smile. Even with cuts and bruises, and exhaustion lining her eyes, she's still the most beautiful woman in the world to me.

"Hey there," I whisper, but she's not smiling back.

"What are you doing here?" She looks around the room as if searching for someone. "I told Chelsie...."

"Chelsie went home to get some sleep. But it's okay, I'm here now." I reach for her hand again, but she pulls it out of my reach and shies away from me. I don't understand what she's doing. "Are you okay? What's the matter? What do you need?"

"I need you to go."

She's avoiding my eyes and practically cringing in fear from me. "What? Go? Why would I leave you?" She's not making any sense.

"Because I'm telling you to, that's why." *What the hell?* That's not fear in her voice; that's anger.

"Normandy, what are you talking about? Why are you saying this? I don't understand." I can feel it. My happiness slipping away. Ripping seams as it goes. And I don't know why.

"I shouldn't have to explain myself to you, Brandon." She grabs her injured arm with tears in her eyes that I can tell she's fighting to keep from falling down her bruised cheeks. My heart lurches as I watch her mentally building a wall between us. Brick by brick by brick.

"Well, I think you do since I have no idea why you're acting like this." My words are coming out angrier than I intend, but once they're out, they're out.

"I'm 'acting' like this because you proved yourself to be just like everyone else. But don't worry, I don't blame you. I blame myself for actually believing you. Actually thinking you could keep a promise to me. Trusting you with my life. With *my life*, Brandon." She's starting to shake uncontrollably, and I reach to pull her to me, but she puts her hands up, fending me off. "Don't. Don't touch me."

"Normandy, I did everything I possibly could to transfer that money. I swear to you. After that gunshot, I thought you were dead for almost two hours afterward. I was ready to jump off the Brooklyn Bridge, thinking my failure killed you."

"That's just it, Brandon. It almost did. I would be dead if Max Calnetta didn't take his brother down." She shudders, and goosebumps rise on her arms. I can only imagine how horrifying that was for her.

"I am so sorry. I don't know what else to say. I did everything I could. I had no idea that Frank wasn't FBI. There was no way to know that. I also didn't know that the government would hold up the payment like that. When I talked to my banker the day before, he said it would be fine and go through without an issue. I couldn't foresee some random government agency I'd never heard of popping up and flagging the transaction for investigation. All of those things were out of my control, Normandy. You seriously can't blame me for those things." *Does she think I made everything go badly on purpose? That I wanted her to get shot?* She can't be that crazy.

"I can, and I do." She's staring me down now, not afraid to look at me anymore. There's a fire behind her dark eyes, a flame that would fry me on the spot if she could. "I trusted you. Something I swore I would never do again, but you sweet-talked me into it. You told me you would take care of everything. I had nothing to worry about. Everything would be fine. But all you've done is confirm exactly what I've been telling myself for years. The only thing I can count on are my scars. They don't go away. They tell the truth. And now, thanks to you, I have another one," she rubs her bandage lightly, where I'm sure she'll have a scar from the bullet wound. "But this is my last one. This reminds me that I cannot trust anyone but myself."

"You can trust me," I say, but I know it's falling on deaf ears. She doesn't want to listen to me, no matter what I say.

"I'm sorry you flew all this way for nothing. Goodbye, Brandon." She looks away again, clearly showing that she's done with me.

So that's it. Everything we've been through is just tossed aside like litter on the side of the road. I stare at her for a long moment more. Taking her in. She looks so tiny and fragile in that hospital bed, all the wires and machines hooked up to her, but when I look at her face, I see her strength. I see the self-determination that has gotten her through some really tough times and the fortitude she possesses to keep moving forward. But she's wrong now. She's got it all wrong.

I know in my heart that I tried to move heaven and Earth to keep her alive today. I did everything that I could to transfer that money to the Calnettas. And I was utterly devastated when I thought she was dead. I was inconsolable, and Taylor was seriously worried about me. And he was almost equally upset at his own failure. We couldn't have done anything any different except breaking the law. Maybe I should have. I'll never know.

There's nothing I can say that is going to change her mind. I can see it on her face. She's done with me. So, I say nothing. I can feel the ache in my chest start before I even turn to leave the room. My heart, which was so full of love, worry, loss, and then relief, is now empty. Everything that filled it up, everything that was Normandy, is gone. I can almost hear my heartbeat echo in the cold void that is left. Knowing that nothing in the world will ever fill me again, I leave.

Chapter 38

Spinning Wheel

Normandy

My mother is tracked down just before I'm released from the hospital the next day. She was apparently on a cruise in the Gulf of Mexico with a gentleman friend nobody knew about. Well, I didn't know about him, anyway. My mom doesn't talk to me about her love life, and I don't speak to her about mine. We have an unspoken agreement that we'll stay out of each other's business. It works for us, though there are times when I wish we did have those conversations. Like now.

Chelsie's staying with me temporarily since I'm still

afraid to be alone, and her apartment is too small for the two of us, but she heads to the depot so that my mom and I can spend some time together. She comes to see me for lunch when she's back from her trip but hesitates when I answer the door to let her in.

"What's wrong?" I don't understand why she wouldn't want to come into the house.

"I'm sorry. I haven't been in this house since...."

"Since what?" I recognize the look on her face. It's fear of a memory.

"Since I went through what you just did." She straightens her shoulders, steps into the foyer, and lets out a deep sigh. "There. I've done it. It's about time, right?"

I hug her with my good arm since I can't lift the injured one very well. "That was fantastic."

Leading her back into the kitchen where I have lunch prepared, I notice her taking in the rooms we pass with curiosity. I try to remember the last time I saw her here, but I can't picture it. I was too young when we moved out. It's hard to believe she's not been here in so long.

"I begged your father to get rid of the house. He couldn't understand why I couldn't come back here, so I left and took you with me." She sits at the kitchen table, still looking around as she talks. I don't interrupt her either. I'm afraid if I do, she'll clam up. "He told me later that letting me leave was his biggest regret in life."

I can't help but scoff at that description. "*Letting* you leave? It sounds more like he chose the house instead of you."

"It was a little of both." She nods her head from side

to side, not completely disagreeing. "We were so young, and he was just starting to make a name for himself. Mischief Motors was getting a lot of attention, and wealthy clients kept pouring in. It was a lot for him to handle. He'd never known success like that before, and he let it go to his head."

"Yeah, but mom, you were kidnapped by his business rival. I'd think that would smack some sense into him." I still can't believe my dad would be so callous.

"That situation started before I even met your dad."

"Whoa. What? How so?" This sounds intriguing.

She shifts in her seat, wiping her hands on her jeans. "Well, it's no secret between us that I used to be a dancer, right?"

"Right. I told you I met Sophie, who owned the club, at that gala Brandon took me to." Memories of our time in that side lounge try to invade my thoughts, but I push them away. I can feel the tops of my ears heat up just thinking about it. *Damn it.*

"Did she tell you what kind of club it was? I don't think we ever really talked about it."

I shake my head with a shrug. "No, I didn't ask either. I assumed it was a strip club."

She laughs, almost spitting out her sandwich, and nearly chokes swallowing it. "A strip club? You thought I was a stripper all this time?"

"What? There's no shame in that." And there isn't. Not in my mind, anyway.

"Yeah, but for you to think I was a stripper, and.... Oh, never mind. No, I wasn't a stripper. I was barely a

dancer. It was a neo-burlesque club with *no* nudity."
She's still chuckling to herself. "Each of us had a schtick.
Mine was a bit of a Marilyn Monroe kind of act. I had the
blonde thing going on, the curves, and couldn't sing for
shit. But I was a tease-artist. We all were."

"So, what does that have to do with Dad and Louie?"
I love that she's talking about this, and I'm getting a
glimpse into her history, but I also don't want to forget
why it came up in the first place.

"Well, Louie was a regular at Sophie's long before
your dad stepped foot in that club." She takes a sip of her
iced tea, choosing her next words carefully. "Louie was
persistent in asking me to go out with him. I always got a
bad vibe from him, so I always put him off. Nice like,
though, so as not to offend him, you know how us women
have to do. Finally, one night I gave in and agreed to have
a drink with him in the club after my set. I wanted to stay
on my territory since I wasn't comfortable being alone
with him. I figured one drink wouldn't hurt, and I could
get him to stop asking me out."

"He sounds like a real creeper. Weren't there
bouncers to handle jerks like him?" I remember him
grabbing my arm after the funeral and shiver.

"There was nothing to bounce. He hadn't done
anything out of line at that point. It was just a feeling I
got from him." She shrugs as if it's just how things were,
and it's not something to question. I guess she's right.
Things were different then, I'm sure. "Well, like I said, to
that point. Things changed when I sat with him at the bar
and had a drink with him. He decided that was a great

time to get handsy with me. Suddenly, this tall, gorgeous man is punching Louie in the face and telling him to get off me."

"Dad?"

"Yup. And Sophie saw the whole thing. Banned Louie from the club and gave your father free drinks all night. And the rest is all crazy history."

"He didn't do anything to you, did he? Louie? When he...."

"No. Nothing like that. I barely saw him, actually." She waves me off like it was no big deal, but I can see in her eyes that she's playing it down for my benefit. "I was kept in some basement by his toadies and scared to death. But nobody touched me."

"So that's why Louie's been after Dad all these years? He was jealous of Dad because you chose him?"

She sighs heavily, staring at her glass with a melancholy I've never seen from her. "Who knows why that man does anything? Maybe if I'd told you all of this earlier; warned you about Louie, you wouldn't have gotten...."

"Nonsense, Mom." I round the table to wrap an arm around her. "There's no way anyone could have predicted he'd come after me. And it had nothing to do with you or Dad. And honestly, he had plenty of opportunities on my weekends and holidays with him to tell me all about it himself, instead of leaving a stupid vague letter in a folder."

"It still feels like my fault somehow."

"Well, it's not. So, get that thought right out of your

pretty blonde skull." I give her a quick kiss on the top of her head, then start clearing our lunch plates from the table.

"So, what are you going to do about Sacramento? Anything?" A clever subject change and deflection from her. Thanks, Mom.

The dreaded life plan question. I've avoided it in my head too, but with all that has happened, I might reconsider getting out of Vegas and back to the safety and security of my townhouse.

"I'm still considering my options. I have associates that are temporarily handling things for me, so I have time to make up my mind. It's tempting, but it's a big decision."

"And what's going on with your Brandon?" There it is. I knew it would be coming eventually. The *'what happened?'* portion of the discussion.

"Nothing's going on." I haven't heard from him since that night in the hospital. There's still security protecting me at home and work, which I didn't ask for, but I appreciate immensely. But we've not communicated since I sent him away.

"That's too bad. He seemed like a great guy. And the two of you together are just adorable." She's got that interfering-mom tone in her voice that I know all too well. She'd like nothing more than for me to get married so I can give her a soccer team worth of grandchildren.

I miss Brandon. Like crazy. But I had to break things off. There's no way I could trust him again. I don't even trust myself anymore. I can't seem to make the right choice about anything, especially when it comes to men.

And especially Brandon. I fell too hard and fast with him, clouding my judgment. So much that I almost got myself killed because of it. I can't ignore that. No matter how much my heart wants to. I'm just not made that way.

"Yeah, adorable isn't enough for me anymore, Mom."

Chapter 39
I Can't Believe You're Gone

Brandon

B ack in New York, I throw myself into my work. It feels like I abandoned it entirely since I was so wrapped up in everything Normandy. I pull twelve-hour work days just to make myself exhausted enough to sleep. Even then, I put off going to bed until I can't keep my eyes open any longer because the bed, the room, and everything at that end of the apartment reminds me of her. Half the time, I pass out on the couch and stay there just so I don't have to face the empty bedroom.

Eve and her husband were indicted for their involvement in the real estate money laundering scheme they were running. It's still unclear why she got in a relationship with me, but I can only assume it was some sort of cover for their illegal activities. Luckily, I'm not under suspicion for any involvement in their crimes. That's the last thing I need right now. With all of that behind me, I can move forward.

I keep telling myself those types of things. *Move on. Let it go. Focus on the future.* I can't seem to listen to myself, though. When I do think about the future, I only think about what could have been with Normandy, not what it's going to be like without her. I can't imagine my life going forward alone now that she's been a part of it. It just feels *wrong*.

We were just getting started. Everything was new, but everything was completely natural too. I could feel myself falling deeper in love with her at various times, and I would note it in my head, *'Here's where I fell in love with her laugh,'* or, *'We'll joke about this dinner conversation twenty years from now.'* It would hit during the tough moments too, and I'd think, *'I never want to be the cause of that pain in her eyes,'* and, *'I want to take that pain away and feel it instead of her.'* Every interaction with her multiplied those inner thoughts and exponentially increased my feelings for her. But she didn't reciprocate the emotions like I thought she had.

Or maybe she did, but breaking my promise to her, even though it was out of my control, did enough damage to erase it all. That is one area where Normandy and I are alike; once someone has broken my trust or offended me or someone I care about, our relationship is never the same. I may not cut you out of my life completely, but we are no longer anything more than acquaintances. So, I can see where Normandy is coming from, especially with her history. But I can't stand the thought of only being her acquaintance.

"Mr. Carmichael, I have Sophie on line one for you." Diane's irritated voice on the intercom pierces through my inner monologue, slinging me headfirst into the present.

It's odd that Sophie would call. I hope she's okay. "Thank you, Diane."

When I answer, Sophie sounds out of breath. "Brandon, is that you?"

The skin on the back of my neck prickles. "I'm here. What's the matter? Are you okay?" My brain smashes into hyperdrive with horrible imaginary scenarios.

She laughs. "I'm fine. I'm at the youth shelter and just jogged up three flights of stairs. I guess I'm not eighteen anymore after all."

Relief floods through me. I don't think I could handle another emotional grenade right now. "Well, what's up? It's got to be early there still, right?" It's just after nine here in New York.

"I need your help, Brandon."

That sounds ominous, but Sophie never asks for help, so it must be serious.

"Of course, anything you need."

"I knew I could count on you." She pauses to take a deep breath and then continues. "We're getting ready for our spring food drive, you know, the big one we do every year. Well, almost all of my usual volunteers have other commitments. So, I was wondering...."

"When is it?" I can't say no to this woman. Not when it comes to her passion project. There is no denying Saint Sophie. Plus, it's something else to distract me.

"Two weeks from tomorrow. Is that too short of notice for you?"

I check the calendar on my laptop and only see a haircut scheduled, which is easy enough to move.

"Nope. I'll be there."

"I knew you'd answer the call if I put up the bat signal."

"Still not Bruce Wayne, Sophie." I can't help the smile. "But I do appreciate the sentiment."

"Anytime, Brandon."

The following two weeks seem to drag by, and I get antsy to return to Las Vegas. Antsy and nervous. The nerves come with hiring Mischief Motors for transportation from the airport, as I usually do, but this time it feels different, like I'm sneaking around behind Normandy's back, but at the same time like I'm taking advantage of our relationship. Neither of those makes any sense.

I received a chilly greeting from Bianca when I arrived, but I didn't expect a warm welcome, to be honest. I had hoped for at least neutrality but understand the hostility. Bianca is Team Normandy if we're picking sides; I don't blame her. I'm Team Normandy too. I'd join if I could.

Bianca leaves the divider down and gives me a quick

glare after getting behind the wheel. She still hasn't said a single word to me, making this even more awkward than it needs to be. There's no reason we can't be cordial with each other.

I try to break the ice. "How are you, Bianca? You're looking well."

Another frown in the rearview mirror, deeper this time, and continued silence.

I give up. If I get the cold shoulder from everyone, so be it. We'll keep it strictly business then. I lean back in my seat and stare out the window, resigned to a quiet car ride. Maybe I should consider using another car service if only to avoid moments like this.

"You broke her heart, you know," Bianca calls back to me, her words threaded with protective anger.

I glance up at her, surprised. I wasn't expecting a relationship therapy session on the way home. I'm also taken back by the accusation. My heart is equally broken, if not more. Meeting her eyes in the mirror, I only nod in acknowledgment. Not agreeing or arguing with her statement. I steel myself for the rest. A remark like that never shows up alone in a conversation.

"If I might be so bold...You can't promise someone complete safety when you can't provide it." She shifts her eyes to the road in front of her but continues. "You don't guarantee solutions when you don't even know the whole problem. And when you care about someone, you certainly don't travel across the entire damn country and leave them to fend for themselves in a life-or-death situation." She catches me in the mirror again when we stop at a red light. "These are all my personal opinions,

Mr. Carmichael, and not necessarily those of my employer. But I'd wager that they would agree with me."

Each sentence rings so loudly with truth my head starts to hurt. I think the pain is mainly from the guilt echoing in my bones. I did all the things she just accused me of. I said whatever I thought necessary to make Normandy happy. I promised her security I couldn't give. I failed to protect her when she needed me the most. And I left. I fucking left. That part alone is unforgivable.

All I can do is stare back at Bianca and nod my agreement. She's right about everything, and I will not argue with her. There would be no point since I feel the same way. She can't beat me up any more than I have about any of it, but hearing it all said by someone else just confirms that every bit of my self-loathing is justified.

The car behind us honks once the light turns green, and she shifts her glare to the side mirror. A few seconds later, the divider between us slowly rises. *I guess our therapy session is over.*

Chapter 40

It's Only Love

Normandy

When I got the call from Sophie asking if Mischief Motors would co-sponsor her charity food drive, I agreed immediately. The business is financially in a place where we can do things like this. Especially now that protection money isn't being siphoned out of the coffers. When Sophie and I discussed her youth homeless shelter at the benefit gala, I was impressed by her work for the community and the difference she's making in so many lives. Plus, Sophie is just the sweetest woman. I don't think anybody can tell her 'No.'

I arrive early, the growing heat of the Vegas spring is

already rising, and Sophie puts me to work at once, organizing and labeling the shelving units where the donated food will be stored. It's a reasonably large area to fill, but Sophie is confident there will be a big turnout. A few of the teenagers from the shelter have been recruited to help me as well, so we chat for a while and divvy up the responsibilities.

About fifteen minutes into the scheduled start time, we're already super busy going through bags and boxes of food and sorting it properly. One of my recruits brought a little wireless speaker with a playlist we're all dancing and singing to as we work. It's nice to be able to laugh again. It's been too long.

After sorting the first round, we return to the drop-off area to gather more donations. I'm crouched down behind a table when I hear a voice that could charm the skin off a snake. *His* voice. I peek over the table, and sure enough, there is Brandon, smiling and greeting the donors as they drop off boxes or bags full of food. I drop down a little bit to avoid being noticed and watch him for a few minutes as he interacts with everyone. The dimples are out in full force, and his hair looks like it could use a trim, but the slightly overgrown style suits him somehow. He's wearing a tight black t-shirt and jeans that emphasize all the right places. He's as impressive as I remembered. And not just his looks. He's genuinely grateful to everyone he deals with; that type of honesty and humility warms my heart. But he looks different. He seems *colorless*. I don't know how else to describe it. Everything about him isn't as shiny and bright as it once was. I might be imagining it or projecting my own despondency onto him, but I see it. He's still gorgeous in my eyes, though.

"Is everything alright, Normandy?" Sophie asks loudly beside the table, catching me spying on Brandon. *Shit. Busted.*

I do my best to look busy doing something important, not like I was just staring at Brandon for too long. I'm definitely not fooling Sophie.

"Normandy? What are you doing here?" My shoulders tighten as I hear his question. Damn it. After seeing him, I was hoping I could go unnoticed and not have to interact with him. No such luck.

"I was helping Sophie with her homeless problem. I mean, project. She asked if we wanted to co-host the event. I mean, co-sponsor, not co-host, because that would be stupid. So, I said sure, that sounds grapes...*great*, and here I am. I'm working in the back with a few kids sorting and organizing the food. They're really great kids. We've been singing...." I let my diatribe fade out as I run out of breath. *Holy shit, woman. Shut up.* As I spoke, the smile on his face grew bigger and bigger, and I can't tell if he's laughing at me or not.

"I'll let you two catch up..." Sophie says, and it's clear to both of us then that she set this whole thing up for the two of us to be face to face with each other. We watch her walk away in stunned silence as she hums a song to herself. What an evil trick. *Saint Sophie, my ass.*

"I should get back...." I turn and start walking to the storage area, away from Brandon, as quickly as possible.

"Normandy, wait." He catches up to me, touching

my shoulder, and even that slight contact sends a shiver through me.

I force myself to stop and turn to him, but I have difficulty meeting his eyes. I didn't know how I would react if we ever saw each other in person again because I didn't think we would. We don't exactly run in the same circles. I am unprepared for this, and I can still feel the blush on my cheeks that spread over me after my super long run-on sentence. One more round of me speaking should make my mortification complete.

I tell myself to use small words and short phrases from now on. "What?" I stare at his chin. It's a safe space to look at. He has a great chin. Squared a little. Strong. A little rough when he needs a shave. *Stop it.*

He hugs himself a little and rocks back and forth on his heels, just as awkward as me. "How are you? How is your arm?" Genuine concern edges his voice as he points to my bicep, where the bullet wound is still healing. The bruises peek out a little under my short sleeve. I instinctively cover it with my hand.

I don't like talking about what happened. I still have nightmares every night reliving it, and that's only if I fall asleep in the first place. My anxiety keeps me up with irrational fears of being taken from my bed in the middle of the night. I'm sure I look like death warmed over with the shadows that are now constantly under my eyes that no amount of concealer can hide.

Still staring at his chin, I say, "I'm fine." Short. To the point.

"Good...I'm glad to hear it." He leans forward slightly as he shoves his fists into his jeans pockets, catching my eye. "I'm doing fine, too. Thanks for asking."

I narrow my eyes at him. I don't like being called out like that. I would have asked if I'd wanted to know how he was. Actually, no, that's not entirely true. I'm too flustered at the moment to think straight, let alone make polite conversation with an ex-boyfriend I can't stop thinking about. So, yes, I should have at least returned the courtesy, but for some reason, I double down.

"Good," I say nonchalantly and continue my trek to my work area.

He must freeze for a moment, but he recovers quickly and runs past me to block my path, hands on his hips. *He'd make a great Superman. Or Batman. Stop. It.*

"Can we talk?" His pleading tone matches his eyes, which are incredibly dark today. "Normandy?"

I'm caught staring at him again for the second time in so many minutes. My mind finally catches up to his question. "We have nothing to talk about, Brandon."

I have fought myself so many times not to reach out to him to talk things over. To apologize for lashing out at him right after the shooting. He was a convenient target for my rage, but once that wore off, I was just left with the truth. I still care deeply about him. But acting on it seems foolish somehow. It's been better for me to shove my emotions down to where they can't be felt and leave them there in the dark rather than deal with them. But I've also been taking steps to deal with that aspect of my life. Facing my truths. It's not been easy by any means.

"Please. Let me at least take you to lunch or something." There is so much charisma in that smile that

I have to force myself not to automatically smile back at him. "If afterward, you still want nothing to do with me, I'll never bother you again."

"Did you put Sophie up to this?" I cross my arms, unsure of what to do, so I'm stalling as my mind fights a war with my heart over the decision to go or not.

He clutches at his chest as though offended, but I can't tell if he's overreacting as a joke or not. "Me? I would never dream of it." He straightens and grows serious. "No kidding, I'm as surprised to see you here as you are me. I didn't know Sophie was this diabolical."

That makes me chuckle. Sophie is anything but diabolical. Meddling? Absolutely. But not an evil bone in her body.

"I don't know...."

"I promise, I won't offer you any money." He tries a smile, but a shadow crosses his eyes as he realizes his words. *A promise.* He tries a recovery. "Actually, I may offer you loads of cash should I find it's my last resort to win your favor." His smile dies a slow death as the atmosphere around us grows uncomfortable, and I don't respond. "Normandy, I'm flustered. I wasn't expecting to see you here, but you *are* here, and seeing you has stirred up all kinds of emotions in me that I don't know what to do with. Can we please just talk at lunch? I have some things I need to say but need to get my thoughts together before I stick my foot in my mouth again."

His admission of being flustered and confused is a massive step in the right direction for me. I've never had a man admit something like that to me. It's usually bravado bullshit. But not with Brandon.

"Fine. I'll go to lunch with you, but can we go somewhere without photographers?" I glance toward the front of the building, where a small legion of the press is gathered to cover the event.

"We could go to my house." He notices me flinch at the idea, even though I thought I hid it well. I haven't been there since I was taken in the middle of the night. I don't want to go back there. "Or we could go to yours. Grab some takeout on the way. Your call."

"Okay, lunch at my house then."

"Okay."

Fantastic. I hope I don't regret this.

Chapter 41

After Hours

Brandon

We stop for sushi to take back to her house for lunch, and as I pull up to her gate in my Impala, it's nice to see that it's clear of any paparazzi. She's still got a security detail that she can't see, as do I. And even though I'm out driving around on my own today, I'm never really "on my own" anymore. It's just something that I've had to get used to.

In the kitchen, we seem subconsciously aware of each other's bodies because we orbit around each other with perfect synchronicity, getting plates, glasses, drinks, and the like. It's as though we've done this dance with each other a million times, and we don't even have to think about it. Of course, as soon as I think about it, everything goes to shit, and I get in her way several times, causing her to run into me. I don't mind the closeness, but it makes things awkward, so I sit at the table to simply get out of her way.

The small talk while we eat, is relatively comfortable, with little dead air between us. That's one thing we've never had a problem with, and after all of my business dealings over the years, random discussions about nothing in particular are my specialty.

When we finish eating, the air in the room becomes charged, and the anticipation and anxiety for the oncoming talk are tangible. I start washing a few dishes out of nervous habit. Normandy seems slightly surprised but grabs a clean dish towel and joins me at the sink.

"Do you always do chores when you visit someone's house?" If I didn't know better, I'd think there was a hint of a laugh in her tone.

I grin. "Only if I have extreme amounts of groveling to do." I hand her a freshly washed glass to dry. "You should see me with a vacuum. The symmetrical lines in the carpet are my forte." This gets a small laugh out of her. That's a good sign. I think.

It falls quiet between us again, but we're back to doing that awareness dance with each other. After a while, I need to stop it. We have too much to talk about in a short time, and if I want to have any chance of fixing things between us, I need to get started.

"I put my house up for sale yesterday."

She almost drops the plate she's drying. "You what? Why?"

I don't know why I brought that up first. It's going to drag us right down to the bottom line of our problems. I had time this morning to figure out how open I want to be, and it's absolutely all the way. This will either stand or fall with all my cards on the table. I'm not holding back.

"Because I came home from New York to find your blood on the driveway." My chest constricts, remembering Taylor pointing it out to me. My blood had chilled and then burned at the sight. "The sanctity of that house was violated, and you were hurt there. I don't want that reminder."

She gets an odd look on her face that I can't read but nods. "Okay. That makes sense, I guess." Her brow furrows with worry. "Will you find another place? Or...?" She cuts off, not listing options.

"I'm not sure what I'm doing yet. I have some traveling I need to do for business coming up, so I'll have time to think about it."

She nods again but doesn't say anything else. This is not how I pictured this going at all.

"Normandy, I'm just going to put everything out there, and if you listen to everything I have to say and then tell me to get lost, I will. But I won't be able to move forward without telling you some things, okay?" I indicate for us to sit back down at the table.

She sits across from me and says quietly, "I'm listening, Brandon."

The knots of anxiety in my chest loosen a little, knowing that I've got this chance.

"First, I have to tell you that I know I was wrong. I

never should have promised you anything I didn't know for sure I could deliver. I don't know if it was hubris, ego, overconfidence, or who knows what. I should have been realistic and honest with you about the situation. Not that I lied, because I didn't lie. I would never lie to you. But I didn't understand the reality of the problem and thought I had it under control. I was obviously wrong. So, that's the first thing; I was wrong. I know I was wrong. I am an idiot and am incredibly sorry for being so wrong about something so important like your safety."

She doesn't say anything or move a muscle. Just stares at me with blank dark eyes, taking in everything I say. So, I go on.

"Second, I never should have left you alone to face everything on your own. I should have been here with you and not selfishly all the way across the country, covering my own ass while you were nearly killed because of my stupidity and ignorance. I am going to regret that decision for the rest of my life. I *do* regret that so much more than I could ever express to you."

Her eyes are welling up with unshed tears, and I dare to reach across and take one of her hands in mine. Her fingers are cold, so I fold them into mine to warm up.

"Lastly, I am in love with you, Normandy. I don't know when it happened, but I don't care either. I just know that I'm there. I can't picture my future without you in it. When we heard that gunshot, and I thought you were dead, my life was over. All I had in front of me were shadows of what life was supposed to be like. Even now, I can't sleep. All I see when I close my eyes is you hurt, scared to death, and alone, and I can't get to you because

I'm too far away." I shudder thinking of it. "I don't want to live without you."

The tears finally overflow and start to run down her cheeks, and it kills me that I have any part in their falling, that I am any cause for her pain. I reach up and wipe the tears away with my thumb.

"Tell me if there is *anything* I can say or do to fix this because I will do it. I will do anything to repair the damage I've done. But if you really have no feelings for me or want nothing more to do with me, then tell me. It's not what I want to hear, obviously, but I will respect your decision either way."

She stays quiet for a long time, staring at our connected hands. The tears have stopped, but I can't tell what she's feeling now. I've said my peace, and regardless of what happens next with us, I'll know that I tried my best.

"I can't sleep either," she says, still not tearing her gaze away from our hands. "I jump at the slightest noise. Chelsie had to move in with me since I'm too scared to be alone. And I've started seeing a therapist to help with all that since I'm such a mess."

"Don't say that. You are not a mess. Anyone who went through what you endured would have the same issues. But I'm glad you're talking about it to someone. I hope it's helping."

"It's going to be a process. There is something that I've already figured out, though."

"Oh? What's that?"

"I don't blame you. I know you did everything you possibly could to save me. Right after it happened, I needed someone to direct my anger at, and you made the most sense to me at the time. I had blinders on to anything bad that could happen and bought into your confidence. Because I wanted to believe the platitudes. I should have been realistic, knowing it would never go as smoothly as we hoped. That was a pipe dream. I can't blame you for my choices."

"I am ready, willing, and able to accept any and all blame if it means we can start over." I can feel the undertow of the tide shift around us, and a glimmer of hope bubbles to the surface. "Tell me what I need to do."

"Well, you need to stop blaming yourself too. It's not helpful."

"The best I can do is work on that."

She squeezes my fingers. "That's a good start."

"What else?" Now that we've chosen the road less traveled, I want to map it out.

"There's something we never really talked about before."

"What's that?" We've had a lot of great discussions. I can't imagine something major that we missed.

"Well, you primarily live in New York, and I live here. And now you're selling your house...How are we going to make this work?"

My heartbeat picks up. We're talking logistics. This is fantastic.

"You may recall I happen to own a flying chariot that swims through the air at extremely high speeds?"

"Oh yeah, what's that called again? A bird of steel?"

"Well, that's definitely what I'm going to call it from now on."

"Seriously, though. You've got a huge company to run. You can't be flying here from all over the place just to be with me." The doubt creeping in needs to be stopped before it spreads.

"Yes, I can. And I will." I gently pull her hand to my mouth and kiss the back of it. "I'm willing to do whatever it takes to make this work. And if that means more time on a plane, so be it. I mean, what's the point of being a billionaire if I can't use that money to be happy?"

She smiles, and her whole face lights up, and at that moment, I know deep down we will be okay. It's not going to be easy by any means, but we have crossed through the desert of pain and mistrust and now see there's an oasis right in front of us.

Chapter 42

Lovesong

Normandy

Two months later

That steel bird has taken me places I never imagined I would see. We went to Japan, where we visited the Shibuya Scramble Crossing, the world's busiest crosswalk in what can only be described as Tokyo's Time Square. Since it was cherry blossom season, we spent a breathtaking day meandering through Ueno Park. I was surprised to learn that Brandon knows how to speak fluent Japanese, and he explained that a lot of his business is conducted there, so he needed to learn how to communicate effectively with his suppliers and customers.

We then spent a week in Australia, traveling to Sydney and Melbourne. We rambled around Newtown and saw incredible street art and murals. Then on Phillip Island, we took a private tour to see the little blue fairy penguins parade across the beach back to their nest in the moonlight.

It was the most incredible two weeks of my life. While I have a passport, I've never been out of the country. The furthest I had been from home up to that point was Niagara Falls when I was a teenager with my mom, and we didn't even go to the Canadian side. Besides the colossal jet lag from the trip, the culture shock of being back in Vegas is a bit jarring. It's taking me a few days to regain my bearings.

Not long after we return, I receive a lunch invitation from Sophie. My mother is invited as well. Apparently, the two women haven't seen each other in years and keep missing each other when my mom is in town. Brandon is more than happy to fly my mother to Vegas for the occasion. She's also highly impressed with the steel bird, but she refuses my offer to stay with us at her old home. I don't blame her, as I know the memories it holds for her more than most.

We meet at an Italian sandwich restaurant which luckily has good air conditioning since it's scorching outside, and when my mother and Sophie see each other, tears and long hugs are shared. I'm reminded of how much Sophie helped my mother way before she met my father. My mom's young life was difficult, and she found herself a little lost when she came to Vegas. Sophie took her under her wing and gave her a push in the right direction. I should be grateful for that too.

"Look at the two of you," Sophie says, holding my mother at arm's length. "You could be sisters."

"Oh, stop it." My mother waves a hand at her dismissively. It's not the first time we've heard this; I'm sure it won't be the last. My entire life, I was a "mini mom" or, once I grew up, a twin. I take it as a compliment since I think my mother is beautiful.

Over lunch, I hear some fantastic stories of my mom's burlesque career and the crazy shenanigans that took place at Sophie's club over the years. The '80s were definitely a wild time to be in Vegas, that's for sure. And from the sounds of it, a hell of a lot of fun. I don't think I've ever seen my mom blush so much, and I can't help but laugh at all the trouble she got into.

Our conversation dances around Victor and Louie and the kidnapping, but I can feel their weight hanging around us as we laugh and joke. Avoiding the bad times is fine by me. The reunion of these two strong and independent women makes my heart sing as I watch them interact. It's as though time hasn't passed, and their friendship remains as strong as ever. I hope it does continue for them, and they stay in touch with each other after this.

"And what about you and Brandon?" Sophie asks me, an eyebrow raised.

"Yes, do tell," my mother chimes in, taking a long sip of her mimosa. "Inquiring minds want to know."

I glare at both of them. I knew this would come up

eventually, but I didn't want to get into my love life during their reunion.

I shrug a noncommittal shoulder. "There's not much to tell. We're having fun."

"Fun is good...." My mom leaves it open-ended, waiting for me to expand on my answer.

"What's wrong with fun?" She makes it sound like it should be a lot more than that. It's only been a couple of months that we've been together, and I don't like labels. And ever since the kidnapping, I take everything one day at a time and try to enjoy each one to the fullest. That just happens to always include Brandon somehow.

"Well, if you ask me, which you haven't," Sophie starts, refilling her own mimosa from the pitcher, "I think Brandon is head over heels in love with you."

My mother giggles at this. *Giggles.* "Do go on, Sophie. I appreciate hearing stories about a man in love. Especially if it includes a handsome billionaire in love with my very own daughter."

Sophie giggles along with her, and I can tell they both need to be cut off from any more mimosas.

I roll my eyes. "You guys are seriously embarrassing me." They're not, but I do feel heat spread into my cheeks. Part of me wants to hear what Sophie sees in Brandon to make her think that, but there is no way I'd ever ask. He constantly tells me that he loves me, and I haven't said it back to him yet. But it doesn't bother him at all. He says he knows I love him in the ways I show him. He doesn't need to hear the words. He's been so patient with me; there's no way I *couldn't* be in love with him.

"I've never seen him so focused on anything outside his company the way he centers his life around you, Normandy." Sophie sighs with a hand to her chest, a small smile playing on her lips and a dreamy look in her eyes. "Not to bring up his old girlfriends, the few I saw, but they couldn't hold a candle to you. Everything Brandon does now, and I mean *everything*, is done with you in mind. He considers you in every decision he makes now, like selling his house. He built that house. And I don't mean just 'had it built.' I mean, he joined the construction crews in literally building it. And for him to sell his dream home because of what happened to you there? That's love, honey. That is love."

My mother gets misty-eyed listening to Sophie, and I'm reminded that my father refused to sell their house after she was kidnapped. My heart aches for her and my dad, knowing things could have been so different between them if he had just done that one thing for her. It makes me appreciate Brandon's actions even more.

"I know," I say quietly with a nod. "I know."

All of these aren't things I don't know about Brandon. I know how much he cares about me because he shows me every day and in a million different ways. Selling his house is just one of a dozen grand gestures he's made to prove his love for me. And I don't take any of it for granted.

So, I tell him that night. And I don't stop saying it to him whenever I get the chance. I tell him first thing in the morning, the last thing before we fall asleep, before we hang up a call, or as one of us leaves or returns, and the best time to say it is whenever I damn well feel like it.

Out of the blue and in the middle of a conversation is the greatest because it always throws him off his game. More often than not, that will lead to incredible sexy times, but that's just a bonus. I was stupid for holding back the words because it makes *me* feel good to tell him what he means to me. Yes, showing him is most important, but saying it and hearing it confirms it. I don't ever want him to doubt us, or me, or himself. *This love is real.*

Three Months Later

"Be careful with that. It's an original Charles Rennie Mackintosh," Dennis, Brandon's interior designer, says to the movers, carrying a gorgeous painting of a Fae woman standing among flowers. He has excellent taste, not only in art but in furnishings too. He's duplicating the feel of Brandon's New York apartment in the house that we're now going to share. I was more than happy to hand over the reins and let him do his thing with the house. As long as Brandon and I are together, I don't care what the place looks like, but it's a bonus that it will look nice.

Last week I said my final goodbyes to my life in Sacramento, transferred my clients to colleagues I trust, sold most of my furniture, and broke the lease on my townhouse to move in with Brandon. I think I knew deep down once I returned to Vegas to deal with my father's estate that I was back for good.

Chelsie is ecstatic since I signed over our dad's house to her. When I realized what had happened to my mother there and her reluctance to visit because of it, I knew I had to find somewhere else to live. Conveniently, Brandon is going through the same thing, and we can just meld our lives together for the same purpose. Well, there are other reasons too: mainly, we want to spend as much time together as possible when he's in town. He's arranging for a satellite office of LC Consolidated to be established here in Vegas, so he won't need to be in New York as often.

This house is a temporary stop, as Brandon wants to build another home along the Red Rock Canyon, this time including things I want, which is sweet, but I keep trying to tell him I'm not picky. I'm sure Dennis will be decorating that house too, and Brandon wants to get hands-on with the construction again. I can't wait to see hot Brandon the Builder in action.

"I see Dennis hasn't strangled any movers, so that's a sign of a successful day." I feel arms wrap around me and Brandon's breath in my ear as I watch the finishing touches go into place. Art pieces are hung, and furniture is rearranged several times until Dennis is happy with everything.

"It was a near thing when they almost dropped your office desk a little while ago," I chuckle, pulling his arms tighter around me. "I thought for sure we'd need to start a cemetery plot in the backyard." I glance at my watch. "You're early. Did you finalize the office space you were looking at?"

He squeezes me again, pressing his arousal against my backside, making my core instantly ache for him. I need to stop myself from reaching around to touch him with other people in the room.

"I did. And now I want to start christening every fuckable surface in the house with you as soon as possible." The low growl in his throat sends my blood singing through my veins as my pulse quickens at his words. And suddenly, I want that too. I want that so bad; my anticipation crests, and I can't take much more.

"Dennis!" I interrupt him instructing the movers for yet another change in the furniture placement, but I don't step away from Brandon. I don't think he'd let me move if I tried anyway. "That looks great just where it is. It's perfect. Thank you so much for everything. Really, the whole house is fantastic. You've outdone yourself."

His initial confusion turns to bashful modesty as the compliments are laid on thicker. I'm not lying. The house looks great. But he needs to leave it. Now. It ends up taking another entire half hour until we have the place to ourselves.

"Finally." Brandon pulls me to him after seeing the last person out the door and gently presses his lips to mine, letting his lips linger as he smiles. His fingers are tracing a teasing line down the center of my back, his touch delicate.

I am *not* in the mood for delicate. Not after the provocative way he's been tempting me for the last half hour surreptitiously in front of everyone. I reach down and firmly seize him with insistent fingers, making him gasp into my mouth, his smile widening. And those goddamned dimples do me in. The next thing I know, the inside of the front door is christened, the foyer echoing with our feverish cravings. And then the library, his office, and finally, our master bedroom.

"That was a decent opening salvo," I say, running a finger down his chest and swirling a lazy circle around his belly button. He twitches under my touch, ticklish.

He raises an eyebrow. "That wasn't enough for you?"

"It was a good start. But there's a lot of house left."

Chapter 43

Wild Love

Brandon

Four Months Later

"You're positive you want to do this?" I ask Normandy, my finger hovering nervously over the Enter key on my laptop.

She bites her bottom lip but nods. "Yes. Absolutely."

I hit the key and take a deep breath, expelling it slowly. We've just applied for a marriage license. We're getting married. *Tonight.*

Normandy proposed over dinner this evening. Actually, no, she didn't ask. She told me, *"We should get married."* And when I asked when, she earnestly said, *"How about tonight?"* So, here we are, applying for a marriage license online and making extremely last-minute arrangements. As neither of us has been married before, outside of the license part, we are like the blind leading the blind.

"I just texted Chelsie and Bianca to meet us at the chapel at eight, but I just gave them the address and didn't say it was a wedding chapel. Just mentioned they might want to dress up a little." She snickers to herself with a devious giggle as she scrolls her phone. "Can you text Sophie and your brother to meet us?" Watching her evil amusement at the situation pushes buttons in me I didn't know I even had, and I'm almost beside myself that I will get to spend the rest of my life with this woman.

My brother Jon has been in town for about a week to visit; surprise, he's about to be my best man. I text them both and confirm they can make it. Sophie guesses what might be happening, but I won't confirm or deny it. Normandy would have my head on a platter if I gave it away. Why we're surprising anyone with this wedding is beyond me, but whatever the bride-to-be wants, she will get.

"And what are you doing so intently on your phone?" I try to sneak a peek at her phone screen, but she yanks it out of my view.

"No way. You're not supposed to see the dress before the wedding. It's bad luck." She jumps off the couch and out of my reach as I grab for her. *Damn, she's quick.*

"Fine. Keep your secrets. Can I get by with a regular suit? Or do I need to pull out the penguin?"

"Penguin, please," she shouts from the hallway, sounding almost offended. Luckily, I happen to own a tuxedo or two. Unfortunately, it's the end of summer, and still hotter than hell in Vegas. Not ideal tuxedo-wearing weather. "We need to get a move on. I've got shopping to do and not a lot of time."

"Remember, this was all your idea...." I call after her, shaking my head that this is actually happening.

"I know; I'm already regretting it." She's back in the living room, shoes on and purse in hand, ready to get married. "I'm kidding. I don't regret anything...yet."

"Give it time," I say with a grin, joining her and pulling her into a passionate kiss. I get to do this with her for the rest of my life. *How the hell did I get so lucky?*

I had some shopping of my own to do before the ceremony. Since we didn't have a real engagement, we didn't have rings. When I arrive at the chapel, Normandy is already there, and I can hear her laughing with other female voices on the other side of the door to the bridal suite. As this is all kinds of unconventional, I guess our engagement will have to be too.

I find some paper and a pen and write a quick note to slide under the door. I put the diamond engagement ring in the center and wrap the message around it.

'Picture me on one knee outside the door (because I am). Will you marry me?'

There are a few gasps and some more laughter before I hear Normandy say *'Yes!'* loudly through the door. *Bam. I have a fiancée.* For a few minutes at least.

Chelsie is Normandy's Maid of Honor, and when

she walks down the aisle with tears in her eyes, my heart lurches. She's seen us at our best and worst and has always cheered for us to work out. When she catches my eye, she gives me a big thumbs up from under her bouquet, and I can't help but laugh.

Then Normandy appears, and I forget how to breathe. She is positively devastating in a white lace dress, carrying a bouquet of white roses. I barely see any of that, though, because my attention is on the massive grin on her face with her eyes dancing brightly at me. Not a tear in sight. And not an inkling of doubt. She's as sure about this as I am, and I have to pinch myself.

We agreed beforehand to say our own vows, and even though we had such a short time to prepare them, I don't hesitate to express how I feel in the moment.

"Normandy Blake, I can't believe you picked me. Out of every other person on this planet, you are choosing me to spend the rest of your life with, and I am so honored. I get to show you every single day from now on how much you mean to me. And I'm grateful. I'm thankful for your grace, patience, and love. Things I hold dear and vital above all else. You see me for who I am and love me anyway. I promise to do the same for you, with all of my heart from this day forward, for as long as I live."

As I slide the wedding ring on her finger, a single tear starts to trickle down her cheek, but she smiles as she wipes it away quickly.

"Brandon Carmichael, of course, I chose you. How could I not? When you show me every single day how much you love me. I can only hope you see how much I return that love. *You* are patient, and *you* are kind, and yes, I'm just repeating what you said back to you because I'm nervous and totally forgot what I was going to say. Just know that I feel like the luckiest woman in the world that you are choosing me too."

She puts the matching ring on my finger and squeezes my hand. And as the officiant pronounces us husband and wife, I get to kiss the woman of my dreams. The woman who has enriched my life in so many ways that money never could. The person that makes me happier than I ever thought possible.

Never in a million years did I think I could be this lucky, especially in Vegas.

Epilogue
The Sweetest Gift

Normandy

Three Weeks Later

We're back from a whirlwind honeymoon in Europe, where we barely saw a single tourist attraction since we spent most of our time in bed. I am *not* complaining.

I had lunch with Sophie earlier in the day, as we've started doing recently, and she remarked on my being pale, asking if I was sick. *I'm not ill, just jet-lagged*, I think. But I could barely eat the lunch I ordered as nausea crested over me like a wave every single time I looked at my plate.

On my way home, I buy a pregnancy test. You're

supposed to wait until first thing in the morning to take it, but I can't wait that long. I force myself to wait the full three minutes the test requires for the results to show, and it's the longest three minutes I've ever lived through. I almost throw up from the anxiety.

What if it's positive? We've talked about having kids, and we both agree that we want a family sooner rather than later, but *this* soon? We haven't even been married a whole month yet. A significant life-altering change like this could upset everything we're just starting to build together.

And what if it's not? I honestly think I'll be disappointed if it's negative now that I've had the thought put in my head that I might be pregnant. Suddenly I want nothing more than to be carrying Brandon's baby. To have growing inside me the culmination of our love for each other would be the most beautiful thing I can think of.

Brandon will be the best dad someday, whether it's now or later. The patience that man has for all things, especially people, is one of the world's natural wonders. A baby will need a lot of it, and he's got enough for both of us. I know in my heart he will love and protect our child, whenever it comes, with a fierceness and passion that not many men could match. These qualities are only a few of the reasons I married him in the first place.

The alarm on my phone sounds, and I shut it off with a nervous exhale. This is it. Positive or negative, I need to accept whatever it is because either result is fine. If it's positive, we'll start on a new adventure together, and if it's negative, I get to spend more individual time with the man I adore. I'll be happy either way.

I shut my eyes tightly and pick up the test stick, feeling my hands shake as I grab it. Slowly, I open my eyes, peer at the result, and smile.

When Brandon comes home from a meeting, he finds a card on his plate at the dinner table. He eyes it curiously, then me.

"What's this?" Now confusion clouds his bright eyes. "Is this a special occasion I didn't know about? Or did know about but forgot?"

I laugh and wrap my arms around his waist, resting my head on his chest. "No, but it is a special occasion. Open the card."

"Okay...." He slowly opens the envelope and pulls out the card. "A Father's Day card?" He gazes at me in confusion, but I smile up at him silently, watching the realization dawn on him. The grin that spreads on his face, displaying those gorgeous dimples of his that I hope the baby growing inside me inherits, is so heartwarming and fills me with so much joy I almost burst. "Are you being serious?"

"Uh-huh," I nod.

"Really, truly serious? You're pregnant?"

"Yes."

"How? I mean, I know how, obviously.... but.... what? We're pregnant?" He tosses the card, lifts me up with his strong arms, and twirls me around the living room while laughing.

"We're pregnant!" I cheer, framing his face with my hands and kissing him.

He sets me down carefully, patting his pockets like he's looking for something. "Right. I need to go get ice cream, pickles, saltines, and what else? Ginger ale? Are you craving anything yet? What do you need? What can I do? Do you need a back rub? A foot massage?" He's torn between stricken and excited, and I can only continue my smile.

This is why I love this man and why I married him. And why our life together with our family is going to be the most incredible thing this world has ever seen.

--THE END--

Ms. Fortune Playlist

https://open.spotify.com/playlist/
6xC6LqzJAuLewzU7BHAdP8?si=c54795c970cf4904

1. Nothing But Thieves, *Is Everybody Crazy?*
2. Soundgarden, *Fell On Black Days*
3. Thrice, *Black Honey*
4. Wilco, *Hearts Hard To Find*
5. Normandie, *Babylon*
6. Jackie, *Unspun*
7. Royal Blood, *Boilermaker*
8. Wolf Alice, *Smile*
9. Faith No More, *From Out of Nowhere*
10. Alice Merton, *Vertigo*
11. The Wombats, *Lemon To a Knife Fight*
12. Asking Alexandria, *Vultures*
13. Arctic Monkeys, *Stop the World I Wanna Get Off With You*
14. Bexley, *Run Rabbit Run*
15. Arctic Monkeys, *Do I Wanna Know?*

16. YONAKA, *Seize the Power*
17. Soundgarden, *Hunted Down*
18. Twin Wild, *Willow Tree*
19. The Black Keys, *Your Touch*
20. Maggie Lindemann, *It's Not Your Fault*
21. Anson Seabra, *That's Us*
22. K's Choice, 20,000 *Seconds*
23. Seafret, *Be There*
24. All About Eve, *Wild Flowers*
25. FINNEAS, *Angel*
26. PJ Harding, Noah Cyrus, *Dear August*
27. David Gray, *Please Forgive Me*
28. BANKS, *You Should Know Where I'm Coming From*
29. Foals, *What Went Down*
30. YONAKA, *Call Me A Saint*
31. Lonely The Brave, *Bound*
32. K's Choice, *Quiet Little Place*
33. The Sherlocks, *End of the Earth*
34. The Mayan Factor, *Warflower*
35. Twin Wild, *My Heart*
36. The Blue Stones, *Black Holes (Solid Ground)*
37. Electric Enemy, *Hollow Eyes*
38. Black Honey, *Spinning Wheel*
39. Trade Wind, *I Can't Believe You're Gone*
40. Tigercub, *It's Only Love*
41. The Weeknd, *After Hours*
42. Adele, *Lovesong*
43. James Bay, *Wild Love – Acoustic*
44. Sade, *The Sweetest Gift*

About the Author

Amy Booker is the International Bestselling Author of the Near Miss Rock Star Romance series (*Almost, So Close, Barely*), which follows the exploits of the members of the band Indigo King. Her next series, Drive Me Wild (*Ms. Fortune, Ms. Chief, Ms. Lead, Ms. Take*), are Vegas-centered stories of strong female main characters and the men who *think* they can handle them.

When she's not writing, Amy can be found listening to or writing music, enjoying an audiobook, chasing her crazy dog, or traveling.

Sign up for release notifications or view bonus content at http://www.amybookerauthor.com